# SIGHT UNSEEN

E. L. CALLOWAY

*For the ones who believe love is the healer of all wounds.*

# Soundtrack

Charlotte Day Wilson - Take Care Of You

Sergio - Lie To Me

Sir Travis Knight - Tell Me

ESTA., Leon Thomas - dangerous game

Devon Culture - Ebony

Anthony Q - Try Loving Me

IAMTHELIVING - Can't be replaced

Teeks - First Time

# CHAPTER *ONE*

## *Darrell*

"You're not getting any younger, DJ," my grandmother rambles on, "I'm just saying, I'd like a few grandkids before I have no energy left to give them and I become the toothless Honey they're afraid of."

"You're already a grandmother, Honey," I remind her as I myself am her grandchild.

She brushes off my reminder with a wave of her hand.

"You know what I mean. I raised you practically for your entire life, you're more my child than your own mothers," She walks past me as we dance around each other in her kitchen of her country-side home that became a safe haven for me at a young age.

She goes to the stove to stir her homemade concoction of whatever magical soups grandmothers make.

A potion of rice, lima beans and whatever else she adds in there to take you right back to your favorite summer nights as a 9 year old who just came in from a day's long play.

"I've got plenty of time to procreate, Honey. I don't understand the rush. Plus, you're skipping over the important part of needing someone to create these said grandchildren with in the first place."

I take a seat at the small kitchen table that was mandatory to join every morning before school.

"No ones forgetting about the part a woman plays, boy, no one could."

She dips her wooden spoon into the now bubbling pot and slightly cools off the sample she pulls up, motioning me to come for a taste test, my job for a little over 20 years now,

"While you may have plenty of time, I, on the other hand, do not."

I smack my lips at the savory taste of the soup, but frown in the same instant, "You know I hate when you talk like that. You aren't going anywhere, anytime soon," I plaçe a kiss to the crown of her head, as I tower over her.

She hums with eyes closed in response.

"Tomorrow is never promised to us, DJ. You know that just as well as I do." Trying to ignore the wince she made, my eyes instinctively go to the photo of her and Gramps.

They're sitting on the swinging chair on the front porch, the one that still sits there today with its rusted legs.

His arm wrapped around her shoulders, her head leaned into his chest, too lost in the comfort he brought her to acknowledge the camera pointed at her.

He looks at the photographer with a toothy grin, the physical depiction of bliss itself.

*"Gramps, Honey, look at the camera!" Sy'Asia yells at them from the bottom of the steps.*

*"Girl, turn that camera away from me, I've taken enough pictures today to fill a photo album." Honey retorts, taking a seat next to an already sitting Gramps.*

*The sun has more than kissed his skin this summer, his already deep brown complexion tanner than I knew possible to be. All he does is laugh at his snippy wife who's been hosting our family cookout on this hot summer day.*

*"Right, so what's one more? Come on Gramps, say cheese!" Anthony says from his spot next to our oldest sister who's still waiting to press the shutter.*

*"Come on doll, take one more with your old man. Then I'll make sure these children of yours leave you be for the rest of the day." He says with eyes squinted despite sporting the thick glasses that rest high on his nose.*

*Honey kisses her teeth, you can see that natural rebellion of hers at war, she can never win against her gentle giant of a husband.*

*6 foot 3, though with old age and bad back he stands a bit lower, gravel for a voice but made of nothing but the soft stuff inside. He's the only voice that's been able to get through those ears of hers.*

*He whispers something in her ear during this internal battle of will, when she looks up at him, in all my 25 years I've never seen such love in just one look.*

*Sy'Asia finally gets her picture.*

I will myself back to the present, and not losing myself to the memories the last photo they'd taken together 4 years ago stirs up.

Not thinking for too long about her laughter and how it isn't belly deep anymore or how her smile doesn't quite reach her eyes the same way anymore.

No.

I focus on the woman that's before me.

5 foot 2 with a graying braid thrown over her shoulder. Freckles on her face where the sun kissed her more than her own family did, and the only mother I've been truly loved by.

The woman who has been persistently and increasingly pestering me about starting my own family, as if I don't have more important things to worry about.

# CHAPTER *TWO*

### *Moriah*

*I* never pass up Sunday Brunch with Anastasia, even though the places she picks are the opposite of relaxing.

Tribune Heights may not be a hot spot like our neighboring city Baltimore, but its downtown area does have its gems. You just have to know what to look for.

I don't know if Anastasia does.

After waiting 20 minutes, in heels, to be seated, we finally receive our drinks and place our food orders. After such a long week, I'm pretty sure I'll be having a liquid lunch.

"Your parents mean well, Stasi. You know the story they've told you time and time again, they prayed for a daughter. They're not going to give you anything less than the treatment of a princess," I remind my best friend of 14 years who is yet again on verbal rampage because her parents treat her as if she's incapable.

They see it as treating her like she's royal.

"It isn't that I'm unappreciative Mo, you know that. I admire them so much. They've worked so hard to build what they have for themselves and for me before they even tried to conceive. Their struggles aren't lost upon me," She says to me, but I believe it was more of a reminder to herself.

"It's just that I'm in my late twenties now. The few skills I have acquired, I've had to do so on my own and not because I've gotten out there and really had to work for anything. I feel so behind and not only behind but not respected for what I actually can do already."

Her shoulders slump as she sips her margarita, "I know you're probably thinking *ugh, what a spoiled, rich girl complaint*,"

I smile at my friend, because it is exactly that.

Her parents wanted to have a name for themselves before planting their roots and expanding their family.

They're the owners of a luxury traveling business, something I had no idea was a thing once I'd met Stasi and didn't realize was so lucrative.

I can see her perspective.

Anastasia was never one of the rich girls who wanted to be rich, she wanted to earn her keep unlike so many of her peers growing up who loved having their things handed to them on silver platters, deserving or not.

"While it is absolutely a rich girl's complaint," I laugh at her audible sigh, "It's an honorable one. I don't have the same… struggle, if that's what we're calling it, as you. But, I respect that this is your struggle. Women wanting to build themselves up instead of looking for a handout is something I'll always stand behind. Plus, no matter your complaint, I'll listen to you ramble on about anything for as long as you need to," I place my hand on hers, "As long as the topic of men is limited to two sentences."

She laughs.

"Speaking of men…"

I can't hide my eye roll, we can never escape the topic for some reason.

"That guy that brought our drinks, you know he wanted you right?" She says, discreetly scanning the crowd for the man who treated us only moments after we'd been seated.

"And you know I don't care, right?" I reply and sip my free tequila sunrise.

"Moriah," she sighs, "I'm not trying to push you any faster than you're willing to move, or push you at all really. You don't need a man for stability or finances, you've been doing so well on your own," She acknowledges, and hell right I have been, "But…"

"There's always a but," I drink a few more sips.

"You deprive yourself of experience, of love, of the feeling a man with strong arms can give you," She wraps her arms around herself and closes her eyes as if she's soaking in someone else's embrace, "Hell, you deprive yourself of some morning glow after you've been going at it all night," She unnecessarily adds.

My face unavoidably contorts from disgust.

"I'm just saying, it's nearly impossible for a man to catch your attention. And the ones that do, you pick apart with a pair of the finest tweezers until his own mother wouldn't like him anymore. I get you have your reasons Mo, but I'm just saying, you're missing out on so much."

I hear her talking but all I'm worried about at this moment is kissing the person who made this drink.

"Stasi," I take another sip, "I quite literally do not have time in my schedule for love right now," Our waiter finally arrives with the food we ordered 40 minutes ago, "And I don't need to. I have you," I smile.

"Yeah, but I'm not putting a strap on for you when you need to release tension," She replies.

I nearly choke on the forkful of omelett I just put in my mouth.

She and I have always differed in many ways. One of those ways is despite her being the one whose attended balls and cotillions, she could fool people into thinking she has no decorum with the things that freely fly from her mouth.

"No, but I'll have plenty of time to be traumatized by love and mediocre sex later. I have more important things to do right now, like getting at least two more drinks," I wash down my food with another sip.

Anastasia gives me a thoughtful stare, and then begins her food as well.

With love constantly on the mind, people tend to act like they have no time for anything else. For goals, for family, for themselves.

Love, or what they think love is, always leads someone to a bad decision.

I don't make bad decisions, and I don't plan on making them any time soon either.

# CHAPTER *THREE*

## *Darrell*

"*This* foundation isn't some gimmick to look good while we also get a tax write off. This was founded in love, its purpose comes from a deeper place. We aren't going to agree to some thrown together offer."

The man sitting at the opposite side of my desk says.

His suit is too expensive for him to convince me he's only in this business out of the kindness of his heart.

However, my job isn't to figure out why he's in the position he's in, my job is to be the middleman between his organization and the grants they're looking for access to. More specifically, my company looks for me to be the person who assures the clients we care about their mission enough to work our hardest to get them what they need.

"Mister Nolan," I say to him calmly, "As an Intermediary, we focus on the needs of our client and we give one hundred and ten percent to their needs. With us being privately owned, we have the liberty to be a bit more hands on with the clients we accept and or reach out to. And, with that being the case, we tend to aim for collaborations that we truly believe in."

I can see the conflict between tension and ease in his face just enough to let me know that he's been run around by other companies that were looking for their own benefits for far too long, and his guard is up. Rightfully so.

"Mister Washington," He adjusts his suit jacket.

"Please, call me Darrell. Mister Washington is my older brother," I offer a disarming smile.

"Darrell," He corrects, "I do appreciate your authenticity. I can't tell you how uncommon it is these days, in any industry honestly," He huffs out a breath as if he's exhausted. "I would say I look forward to working with you and your team, as I've heard much about your company."

"All good things, I hope," I say, again with a smile.

"Good things about you specifically, I can assure you," He places emphasis on it being about me. I'm the friendly one out of my siblings, my older brother Anthony, who is the president of our company, he's the hardass. "But, while you may have sold me, I'm barely half of the battle."

The reputation of his partner, co-founder of their organization Love Unbound, is not lost upon me.

It's said that getting through to Nolan is a cakewalk compared to his partner, Jackson. But, I've dealt with my fair share of difficult people and walked away unscathed, so there will be no shaking in my boots.

"Ah, yes. Jackson, correct?" As if I have not done as much research as I could have upon reaching out to them when I heard they were in search of an intermediary.

"Yes. Jackson… Well, Jackson is the true founder of this organization, the idea of it being born due to Jackson's own story," It must be a story that hits home, because Nolan's eyes cast down as if he's recalling it in his head.

"So, because of that, I'd put on your best selling voice and strap up your boots. The lack of authenticity may be one of the reasons we've been on a search for so long, but my partner's… fastidiousness has also played quite a part," He tells me as candidly as he can.

I give an assured and confident nod, "I understand, being particular can certainly be both a strength and hindrance," I respond.

"Certainly," He stands from his seat, and I mimic the action,

"I provided Jackson's email address in the folder I handed to you earlier. I'll make sure to return back to the office with a great report, but it'll also be beneficial if you reach out on your own requesting a meeting," We stand at the door of my office.

"Will do. Thank you again for meeting with me Mr. Nolan, I look forward to working together," I shake his hand.

"Hopefully that happens, Darrell," He exits.

I take my seat back at my desk and moments later Anthony enters my office, opting to stand opposed to sitting.

"So," He picks up the folder Nolan handed to me earlier and casually flips through, "How did it go?"

"As well as I anticipated," I respond, not looking up from my computer as I tend to unread emails I missed during my meeting.

"Good," He sits the folder down, "You alright?" He asks with as much of a concerning voice as my stoic brother can manage.

"Yeah. Why?"

"I don't know. You've seemed a little off kilter lately, a little low in spirit I guess. Just checking," He observes.

I lean back in my chair, finally meeting his gaze, "I won't lie, I do feel a little strange to say the least. But, I can't exactly tell you why."

He only continues to look at me in response, my brother is a thoughtful speaker, he doesn't waste time on words that he doesn't deem necessary.

"Can I ask you something?" I look at him again.

"What's up?"

"Has Honey been talking about death to you, recently?" The words Honey and death in the same sentence is enough to make my chest tight.

He doesn't respond immediately.

"Why do you ask?" Not answering my question.

"Because she's been causally, I don't know… joking about it or saying it lightheartedly to me more than I'm comfortable with lately. Like she's preparing herself… or me," I avert my gaze from him, feeling an odd pressure form in my chest at the implied possibility.

"Well," His brow furrows, "She is getting older Rell. As much as we would like for her to, she isn't going to live forever. Maybe she's just accepting that."

I look at him as if he just told me he wants to fight me.

"What is wrong with you man? Why would you say that?" I try to keep my voice even.

"Because Darrell, death is a part of life. We all face it at some point, rather it's losing someone we love most or our own fate. No one escapes it," He says, with brows still furrowed, like he's confused by my reaction.

"I'm not saying anyone is on their deathbed, but what I am saying is, maybe now is a good time to start preparing your heart for something like that."

With his hands in his pockets, and a look of pity, he turns on his heels and walks out of my office leaving me with my nightmare as my daydream.

The thought of losing the only woman who has been an actual mother to me is something I will not sit here and entertain, no matter what anyone says.

# CHAPTER *FOUR*

## *Moriah*

*I* sit at the island in our kitchen, getting my daily dose of social media scrolling when I hear my favorite man enter through the front door.

"I'm 67 years old, I don't need nobody that's read a few books telling me how I need to eat. I've been feeding myself since I was 7 years old, I ain't dead yet." I hear him crankily rambling to my older sister as she sits the keys in a dish by the door.

"Daddy, the few books the doctor read made him qualified to be your physician. He knows what he's talking about." Adella says with an exasperated tone, but she isn't as tired as she sounds. She's been his primary care taker for 4 years now, this is a conversation that is well practiced.

"Hey old man." I place a kiss on his prickly cheek as he enters the kitchen, Adella following behind him with his bag of refilled prescriptions.

"Hey MoMo." He responds to me with a smile.

"Mo, please get your father." My sister says, getting out his pill organizer as she begins to place the proper medication in its prospective places.

"Nobody needs to get me, AJ. I'm grown." He huffs as he slowly sits at the island in my place.

"You're grown but sound like the wind is being knocked out of you if you try to talk and sit at the same time." I retorted. "What are you giving the doctor a hard time about now Big J?" I ask him.

The way my sister and I interact with him differs from one another.

Where she's his caretaker slash mother, I talk to him like we're friends. My father has always been an independent man, taking care of my sister and I all by himself since I was 2. He's not used to needing someone to care for him, so it's a bit of an adjustment.

"No, you mean what is that doctor giving *me* a hard time about," He corrects me. "Telling me I'm in the running to become a diabetic if I don't change my eating habits."

He lets out a 'pfft' sound as if what the doctor told him is absurd.

"I've been eating the exact same way most of my adult life, and some kid who hasn't been on this earth longer than these shoes I have on my feet is going to tell me I'm wrong all of a sudden?" He rolls his eyes.

I can't help but laugh.

He always wonders where I got my stubbornness. I should record him so that the next time he asks I can play a real life example.

"That 'kid' may be younger than your shoes, but because of his field of study, he's in better condition than you and those talking loafers." I nod to his worn out shoes.

My sister snickers as she finishes up with his medicines.

"Man, I'm not hearing that. I'll holler at him once I actually need him. Seeing him once every three months is a little too frequent, wait until I get an issue I actually need his help with." He takes a sip of the water bottle he's been holding on to.

"That's exactly the opposite of what you're supposed to do, Daddy." AJ responds to him as she begins to prepare his favorite snack, a peanut butter, banana, and jelly sandwich.

He turns his attention to me, "Enough about me, how was your day MoMo? Better than mine I'm sure." He scoffs.

I smile at him, he's always made sure to ask us about our day, since preschool. He's always been interested in us.

"My day was good pops, nothing too crazy has happened thankfully. How about you AJ? Aside from the grouch over here giving you a hard time." I point a thumb at him while talking to my sister who's sitting his freshly made mid-day snack in front of him. Same snack every day at this time and he still practically salivates at the sight of it.

"It was fine, not too much ruckus to be honest. Thank you for asking sissy poo." She smiles at me.

We may be sisters, but we are also best friends.

We've always stuck close to each other and stayed close to home, skipping out on most of the things our peers were doing. Not out of obligation, but out of choice.

With us understanding more and more as we got older the sacrifices he's made on our behalf, we both silently agreed that we needed to carry our end just like our father carried his for us.

So, we kept our heads in the books and out of trouble.

"Mo, why don't you take some time off soon and spend a day with us? Since work has been slower lately. We could all go to the park y'all loved so much growing up, or go get something to eat. Y'all loved doing that." My dad says in between inhales of his sandwich.

"I'd love to do that daddy." I smile so hard it makes my cheeks sore.

Only he can get such emotion out of me and only he can get me to agree to step away from my desk without having to attend to an emergency, a true daddy's girl at heart.

"They're hosting a flower show at the park soon too, maybe we can go that day." Adella says from her side of the counter. Even now, at our big ages, we'd give anything to spend time as a family with the man who gave up his life for us.

When my mother met my father, he was a budding, promising attorney. Just getting his footing in his career, and she was no bum either. She'd taken a year off from school, practicing medicine to become a child psychologist.

One year off became five, as she'd fallen pregnant twice with my sister and myself.

One day, she decided she didn't want to do it anymore. Leaving my father as our sole provider.

Instead of doing what he loved, fighting for justice in the courtroom, he became a law professor at our state college. He gave up his passion and changed his life course entirely for us.

Though it wasn't our fault, we still carried guilt with us. So, in every way we can, we pour into him the same way he poured into us all of our lives. There isn't anything we wouldn't do for him.

"Well, I'm going to go grab us some dinner. I don't think anyone feels like cooking today." I kiss him on his cheek, "How does chinese sound?" I ask AJ .

"Fine for tonight, but we also have to cut down on our sodium intake." She arches an eyebrow in our dads direction.

I laugh. "Gotcha, the last Chinese meal of our lives. I'll make it a good one." I wink at my dad and head out the door.

# CHAPTER *FIVE*

## *Darrell*

*Sy'Asia,* my oldest sister and also our company's project manager sits across from me in our office's flex space. She texts furiously on her phone to someone about a deadline that's gone unmet, and with the look on her face I'd hate to be on the other side of that conversation.

"What fire are you starting over there?" I briefly glance at her.

Without averting her focus from the small screen in her hands, "One of our reps, a newbie, was supposed to show up at this closer today with that client who's starting that youth nonprofit. You remember?"

"Yeah, the re-entry program." I answer. I loved the idea of helping youth exiting juvie and aiding them back among their peers.

"Yeah, them. Well, the newbie apparently just… forgot?" She shrugs her shoulders like it's no big deal, when if there was ever someone who could breathe fire, it would be her at this very moment.

"That would have been a perfect client, do you know how many grantmakers would've eaten that up? And now, we get nothing. No one gets anything and you know how that makes us look? Like we don't want to help the youth. Would you want to work with a network that doesn't want to help the youth?"

Her tone may be calm, but the look in her eyes is telling me she can have a psychotic break at any second.

"So, I am currently ripping him a new pair and no, I will not feel bad about it." She returns her eyes to her screen, and I believe it's in my best interest to remain silent.

I sit in a lounge chair with my laptop. A reminder pops up in the top right corner of my screen alerting me to send an email to Nolan's partner, Jackson.

Opening my email on the laptop, I begin a new message and type in the address of my recipient: M. Jackson.

The email reads as follows:

To: mjackson@loveunbound.org
From: djwashington@themiddlemen.net
Subject: Extended Offer

Good morning, I hope that this email finds you well.

I had the pleasure of speaking with your partner, Mr. Nolan, and since said meeting I believe it is safe to say we'd both agree that a partnership between us would be beneficial, as we share a common goal.

On behalf of my company, we would like to formally extend the offer of collaboration to you as we pride ourselves on working hard with organizations founded on integrity and purpose, as I believe your organization, Love Unbound, to be.

I do hope the report from Mr. Nolan, as well as this email provide you the comfort and reassurance needed to thoughtfully consider this offer.

Hope to hear from you soon.

Regards,
D. J. Washington

I click send with the utmost confidence that no matter how tightly wound this Jackson person may be, that I've secured this deal.

Though part of my job is to sell us to the client, that doesn't include lying. I don't know about my siblings, but I do actually have personal interest in this foundation. Their mission to help struggling families hits a bit closer to home than they of course know.

Not too many moments pass before I'm notified of a new email.

To: djwashington@themiddlemen.net
From: mjackson@loveunbound.org
Subject: RE: Extended Offer

Hello, Mister Washington.

I was able to debrief with my partner, Mister Nolan, following the perfunctory "meeting" held between the two of you.

Unfortunately, I can not say either the debriefing nor this email provided reassurance.

Love Unbound handles the lives of people everyday and wishes to only partner with those who believe in and support us and the families we assist daily.

Thank you for extending this offer, my partner and I will reach out soon upon further deliberation as to ensure that we are making decisions that are for the utmost benefit of this organization.
Best,
M. Jackson

Who the hell says perfunctory? He must be old as hell.

My face has to be betraying me because Sy'Asia finally looks up from her phone, assuming her thumbs are on fire, and says "What's wrong with you?" Mimicking my furrowed brow.

"This Jackson guy from the foundation I've been trying to secure, is weird as hell," I rub my chin, reading over the email again. And who in their right mind writes out the word 'Mister' - a crazy person, that's who.

"Why is he weird?" She releases a light laugh, not a sound we're often blessed to hear. She's always business only, so to get a laugh or any similar sound out of her is a blessing for us.

"Because he writes out the word Mister," I don't move my eyes from the screen.

She rolls her eyes, "Read me what you said and what he said in reply." She sits her phone down fully in her lap and provides me with her full attention.

I read the email exchange to her and by the time I'm done, I notice a smirk. "Was something funny about that? I missed a joke?" I ask genuinely confused and again scan the email for any missing punchlines.

"The joke is, your crazy 'guy' is a woman and that little suave guy to guy thing you do in your meetings is absolutely not going to work with her," She sounds almost proud.

"How do you know it's a woman?"

"Her word choice, her typing style. Basically telling you to hold your fucking horses because *she* hasn't decided anything yet. A woman knows a woman, little brother." She pats my shoulder as she exits the shared space.

I sit with the email window still open, perplexed. Nolan didn't mention his partner was a woman, granted I guess it wasn't something that would or should matter.

Either way, my confidence won't waiver.

This isn't my first hard-ass client, and it won't be my last. My siblings made me head of relations for a reason, and it's rare that I can't secure the relationship. This will not be one of those rare moments.

Before closing my laptop and heading to the board room, I shoot off one more reply.

To: mjackson@loveunbound.org
From: djwashington@themiddleman.net
Subject: Re: Extended Offer

Thank you, Ms. Jackson for your timely reply.

I do indeed understand the choosing of your partnerships being a precious matter with such a delicate mission at stake.

I encourage you to take all the time needed to come to this decision to guarantee you are making the best decision for your organization and above all, the families you assist.

Do feel free to reach out at any time with any questions, comments, or concerns regarding this proposal.

Nerves are not something I feel often, and with this client it is no exception.

Love Unbound being founded by a woman makes sense now, considering the smaller details it tends to regarding the needs of families, especially children.

I've seen them work to reconstruct rundown playgrounds in lower income neighborhoods, give entire children sections to libraries, offer parent makeovers for job searches, and so much more.

Yes, securing this partnership is imperative for us, as they've made headlines with the good that they do in and around our community, and that's the sort of publicity and connections we need.

But, more than that, I've watched them silently for some time and my curiosity to know who is behind these selfless acts grows with each article I read.

Growing up, coming from a place of nothing but selfishness and thoughtlessness, I'm intrigued by people who just want to do for others.

People like my grandparents, helping those that they didn't have to help but just wanted to.

Those are the types of people I look up to, and those are the sorts of organizations I wish to work closely with. So, yes, this deal is good for business.

But, it's deeper than that.

# CHAPTER *SIX*

## *Moriah*

"*I'm* telling you Mo, we're right up their alley of clientele," Elijah, my business partner says across from my desk.

I'm doing my best to tune out his blabbering while I check my calendar for dates to take off per my fathers request. I typically save all of my PTO every year for emergencies, but when Pop calls, then it is an emergency.

"You may want to give them an actual chance, that's all I'm saying," I wait until it seems that he is absolutely finished with his little sales pitch about this guy he's basically fallen in love with.

Sometimes, he seems so easy to sell that I wonder why I send him as the face. But, then I remember, he actively smiles more than me. People seem to like that.

"I really don't care about their alley, Lij," I don't look up from my eCalender, "Why are they interested in us? What's their true word of mouth reputation, not the one google or yelp tells us. Why are they, or whoever the hell D. J. is, pressing so hard for this?"

"Becau-"

"Because they see dollar signs," I answer for him, "They see dollar signs, they see that we're successful at what we do, and they're clearly trying to build up a portfolio that shows they have humanity."

I look at him instead of my computer screen and fold my hands on my desk.

He doesn't respond, he's learned me well enough to know to let me get riled up *and* calmed down before he interjects.

"So, I do not care about their clientele, their allies, their driveways or their anything else for that matter. What I care about is that they will help us access the grantmakers and the silent partners that we otherwise cannot reach on our own," I take a breath, finally.

And then three more, deeply and silently to regulate myself.

I founded Love Unbound in college and met Elijah along the way in its beginning stages.

It started as us making care packages to give to homeless people in our hometown when we'd visit from school, and there were plenty of packages to give out.

The packages started as toiletries and bottles of water, slowly turning into small boxes with travel size hygiene products. Eventually, with the extra monies we had from our savings and college funds, we included what each specific person on our routine rounds would need.

Some needed shirts, some needed blankets, sometimes they'd just want a new stuffed animal for their kid or treats to feed their dogs.

We were like a shelter on foot.

Me coming from a single-parent home who worked overtime to make a living and never miss a beat in our lives, and Elijah coming from parents who battled with addiction but did their best when they could.

I may be the vocal passion behind this, but Elijah feels just as passionate as I do. He's just less aggressive.

"Mo, I hear you. And you know, more than anyone, I understand your concern and why your guard is up," He finally speaks after seeing the storm has ceased.

"But, I'm telling you, I have a good feeling about them. At least about Darrell, he seems trustworthy and though yes, he was laying on his charm, I know he wasn't bullshitting me about the pride they take in who they choose to work with."

I see the silent and delicate plea in his eyes and I feel guilt. What sort of partner am I to act as if I can't trust my closest partner?

I struggle sometimes to remember, we didn't start this organization because of little ole' Moriah. We started it for the families like ours, and worse, to be the helping hand that the government refuses to be for them.

This isn't about me.

"I'm sorry, Lij," I shake my head. "I'm sorry, I really am. You're my partner, not my employee, and I trust your judgment. I owe you that and so much more."

His empathetic smile tells me that he hears my sincerity.

"So, tell me more about this guy and why're talking to me like he created chocolate stuffed oreos," I say before taking a sip of my barely warm Mocha latte.

I'm sure his eyes got brighter at that moment.

And for the next 45 minutes, Elijah talks interrupted about this guy that he's so impressed with. How he could tell this guy was trustworthy just from the firmness of his handshake, such a guy observation.

He damn near has made an entire presentation, showing me a folder of other organizations that they help, grantmakers and investors they're connected with and literal printouts of real life reviews from other founders we're familiar with and that are well respected within our network.

He eventually takes a breath.

"So, are you going to ask him on a date?" I say while he catches his breath.

He laughs.

"Nah, he's not my type. I'm more of a boob guy, he doesn't have any of those."

We laugh again.

"Seriously though, he *sounds* good. But, it's his job to sound good," I remind him.

"And, it's your job to be a cynic," He retorts.

I smile at my friend and business partner.

"I'm just saying Lij, it isn't his company, It's his family's, and just because he's… pleasant and charming, doesn't mean they'll all be such a joy to work with."

Sometimes my friend is a dreamer and unfortunately, I have to be the one to shake him awake.

"Yeah," he surprisingly agrees. "He and his brother have… differing reputations."

I raise an eyebrow.

"But that's fine, because you'll rarely ever see him. He isn't someone who deals directly with the clients."

He knows my expressions so well that I don't have to voice my apprehension given this information.

"To be fair Mo, you and his brother may have that in common," He says gingerly.

"Uh, no?" I say, offended, "Families love me, literally I still keep in touch with 80 percent of them."

"Yeah, families do. But they aren't the only people we deal with, as much as we wish that were the case. All I'm saying is, we maybe shouldn't be so stuck on who's charming versus who isn't as approachable because you never know what people say about us when our names are in a room without us," He says, and it was a wise point.

"Well…"

It's not often that I don't have a reply.

"What's his email again? There are some things that shouldn't be discussed behind screens, getting lost in translation and all," I say trying to ignore my defeat.

With my eyes back on my computer screen, I can hear the smile that he's trying to hold back, us both knowing I am no easy feat.

I open my email portal and begin a new message, typing in the address of my desired recipient as Elijah reads it off of the card he was given.

The email reads as follows:

To: djwashington@themiddleman.net
From: mjackson@loveunbound.org
Subject: Offer discussion

Good afternoon, Mister Washington.

I appreciate your patience throughout this deliberation process.

Upon further conversation with Mr. Nolan, we agree that it would be wise to schedule an in person meeting to discuss a few further details regarding a possible partnership between the organizations to see if we are a proper fit and how we can be of benefit to one another.

If the offer still stands, we would appreciate scheduling this meeting before the end of this week so as to not drag on this process any further than necessary. As I am sure we all have multiple orders of business to tend to and would like to lessen those plates of ours as soon as possible.

Thank you, again, for your patience and also for your expected timely reply regarding this matter and we look forward to meeting with you and your partner(s) soon.

Best,
M. Jackson

I released a breath I did not know was being held immediately after pressing send.

I look up to Elijah who is occupying himself by removing the jacket from the back of the chair he sat in not too long ago, trying to contain the excitement on his face.

"Elijah," I say as he silently makes his way to the door of my office.

"Why are you pushing for this so hard?" I ask because yes, he's had to sell me on people before, but he's campaigning with passion this time and I can't grasp why.

"Because Mo, I'm serious…" He turns to me before walking out, "I really do have a good feeling about this, even if you don't."

And with that, he leaves my office.

# CHAPTER *SEVEN*

## *Darrell*

*Though* it took a few days longer than I anticipated, Jackson caved and requested a meeting.

Of course I don't think I sealed the deal yet, but I at least have her attention, and with the things I've heard about her, that's enough for now.

After she requested that we arrange the meeting, I was admittedly a bit excited, but you never want to show too much eagerness. Though we had availability this week, I scheduled it for the following Monday instead.

Play it cool.

Sy and myself have just arrived at the bistro Nolan scheduled for us to meet at.

The two of them are already here and seated, though due to the small crowd making up the distance between us, Nolan is the only one I can fully see, whereas I see only the moving arm of his partner.

"Good morning, and thank you for trusting Delectables for your dining experience," The cheery host greets Sy'Asia and myself.

While my sister tells the host the party we're with, I take the time to browse through a few texts I couldn't give my attention to while driving and absentmindedly follow the steps of my sister and the host as we begin to walk towards our designated table.

"Please let me know if there is anything I can help you with, and in the meantime I will grab a couple waters for you."

As Sy thanks the young host, I finally look up from my screen, pocketing my phone and using the manners I was raised with, and I immediately wish I had that water in front of me.

"Darrell, Ms. Washington, it's so nice to be able to meet with you all." Nolan speaks as he stands from his seat.

His partner rises slower, more deliberate, like she wants you to know she won't rush herself on your behalf.

I'm silently upset at the dining furniture between us, as it blocks me from fully soaking in the dictator I've only met through a screen.

She stands about 5 foot 9, but considering she's probably wearing heels, I'll assume she's around 5 foot 6 flat.

A mane of curls surround her face with streaks of gold and brown, speaking to the ferocity she exudes without even uttering a word.

Her skin can be described as a deep copper tone, it looks as soft as silk.

Her eyes speak something of danger and disinterest. They're round, deep pools of chocolate. She looks at you as if she wants you to know she's passing judgment in her mind.

The pants suit she wears tells me that she isn't here to be charmed, and to my dismay, as soon as she looks at me, that is the only thing that I want to do.

“Ehem,” My sister clears her throat from beside me, shaking me out of the trance I was unexpectedly placed in. I notice all eyes are on me, it's now that I realize I haven’t yet spoken during the round of introductions.

The woman’s eyes are trained on me, judging me or awaiting my next move… at this point, maybe thinking I’m mute.

“Yes,” I cleared my throat. *Focus, man.* “My apologies. This is my older sister and our project manager, Sy’Asia Washington. Sy’Asia, this is Mr. Nolan, whom I’ve told you about.”

They shake hands as we still stand over the table.

“And, I take it this is Ms. Jackson?”

I attempt to coolly extend my arm to her from across the table. At least 3 seconds pass as she scrutinizes my hand as if she could get scabies from touching it.

Finally, she takes the offer and I wonder if I’m the only one that feels the air thin around us at the contact we make. But, considering the look she gives me, I’m sure I’m alone in that.

“Yes, this is Ms. Moriah Jackson. Moriah, this is Darrell, whom I met with last week.”

“It’s lovely to meet you Moriah-”

“Ms. Jackson,” She corrects me, with a proud lift of her chin before I can fully finish her name, “A pleasure, Mr. Washington,” There’s a practiced sharpness to her tone.

“Please, do call me Darrell,” I smile as I retract my hand.

Her only response is a tight lip.

We all sit.

As if on cue, our waiter brings out waters for Sy’Asia and I as well as take our orders. Without skipping a beat, as our waiter departs, Mor-... Ms. Jackson gets straight to business.

"I requested that we meet face to face as extended conversation via email can often lose not only its proper tone in delivery but also can just become blinding in a sense. Constantly reading words about the same subject with no direct communication. A lot can get overlooked or lost in translation at some point in time."

Her cadence is just short of robotic. If I thought for a second she builds any of her business relationships on personal connections, she obliterated that idea. I see why she sends Nolan as the front man.

"I can agree to that," I sip the water my mouth desperately needs.

"I'm not sure what of our history was discussed between yourself and Mr. Nolan, so forgive me if anything I say can be deemed repetitive. I believe it's imperative any potential partner or investor knows just a tad about our history as an organization before we discuss anything remotely concrete."

She says more to Sy'Asia than me, though I'm the one that had the meeting.

"Repetition is no issue to me, especially as I wasn't a part of the initial meeting in the first place," Sy'Asia responds.

Moriah nods curtly.

"Love Unbound was founded by the two of us during college. Neither of us were there for humanities or anything regarding the people, however it felt a bit like a calling once the idea was born. We've given countless unpaid hours of our lives to those in need, and would have not dreamt of requesting anything in return. Love Unbound was born out of personal relation to those we sought to help. I feel that to be an important note to keep so that it is understood that anyone we work with, in any regard, we'd want to actually support our cause. No matter any amount of money involved or any gains that can come of it that are outside of the ways our families and communities will benefit."

I wonder if she's ever given public speaking any consideration, she barely took a breath.

I look at Nolan who watches her face as she speaks, I can see the warmth between them and I can only imagine how long it must've taken them to get there if she's always put forth this sort of demeanor.

"Does Love Unbound only focus on low income households or are there other criterias to fit for assistance from your organization?" Sy'Asia asks with her notebook open and pen in hand. As project manager, she likes to fully understand the ins and outs of the companies we work with so as to help manage better.

"We focus on struggling families. Single parent or two parent does not matter. We recognize there's a fundamental or core need within the family that they cannot meet or recognize on their own, albeit clothing, housing, medical expenses - we do our best to help," Moriah answers with not a drop of infliction.

The two of them go question for answer for a few more rounds, long enough that our earlier ordered meals finally arrive.

Throughout their ping pong conversation, she periodically glances at me, I guess to keep me in the involved though I seem to have lost all the words I've had stored in my vocabulary.

Normally, it's me that leads these meetings, being a bridge between my own company and theirs. But no matter how many openings Sy'Asia provides or silent cues Moriah gives me, all I can do is watch her.

At some point Nolan becomes an active participant in the conversation as well while I remain an observer.

Seeing her, you can't help but to simply watch. She doesn't speak with much emotion, but she captivates your attention all the same, conviction and confidence in her every sentence.

"My next, and probably most important question is for you, Mr. Washington," Moriah addresses me directly for the first time since our being seated. Her eyes are low and dissociated, as if it's to remind she's only speaking to me out of obligation.

"You have a question, I have an answer," I respond, wiping my mouth from the bite I took of my breakfast taco. Meeting or not, if food is near, I will be eating.

"Why did you take interest in my organization?"

"Well, as I'm sure Mr. Nolan informed you, our clientele-"

"No," She cuts me off, I'm assuming this is a habit she has. "Why did you, personally, take interest in us?"

I can see in her weighty glare that this may be a test, and if I do not answer the correct way, this entire meeting will have been for nothing. I'm used to leaning on relatability, so all I can think to do is answer her honestly.

I take another sip of my water.

"Well, Ms. Jackson," I begin, "Your desire to help families whose structure at home is far from perfect hits a bit close to home for myself. I will not speak for my sister here, however I find myself drawn to organizations, individuals period, who have a desire to help children have a more healthy or stable home environment, as I was adopted by my grandparents as a child due to my mother realizing there were more important things in her life than motherhood."

Without looking at Sy'Asia, I can feel her posture stiffen. I know this even very slight overshare, will be a topic of conversation later.

Moriah doesn't say much, she doesn't need to when the quick widening of her eyes that she tries to mask do all the talking for her.

"I see, I'm sorry that you experienced that. No child deserves to be abandoned, especially by their mother," Is all she offers.

There's a silence that falls over the group.

"Yes, well, I do feel this meeting can be called productive," Nolan offers one of those young rich guy laughs.

"I agree," Sy'Asia chimes in.

"Ms. Jackson, Mr. Nolan, I do hope that any reassurances that needed to be addressed were soothed during this meeting and that you do take us into true consideration. We'd love to assist you in getting the grants and sponsors your organization and the families you help, truly deserve." She stands and extends her hand first to Moriah and then to Nolan who both mimic her rising.

"Yes, I agree with my sister and parrot the hope that you do take us into consideration to be of assistance to you," I shake Nolan's hand.

As he and Moriah round the table, I can now see just how much her burnt orange pants suit compliments her. My mouth dries again while I extend my hand for a parting handshake.

She stops at an arm's length distance from me.

It feels like an eternity passes with her gaze locked on mine before she meets my hand in the space between us.

"I do hope to hear from you soon, Ms. Jackson," My voice nearly cracks.

"Thank you for the meeting, Mr. Washington," She does not smile.

As Sy'Asia and I turn to depart, all I can think about is how badly I hope that we secure this deal.

# CHAPTER *EIGHT*

*Moriah*

"AJ, I tell ya, it's like cooking was etched into your DNA. You really ought to be a chef," My dad with his full belly sings his praises to my older sister, Adella.

He's not lying either.

Though we're only 5 years apart, she naturally assumed a motherly role during our childhood and despite my disdain for people wanting women to stay in the kitchen all day, it fits her perfectly.

"Daddy, it was no new recipe. You've eaten my jambalaya a thousand times," She humbly responds, she never did know how to take compliments.

"One time or a thousand times AJ, you always outdo yourself girl," Anastasia, who visited us for dinner, chimes in to praise my now blushing sister.

"Help me with the dishes, Stasi?" I began to collect the empty bowls that won't need much cleaning because we definitely did not leave a drop behind.

Anastasia follows me to the kitchen with the dishes I wasn't able to fit in my arms.

"So, you didn't get a chance to tell me, how did your meeting go?" She asks standing aside, waiting to be passed a dish to dry.

I take a deep sigh.

"It was a meeting for sure. At least the food was good," I focus on my hands at work in front of me.

"Oh…" She says. She knows I've been hoping to find an intermediary quickly, as we've parted ways with the company we once dealt with due to a conflict of interest.

"The project manager, who is also the sister, had her wits about her, she seemed to really know her stuff which was refreshing. It's just, the way Elijah praised this guy and then he gets in front of me and hardly utters a word the entire time," I tell her disappointedly, "He's supposed to be the one relating and selling, but he offered literally nothing intelligent the entire… well, almost the entire duration of the meeting."

"You trust Elijah though, no?" Anastasia asks gently.

"I do," Elijah has rarely ever made a bad business call, he's been my partner all these years for a reason.

AJ joins us in the kitchen to take care of the miscellaneous things lying about from preparing dinner.

"Then, just trust him. The worst this will do is put back your search a little, but you guys have been making it happen thus far on your own. With reward comes risk," Anastasia offers.

"I get the risk and reward thing, it's just weird that Elijah's version of this guy and the version I saw didn't align. I was actually a tad excited to meet someone who was even a little bit passionate about what we do, you know? But, the most he said was his introduction and the answer to a question I had to ask him to prompt him to… say anything."

"Not to eavesdrop," AJ says from her place at the island,

I know it was killing her to not speak from the moment she started listening to the conversation from the dining room, "But, just keep in mind, we all have off days, Mo. Not everyone can be on go like you at all times, cut the guy a bit of slack. If Elijah says that there's a different version that sold him, then believe it's there and you just caught him maybe after a rough meeting or something."

To be raised under the same roof, she and I tend to differ in so many ways.

Where AJ is all, 'cut him some slack' or 'sometimes people make bad decisions'... I believe in a one strike rule. You care for that one strike with all you've got, and if you mess it up, that's what you deserve for being careless.

"I hear you. But, 'off days' have no place at work, especially in important meetings with a company that *you* want the connection to. We aren't pining after them, they need us for their portfolio and the good karma our name comes with," I say.

Both she and Anastasia exchange a glance that they try to hide.

"Don't do that, I can literally see you," I tell them, it's like I can hear their thoughts. Calling me a hardass, telling me that everyone deserves consideration or a chance, whatever. I run a tight ship, either you sail or you sink.

"We aren't doing anything babe," Stasi responds on both of their behalf.

I look between the two of them while they stare back at me with so many unspoken offerings of advice on their minds, struggling not to say them all.

This has always been our trio.

AJ, being the mother that tries to get you to see it from a different perspective.

Anastasia, wanting to support you but will let you learn from your own mistakes if you have to learn the hard way.

And me, the one that absolutely must learn the hard way.

"I didn't say I made my mind up about working with them or not," I grow tired of their heavy silence, "I did like the sister though."

They do their silent communicative glance to each other again.

"You guys, seriously stop. I said I trust Elijah. If he thinks this guy and his company can help us, I'll give them a shot. A real one. The worst that can happen is they make us crash and burn and no grantmaker ever wants to give us money again. No big deal, right?"

# CHAPTER *NINE*

## *Darrell*

*I'm* not sure what Sy'Asia said to Anthony, but whatever it was moved him to 'suggest' I take a day off.

I never take a day off.

I won't complain about it today though, it's allowing me to spend some quality time with my absolute favorite lady.

"And another thing," My thoughts are interrupted by the ramble Honey was on, "You all work too hard as it is. One of the many things your gramps reminded me of way too often was all work and no play makes Jane a dull girl."

My grandfather perfectly balanced work and home before he retired a couple years before his death.

He rarely was late for dinner, he never missed a family day and he was always there not only for his wife's needs or "just because" quality time days but he also never missed one of my or my siblings' events.

He was damn near a superhero to us, being in multiple places at once without breaking a sweat or complaining. He never missed an opportunity to remind me that family is the most important thing a man can have.

*"It's your family that makes you a man. That's where you learn responsibility, reliability, integrity... that's where you learn how a man shows love to someone. It isn't all about going out and working overtime for money you won't be able to enjoy. It's about being a part of the foundation your home relies on, and the biggest part of being that starts with showing up."*

There's no man in this world I'd ever admire the way I admire him and there's no one that I wish to make proud more than him.

Losing him shook us in a way that I think we're only just now recovering from, barely.

Honey, especially, has never been the same.

They came from the time where the first person you look at is the one you spend your life with, and luckily for them, it worked out better than either of them imagined.

Well, better than Honey imagined.

Gramps said the minute he saw her, there wasn't a doubt in his mind that she'd become his wife. She just needed a little convincing.

He swore that when the time came, I'd have the same sense of knowing.

"Anyways, child," Honey again pulls me from my thoughts. "I'm a bit hungry. I want something sweet though and I can't think of what I can make around here for that," She stands with her hands on her frail hips and surveys the kitchen from her spot at the sink, as if ingredients will appear in front of her.

"Ah!" She snaps her fingers, "You know what I'll have?" A childlike gleam appears in her eye.

"No, but I figure this is the part where you tell me," I smile and sip her homemade iced tea. Seeing her excited about anything brings me a joy I can't explain, she could ask me to bring a star to her right now and I'd do my damndest to figure out how to get it for her.

"I think I'll have some grits and catfish. Only thing is, I don't have no catfish," She looks at me from the corner of her squinted eyes.

The doctor told her that it's time she starts to wear her glasses full-time, but she feels 76 is too young for her eyesight to go on her just yet. She sticks to readers, sometimes.

"Is that your way of asking me to run to the market?" Already grabbing my keys from the counter to the side of me.

"Well, I surely ain't getting it myself and they won't get here on their own, now will they?" Just as sassy as my childhood, and I'd have it no other way.

I place a kiss on her forehead and with a quiet chuckle head to my car.

---

For it to be an early Tuesday morning, the market is busy.

Not too busy for me to try another store, but busy enough for me to head straight for what I came for and beeline for checkout as soon as I can.

Since this is the neighborhood I grew up in and I'm with Honey so often, I know this market like the back of my hand so I don't have to roam to figure out where I'm headed.

Once my eyes lock on my designated section, I move towards it with vigor and determination to get to it as quickly as I can. I hate food shopping, this is usually my sister's sport.

Once I make it to the frozen section, I approach the counter of their fresh fish area.

Honey uses fresh ingredients only, I learned that the hard way. I once bought packaged fish instead because I didn't feel like waiting in the line and she threw an old shoe right at my head.

I don't take that risk anymore, an angry Honey is nowhere near a sweet experience.

I grab my ticket and step back so that others can easily access the counter for their own dealings.

I stand there scanning the other shoppers, waiting to hear my number called. My eyes land on a bush of curls not too far away, a familiar sense of the air around me disappearing occurs.

I can't see her face, but I know that's her.

The bouquet of curls that were once protecting her face now sit atop her head in what I guess some would call a bun.

She isn't wearing her pants suit, nor is she wearing heels. She looks much smaller but even with her back facing me she still invites my nerves into the room.

She sports a fitted white T shirt and jeans that look painted on but in the most respectful way one could mean that.

On her feet are all white vans.

I wonder if she feels me burning a hole in the back of her head with my eyes, if she does feel it I'm sure it's not a new feeling to her and that's why she doesn't turn around searching for her distant admirer.

Finally, she turns away from the freezer she stood in front of as she searches for vegetables and angles herself in a way that I'm just able to see a slither of her profile.

Even from this angle I can tell her face has that pensive expression it did at our meeting yesterday, and all she's doing is checking for an expiration date.

Before I can stop them my feet are moving towards her, abandoning my spot in line.

Being 6 foot 2 allows me to cover more ground in a short amount of time and thankfully so because I'm able to catch her just as she was pushing her cart to leave the area. But, catching her is all I do.

My eyes register that she's looking at me, waiting to give her an explanation for stopping her but my mind and mouth can't seem to get on the same page about what to say.

"So, it wasn't that you didn't want to speak yesterday… it was that you lack the ability to," She speaks first.

If she were anyone else, I'm sure that comment could've been a laughing point, but it's very obvious from her tone and lack of expression that she wishes to be anything close to comical.

"I'm sorry," I finally spit out.

*The hell is wrong with me?*

"I know I may have not put my best foot forward yesterday and dropped the ball. I'm sure what Nolan told you of the meeting between him and I was not at all reflected well by my… lack of participation."

She doesn't speak, just raises a single eyebrow.

I thought speaking to her in a group setting was daunting, but with it now just the two of us, I feel like a young boy that has to present a project by himself in front of a new class.

At least she hasn't turned away.

"I wanted to extend my apology-"

"You did that already, five seconds ago," There goes that habit of hers.

"Yes," I continue, "I wanted to extend that, but also say that isn't usually my role in any meetings I am a part of. Though this is no valid excuse in the game of business, I was a bit off kilter during our meeting. I take full accountability for not seeming interested or being able to properly regulate myself and show up better."

"Yeah, you left your sister to do all the talking when I'm assuming she was meant to be the listener that you became," She places her weight on one leg, causing her hip to pop out. A curve that looks more dangerous than a wet, mountain road in the dead of night.

*Darrell, focus.*

"You're right," I reply, "I want to assure you that all Nolan reported back to you regarding our meeting was truer to my nature and I promise, my… Our interest in working with you all is genuine. I've followed your organization for quite some time and I do admire all the work that you all do and who it's done for."

She doesn't respond. I'm not easily intimidated, certainly not by someone nearly half my size both in height and in mass, but her glare holds the weight of a bull.

"I-... I just saw you and wanted to say that. Normally, this would've been an email," I laugh, she does not, "But, I do believe that actual human interaction holds power, so I couldn't let you pass without actually hearing my apology."

She continues to stare.

"Number 172!" The worker calls my ticket number from a few feet away.

"That you?" She asks, causing my head to whip back in her direction.

"Yeah, yeah it is. I'm ordering some catfish for my grandmother. She only likes fresh ingredients," I give a half smile that she again does not mimic.

"Anyway," Time to wrap this up before I tell her my favorite comfort movie or something, "I do hope that you still consider us. Yes, we do see financial benefit and notoriety coming from this partnership. But, on a deeper level and beyond portfolios, what you do is something that is selfless and admirable. I meant it when I said I try to connect myself to those sorts of people."

"Organizations," She corrects, I don't catch on, "You'd be connecting yourself to the organization, not any people there," She says pointedly. She leaves no room for a misstep.

I nod, "Correct. The organization."

"172!" The worker calls again.

"Better get your fish before it's no longer fresh," She doesn't smile, but there is something softer in her face that I'm sure she didn't mean to allow slip through. She turns and walks away with her basket hanging from her arm.

I don't know if I convinced her or not, but for my sake I sure as hell hope I did. And if not, I wouldn't mind trying again.

# CHAPTER *TEN*

## *Darrell*

***Though*** I enjoyed my time with Honey, I did not enjoy being away from work.

When I returned home from the grocery store, my youngest sister and also best friend, Rayana, was there.

While my siblings and I all decided to devote ourselves to taking care of Honey, we devote the same care and attention to Rayana.

She was diagnosed with Lupus at the age of 9, so on top of her already being the baby of the bunch, she was also our sickly baby. We're all close, but without a doubt she's the sibling I'm closest too.

I've tried my hardest to help her have as close to normal of an experience as possible like her peers. But, there's always been a limitation and she's always forgotten she's as sickly as she is - so, it hasn't been an easy feat.

Thankfully, she's old enough now to recognize her limitations and while that doesn't always stop her from pushing herself a little too much, we trust her a bit more to make her own decisions. Though, of course, as older siblings it's a bit hard.

I'm back to work this morning and have just finished a board meeting.

While I go over my notes and some new tasks that were discussed in the meeting, a glimpse of Moriah's face flashes before me.

The unforgiving eyes that hold so much intensity she can make you question your own name if you look into them long enough.

Why she's crossing my mind in the middle of my morning I can only assume is because I'm subconsciously awaiting some sort of communication from her or Nolan.

I cannot recall a time I've single handedly aided us to fumbling a client, but I fear that this may be the one time I have.

It wasn't that I had nothing to contribute, hell, I bought a thick ass portofolio full of our prior clients that do similar work and I fully intended to explain why we'd be the perfect partners for them.

But for some reason I froze, and that's not in my nature, so to say I'm disappointed would be an understatement.

I've come across many attractive women at work.

I'm a normal functioning man in all the ways that can mean, so of course every now and again a beautiful woman may take a brief moment to appear in my thoughts.

It's fleeting though, it always is.

Except this one time when it isn't.

But I don't have time or the mindspace to figure out why or allow anything other than my priorities to last longer than a minute in my head, so I shake the flashing images of her face and eyes and lips, out of my head.

While I rest my head on the back of my chair and take a moment to regulate my thoughts, I hear someone enter quietly.

"Alright there?" Anthony asks me and I don't have to see his face to know there's scrutiny in his gaze.

I take a breath but don't adjust my position, "I'm fine. Just buried in emails since I was 'advised' to take a day off,"

"Sy'Asia suggested it, not me. And she still won't tell me why. Is there something I need to know?"

I lift my head to see him standing at my side with both hands stashed away in his pocket.

"No, who knows what she's thinking sometimes. Maybe she just took some pity on her kid brother who tirelessly works day and night and figured I deserved some time to myself," I offer a half smile.

Anthony isn't someone you really confide in with little concerns like having an off day during a meeting.

As kids, both he and Sy'Asia as well as my second older sister, Angeline, chose to stay with our mother, taking care of her while my youngest sister Rayanna and I stayed with Honey and Gramps.

So, while the two of us only had to worry about getting our homework done before dinner, the three of them had to worry about being prepared for whatever man she bought home or taking her to the bathroom quick enough for her to not throw up on the floor.

The only time he was awarded some normalcy was when they finally moved in with our grandparents. Sy'Asia & Ang came first, Anthony took a little longer to follow suit.

He struggled for so long.

It wasn't until a few years later that he finally started to relax. But when we lost Gramps, the walls came back instantly and haven't gone away since, like they never budged in the first place.

I try to show him that he doesn't have to bear the weight of the entire family on his own, but something in his head tells him only he can fulfill the duty as the head of the household, so I just fill in where I can.

"Well, if that was your bid for recognition or something, I do know that you work constantly, and it's appreciated," He says. He's not a sentimental man either.

I chuckle, "Thanks man. You okay?"

"Yeah, yeah I'm good," He responds unconvincingly, but I know my brother well enough to know to accept whatever he offers until he's ready to give more.

He stays for a few silent moments and then turns to exit my office, "By the way, that foundation you're working with, they emailed me accidentally. I think it was intended for you, an M. Jackson?"

I sat up a bit straighter in my chair when hearing her name.

"I forwarded it to you," He says as he exits.

I silently scold myself for hurrying to my emails at the speed that I do, but again convince myself it's solely because I was worried I'd failed my company and my family, for the first time.

Once my emails finally open, it's sitting right at the top.

To: djwashington@themiddlemen.net
From: enolan@loveunbound.org
CC: mjackson@loveunbound.org
Subject: Offer Acceptance

Good morning Darrell,

I hope this email finds you well.

After much intense deliberation, we have concluded that it would be in our best interests as an organization to move forward in this partnership.

As mentioned before, it is imperative that our partners, grantmakers, and investors truly believe in and support our cause and all that we aim to do for our and neighboring communities and the families that reside within them.

Ms. Jackson and myself have agreed that your company does just that and we are looking forward to seeing what this new partnership can lead to.

Please see the attached calendar invite to your next scheduled meeting with Ms. Jackson to discuss next steps.

All the best,
E. Nolan

I release a sigh of relief.

I don't know if it was my dramatic grocery store plea, if she just had a change of heart or if it had nothing to do with me at all.

Whatever it is, I'm glad it worked.

# CHAPTER *ELEVEN*

*Moriah*

*I'm* home early from the office today, a rare sight to see.

My dad and AJ aren't back from their daily outings so I have the house to myself. She tries to keep him active despite his whining about it.

People ask why I live at home still with the success I've made, but honestly, there's nowhere else I'd prefer to be. There's no need to leave the people I love the most just to be alone with my thoughts all day and night in an empty apartment.

College was probably the only time I'd been away from my family for such a long time, and even then I visited whenever I was able to. I tried the living away from home thing right after college with an ex, and… well, clearly that didn't go well.

A therapist once tried to convince me that it was abandonment issues or something like that. That was the last session we had.

It's not that I never leave them, I've gone on vacations and trips with Anastasia. It's just that once I do, I miss them soon after I've left.

I don't see what the issue is with loving your family.

While I still have the house to myself for a few more hours, I make a bowl of my favorite childhood cereal, lucky charms, and plop down on the couch in the living area.

As a kid, dad would sit with AJ and I, picking out all the marshmallows to make these super sticky, sugar filled treats we'd see recipes for on the back of the box.

While eating, I take in my daily dose of social media.

I scroll past pregnancy posts, gender reveals, engagement announcements and people hard launching their new partners. I never really subscribed to the idea of dating and love, I mean look what it does.

My father thought he and my mother were madly in love, thought they'd be a power couple and get married. But instead, she chose to leave him one random weekday afternoon and didn't think twice about how to help him with the two children she laid down with him to make.

Love has too many variables attached to it that I can not afford to juggle.

Just as I was preparing to close the app and turn on the TV instead, a post catches my eye.

It's one of those pop culture newsroom pages, but this time it isn't about some trashy celebrity gossip. It's a video clip of a man and two girls.

"I've been struggling to make ends meet since being laid off," The man speaks into the mic being pointed at him by the journalist. "I was wrongfully terminated and it was written off as a layoff. I have two daughters and they both have individual needs as well as of course our need for food and shelter. I've tried to pick up odd jobs here and there but of course they aren't really making a dent."

The camera pans to the two young girls standing right behind him, holding on to one another by the hand. The older sister protectively gripping her sister's hand a bit tighter than needed, but I recognize the feeling of a need for protection.

The older sister looked around the age of 13, the younger being around 9 years old maybe. Immediately I feel a pull in my chest.

The short clip concluded with the man offering his name and the shelter they were currently residing at, after being evicted from their apartment.

After the video is over, I put my phone and my bowl of cereal down and make a beeline to my laptop that I left on the island in the kitchen.

I waste no time opening my documents app and creating a rough to-do list, starting with finding the address of the shelter the man mentioned in the video.

I create an agenda to discuss for my next meeting with Darrell Washington, and figure maybe he'll be able to truly prove his words in the grocery store after all.

While I'm typing ferociously, AJ and Dad walk in the door.

"How are you home from work early, but still working?" AJ asks, seeing me from her spot in the living area.

Daddy doesn't waste his breath trying to walk from the door all the way to the kitchen, so he takes a seat on the couch instead.

I pick up my laptop and join them in the living room, taking a seat on the lounger.

"I just saw a video of a father and his two daughters. He says he was wrongfully terminated and because of that he's been evicted from his apartment and is staying at a shelter just outside of Tribune Heights while trying to pick up odd jobs."

"Oh my god, that's so unfortunate," AJ says, clutching her chest. It's obvious this is a story that would touch our hearts a little more than it would the average viewer.

"The girls are school age, one could definitely be menstrual age. Can you imagine a young girl having no privacy, going through your period in a shelter? And who knows how often dad is able to be with them," I say without taking my eyes off of my screen, still typing.

"So, what are you typing then?" My dad finally speaks.

"An agenda. He mentioned the name of the shelter they're at, I want to figure out the address and find out how I can help them."

"Of course you do," He responds with a warmth only a proud dad can have in his voice.

"I know they'd appreciate it, Mo, beyond words. And who better than you, of all people, to help them," AJ adds.

I stop typing and meet the eyes that are already on me. There's an emotion in my chest that I feel trying to climb up when I see my two biggest cheerleaders looking at me full of faith in me, but I fight against it.

"Yeah," I say, "I have a meeting with that Washington guy from the company Elijah connected us with. This is going to be our first project as partners."

"And I know you won't stop until they get exactly what they need," Daddy adds.

I offer him a tight smile.

I've helped many families over the years, and given much to the community. But there hasn't been a story that resembles mine this much, albeit a bit more dire than my own.

This may be my most important accomplishment with my foundation yet, and my dad is right - I will make sure they get exactly what they need. Let's just hope Washington proves to feel the same way.

# CHAPTER *TWELVE*

## *Darrell*

*I* sit in my car outside of the small cafe Moriah requested to have our meeting at.

I'm reading over the email for what must be the hundredth time, making sure I'm more prepared than I was for our initial introduction.

The email mentions a homeless family in need of shelter and that the father needs resume building assistance. It doesn't give too many details outside of that, I don't think a name was added either.

Honestly, the email seems like it was typed haphazardly.

It's 12:55 PM and we're supposed to be meeting at 1 o' clock. I figure it's a good idea to head in now, order something and find a seat. Better to be 5 minutes early than one minute late.

I exit my car and head towards the door.

As soon as I enter, the overhead chime takes me into a new world as I leave the quiet street behind me and am met with the hustle and bustle of other patrons.

Some placing orders, some catching up with friends and others seemingly like me, handling work matters.

After I place my order for a hot tea with extra lemon, I turn to browse the crowd and stop short when my eyes land on her.

She looks settled in at her table like she's been here for way more than 10 minutes, with her ipad and notebook already out as well as her food nearly finished.

Instead of waiting at the counter for my order, I roll my neck to release the tension I suddenly feel and make a slow stride towards the table she's seated at.

"Early bird, I see," A hello, thank you for giving me a chance probably would have sufficed, but here I am.

She looks at me through her lashes as she takes a sip of coffee. One thing I've noticed is she rushes for no one, I admire that.

"Early is on time, on time is late," She responds without eye contact as she focuses on placing her coffee mug back on its coaster properly.

"Funny, that's something my Honey used to say to my grandfather a lot," A chuckle escapes me at the memory. Gramps was never in a hurry, while Honey was always darting around. He never understood her urgency because according to him, there was time to spare. Honey believed if you had time to spare, that was the time to get going.

"Your honey?" She repeats back to me.

"Yeah, my grandma. We call her Honey."

She nods.

After a moment, I realize I'm still standing, looking down at her. I only notice this because her eyes ping pong between me and the empty seat across from her, silently asking me to sit down.

I take the hint.

Removing my jacket and placing it on the back of my chair, I take a seat and sit my bag that contains my own tablet and stationery at the leg of my chair.

"So," I begin to pull out the items from my bag and set them up, "Forgive me if I overlooked it, but I don't believe a name for this mystery family was mentioned in your email to me. It didn't provide much information honestly, but from what I gathered it's a homeless family who's been wrongfully treated somehow?"

"Yes, my apologies for that. I saw their story and immediately started typing afterwards. I didn't include much formatting or structure, my mind was moving a bit too fast but I figured we'd take care of the details here."

I hide my surprise at her admitting imperfection in any sense. She doesn't strike me as the type to be easily excited or frazzled, so to know she was too frantic to properly structure an agenda is… sort of comforting, letting one know she's more human than she sometimes appears to be.

"It's no issue, really. We can start sorting through the details now," I offer a tight smile and nod.

The barista I placed my order with brings my tea to the table during our conversation.

"Oh, thank you. You didn't have to do that," I take the tea from her hands, place it on the table beside my tablet and grab my pen to continue taking notes on the family Moriah is talking about.

"It was no problem," She smiles a bit too brightly.

I give her a thankful nod but quickly return my attention back to the woman seated across from me, away from the one clearly trying to get my attention.

She was pretty, very pretty. But women aren't hard to come by for me, and I don't say that to sound disgustingly conceited. It's been that way.

They see me entering a space in my suit with my laptop and folders, they see that as an invitation to start up a conversation, trying to get my attention.

I'm a meal ticket for them, and because being kind is in my nature, it only encourages them. But, it isn't in me to be anything but that, I just navigate it as best as I can.

One thing that stands out about the woman that sits across from me, she doesn't even bat an eyelash my way.

"Um, can I get you anything else?" She finally turns to ask Moriah.

"Yes, actually. Do you mind getting me another cup of hot chocolate please?" She asks in a tone I've not yet heard from her, it's sweet sounding.

"Sure can. Coffee creamer and whipped cream, right?" The barista asks as she takes the cup from Moriah's hand.

"Yes, please," She smiles, and the barista takes the cup away.

"Hot chocolate? I took you as a hot latte kind of girl," I say, offering what I think and hope to be a charming smile.

I can practically see the sweetness she offered our waitress moments ago, disappear.

"Hot chocolate has just always been a comfort drink. That's all," She clears her throat, "So, the name of the family is the… ah, the Henderson's. Markus Henderson is the father, I didn't note anything about girls names as they aren't released anywhere. I did confirm that they are 14 and 8 years old, and I couldn't find anything about their mother."

She reads off her notes as I type into my ipad.

"Okay. What's their circumstance that we know of so far?" I ask with my fingers still hovering my keyboard.

"So far, I've confirmed that he worked at a sheet metal factory and he was laid off. He said there was foul play at hand. Because of the lay off, they weren't to keep up with bills and ultimately got evicted from their place," She pauses for a moment and stares at the screen in front of her.

"The girls have struggled with school attendance because they also don't own a car and their school is a good distance away from the shelter they're currently placed at."

"Okay," I immediately start to jot down organizations that sponsor individuals in their predicament, "Got it. So, how do you plan on going about this? Are you looking to contact them first and help their story gain some traction then see who reaches out to you?"

"No," She says immediately, "Fathers pride aside, those girls are school age and absolutely bully-prone age. I'd never put them in a place of spotlight so that their peers could see them plastered all over the place and make their lives more hellish than it already is."

Her reaction takes me aback, her face twisted as if my question was ridiculous.

"That's actually very thoughtful. Not many people in your position would view it that way."

"Well, it's important to me that they aren't further traumatized than what they already probably are. Who knows what happened to mom, I don't want to place anything more on them than they can bear. Plus, if they have more on their plate that means dad does too, and he has enough to worry himself with, clearly," She adds.

I nod in response.

With her brows furrowed and mouth frowned, I can't help but to take her in more intentionally.

Her hair is tamed into a low bun at the base of her neck, she's wearing minimal makeup opposed to the first encounter we had.

Her attire is slightly more laxed too, as much as she could be I'm assuming, with high waist black pants and a plain white blouse. Walking towards her I noticed she didn't wear heels today but flat's that match her top.

In this meeting thus far I've only seen the same expressions from her. Focused, and more focused as she's kept her eyes primarily trained on whatever she's researching on the tablet in front of her.

The waitress brings out her whipped cream topped hot chocolate. She thanks her with the same sweetness she offered to her earlier, and I find myself wondering what someone has to do to be on the receiving end of her kindness.

"So, what's your course of action?" She finally speaks and immediately disrupts my train of thought.

With eyes on me, she lowers her face to the mountain of whipped cream that sits on the hot cocoa she holds and takes in a mouthful.

"Pardon?" I ask.

I've nearly forgotten why we're sitting here.

"To get sponsors," She enunciates each word the way you would for a small child, "What's your plan?"

"Ah, yes. Well," I take a quick sip of my tea that's now cooled off, "I take this case to my team, primarily Sy'Asia, and we compile a list of organizations and individuals that we know prefer to take on "projects" similar to this. I'm sorry to use that term, as they're people and not a school assignment.

Um, and then we have someone to write their story in the most tear jerking light and go from there."

She nods attentively.

"Okay," She replies, "And, thank you for the apology for using that term. I hate referring to any of my families that way. I hate even more that to a lot of sponsors and organizations, that's all that they are."

"Of course. I wouldn't want to be addressed that way so I'm sure they wouldn't either."

Her mouth twitches, she nods her head and returns to her ipad.

After a few moments of silence, I can't stop myself from asking, "What brought you here? To this career choice and foundation?"

Her hand stops moving, hovering the screen of her iPad.

Her eyes take their time to meet mine, "I care about those who've been let down, abandoned in one way or another." She offers a smile that isn't really a smile, "We support families we see ourselves in, one way or another."

Her answer makes me more curious than I was initially, but I know that's all I'll get so I don't press any further. I go back to writing my own notes.

I know that Love Unbound was an idea born solely out of her own head and she bought Nolan on later.

What I don't know is what her story is or how she acquired such a passion to help families the way she does. Suddenly though, it's something I almost desperately find myself wanting to find out.

# CHAPTER THIRTEEN

## Moriah

After my meeting yesterday with Washington, I've been tapping on the shoulders of resources I've previously worked with to assist the young Henderson girls with clothing and tutoring to get them back on track for schooling.

"So, we get to the restaurant and he orders literally my entire meal from the appetizer to the dessert. As if I can't think enough for myself to decide what I want to have for dinner. I don't even like zucchini!"

I'm meeting with Anastasia during happy hour for our weekly catch up. She's in the middle of telling me about the date she had this past weekend with some trust fund asshole.

This has always been her tribulation, people treating her like a porcelain doll and not like an individual who can make her own decisions.

I've witnessed so many guys come into her life and treat her like a shiny trophy opposed to a partner. She gets enough of that from her family.

"Where do you keep finding these men, Stasi?"

"I'm not, that's the problem. My parents continuously play the bachelorette with me and the sons of their associates. I'm

29, I can pick my own men. Every time I remind them of that, my dad goes into the whole 'I don't want you have to kiss toads to find your prince' spiel. I just-" She sighs.

"To be fair," I say through a full mouth, "They just started letting you pick your own clothes. I highly doubt he's about to let you pick a man." I try to make light of the situation, but the laugh I earn is more sad than humorous.

"Enough about my life in prison, what about you? How's it going with that family you mentioned?"

"Well," I sit up a bit straighter, "I haven't reached out to them yet, I wanted to conjure a plan and strategy before I talk to them. So they know exactly what is within their reach."

"Okay, okay. You and Elijah have been in the lab I'm assuming, figuring out your first steps?"

"Actually, I've talked to Darrell about it more than I have Elijah so far."

She stops sipping her drink to raise her eyebrow at me.

"I just figure since they're our intermediary, I might as well start there, let them know the sort of things we're looking at for this specific family and their needs so that he, or they, can be working on the backend while we're working up front. You know?" I respond.

"Yeah, I know," She smirks at her mimosa, "How did the meeting with Darrell go?" She says in name in a slight singsong cadence.

"It went well," I say pointedly, "By the time I was done running through their situation with the few details that I do have, he'd already started writing down sponsors he thinks would be a good fit."

"That's good. So, he seems like he's interested in helping the family instead of just being interested in the network ladder his company will be climbing from working with you all?" She gives a voice to the concerns I've tried to push to the back of my mind.

"It's still pretty early. Anyone can put on a front, you know?" I push my food around on the plate in front of me, "But, so far he seems to be honoring his word. Plus, he doesn't seem as incompetent as I initially thought he was. He offered some pretty good strategies for when we start presenting the family to sponsors directly." I take a forkful of my food into my mouth.

Her eyebrows shoot to her hairline.

"What?" I try to ask with a mouthful.

She shakes her head slowly, "Nothing," Smirking, she replies, "I'd just be careful. I can't remember a time you've ever commended a man for not being an idiot in some regard."

"I can't compliment someone for having a brain?"

"You absolutely can, it's just that you never do," She smiles as she takes a bite of her own food.

"Don't make me regret it, Stasi," I continue to eat my food, "Anyways, how is the job search going?" I ask to change the subject.

Anastasia has a job of course, but it's for her parents' luxury travel business.

Because it's her parents, they created some unheard of position doing little to nothing, just because they were tired of hearing her complaining about not being a normally functioning adult in the real world.

So, she's planned to go rogue and find a real job with actual work.

"It's… going. Most of the places I've sought out ended up having some sort of connection to my parents. Either the owner knows them or they're regular clientele and once they realize who I am, the door essentially closes after the "does your family know you're applying here" question pops up,"

I nod in response.

"I just don't know what to do Mo. I can't continue to allow them to shelter me at this huge age, but I also can't act like I'd know what to do if I go work in a low-end retail store."

"Well, what do you feel you're most capable of?"

She looks stunned, which I'm sure she is. I doubt anyone has ever asked her of her own talents and skills.

"Well, I like analytics and data. I feel like I'd be really good at note taking, I'm really good with fine details too," She says somewhat confidently.

"How do you think you'd do in office management?" I ask, still feeding my face.

"Um, I guess I'd do well. I was always good at leading projects in college, though that was eons ago. I was always nominated in groups to give out the tasks and stuff," She shrugs her shoulders.

I nod again.

"Well, with our office starting to grow, and Elijah and I having other things to focus on, it's sort of hard managing what's going on as well as focusing on our own tasks," I say.

She just stares at me, like she's waiting for me to continue,

"So, it would be a real help to have someone manage the day to day tasks and take that off of our plate."

Her eyes widened, "Are you offering me a job?"

I laugh, "Yes, Miss I'm good with detail."

"Oh my goodness!" She squeals, "I'd love that Mo, oh my god."

"Now, I can't promise you the same pay as a luxury service job does, but I can do my best to get close to it," Though, who are we kidding, she literally does not need the money.

"Whatever you give is fine, it's not about the money at all. This is like my first step to freedom."

I laugh at her excitement.

For the next few minutes she rattles out all the things she's excited to do in her new position and how she's excited to prove herself.

And while I love that for her, I can't rid my mind of the fact she was right. I rarely have kind words to offer men in any regard and how concerning it is that after having that meeting with Darrell, all I can think of are kind things to say about him.

---

The next day I cash in on that family day request my dad made a little while ago.

The three of us caught a movie, something we definitely have not done as a family in years. Then we went to a small, family owned diner in town for lunch and I had the absolute best fried salmon ever.

We finish off by spending a few hours in the park he used to take us to as children after school or on weekends.

"You know," My dad says after we've all picked a bench to rest on, he may be the older one here but I think all three of us can relate to a lack of stamina than what we had all those years ago, "I'm thankful for you girls." He places either hand on each of our knees, "I really am. You've kept me young when I'm sure I'd be otherwise laid up in a bed right now being spoon fed by some nurse that smells funny." He chuckles.

We both laugh.

If it's one thing my father will do, it's try to refrain from making a sentimental moment too heavy.

"We're thankful for you dad, way more than you should be for us. All we can do is our best to repay you for everything you've done." AJ responds with a hand over the one that's on her knee.

"I second that," I add, "Who knows how either of us would have turned out if it hadn't been for you making all the choices you've made on our behalf? We're just trying to pay you back."

He smiles, "I think you both would've turned out just fine either way. I'm very proud of the women you have become so far."

Silence befalls us again.

"Okay well, enough of the heavy. Let's get to the grocery store before it starts to get crowded," AJ stands from the bench.

"Actually, I can take dad to the store, A. I don't mind," I tell her, standing from my seat next.

"Are you sure? It's fine honestly, this is literally just a part of the routine," She replies hesitantly.

"Yeah, I'm sure. You take a little time to yourself, you never get any," I offer my father a hand, while she takes the opposite one and we help him to his feet.

"Um," She looks to both of us, giving dad an extra once over, "I mean, yeah. Okay. I guess you can just drop me off at home?"

"Yeah, and text me the list of what we're getting. Trusting him to tell me will have us with a cart full of those peanut butter & jelly snacks sandwiches he loves and rice cakes."

We both laugh as we start to walk to the car.

After dropping off my sister, we arrive at the grocery store just as the parking lot looks like it's starting to fill up.

Luckily the list my sister sent me isn't a long one, so despite the crowd that's starting to form, we should still be able to make this a quick trip.

I'm about to exit the car before my dad stops me.

"MoMo, I meant what I said about how proud of you I am."

It was random, so I looked at him a bit confused because I never questioned the sincerity of what he said.

"I know dad," I laugh, "Did I look like I didn't believe you?"

"No, I know you believed me. I just wanted to remind you. You've accomplished so much from a young age and you've been running nonstop ever since you started your business,"

I take this time to settle back in my seat, because I feel there's more to this.

"I just wanted to tell you Moriah… don't forget why you do all this. I know you don't say it, but I'm your father and I know you. While you're moved by love towards others and your heart is in the right place, I know that what's driving you is pain. Resentment."

My shoulders sink a tad. I want to counter his words, tell him he's wrong and this has nothing to do with resentment for my mother and leaving us. But, I can't tell if that's true, so I just listen.

"I know you've held on to that hurt, the loss, sort of speak, of your mother but you can't let that pain be your motivation, Mo. You're accomplishing so many things for people and impacting so many lives with your actions. But, how are you going to really appreciate what you're doing if you're working from a place of vengeance? Making yourself hold on to that, it's going to soil any ground for love. Because you're so focused on making sure no one feels the sort of pain you're feeling, you're going to miss out on letting someone come in and soothe that pain for you."

My father has always been emotionally available to both my sister and I. And he's always corrected our paths when he could spot danger ahead.

But this, this is not a conversation that we've had before nor one that I expected.

I don't know how to respond because I'm too busy fighting off the tightness that's in my throat and the water begging for freedom from my eyes.

"I know you didn't expect all of that, and I know you may not have anything to say right now which is fine. I didn't say it for you to have a response. I just want to remind you, that when you hold on to pain, you take up all the space that's supposed to be held for love."

All I can do is nod my head to my father, who I know worries about me.

I'm too young to remember when my mom left, but I saw the effects it had on us. My father was great, but there are some things a dad just can't do on his own, and that wasn't his fault. It was hers.

Once I realized that difference, my bitterness was born.

I soon thereafter exit the car and help him out of the passenger side.

He holds on to my arm tighter than he'll acknowledge because he refuses to use the cane that was given to him by his doctor, the pride on this man is the size of Texas.

As we enter the market, I leave him for a moment to grab a shopping cart. As I turn around to head back to my fathers side, I bump another moving cart and immediately offer my apologies.

"I'm so sorry, I was moving way too-" I stop when I look up to see who was pushing the other cart and the rest of my sentence fades off of my tongue once I make eye contact with Darrell.

"It's fine." He offers a small smile, "I'm sure you didn't break it."

I don't smile back, but I notice unlike most times, it takes effort to maintain my expression..

"Getting some weekly shopping done?" He asks, as if we aren't in the grocery store both pushing carts right now. I accidentally allowed a small and quick chuckle to escape me.

"Yes, that is what one typically does in the store," I respond.

"Um, DJ." The older woman that stands not too far from my father speaks. "Are you going to introduce me to your friend or can we skip to shopping? My legs won't hold me all day."

I bite back another fighting smile at her snarkiness.

"Sorry, yeah. Honey, this is Mo- Miss Jackson. She's the founder of the foundation we've recently begun to work with."

We exchange smiles and I approach her with an extended arm, "Nice to meet you… Ms. Honey?"

She laughs.

"Honey will do, baby, Miss grandma doesn't exactly have a ring to it. Nice to meet you as well."

"This is my dad, Mr. Jackson," I introduce my father who hasn't spoken but has kept his eyes on Darrell during the entire exchange so far. "Dad, this is Mr. Washington,"

Darrell shakes his hand, "Darrell. Nice to meet you, Mr. Jackson. I do have to commend you on the woman you raised, she's very no nonsense and runs a tight ship," He laughs, "It's been… entertaining, thus far, partnering with her and her company."

My dad takes in a deep breath, "A tight ship?" He laughs, "Yeah, you're right about that. Been that way since she was sharing toys with the kids in the neighborhood. A dictator by nature, but a great one for sure," He adds and looks at me with endearment in his eyes.

I turn back to Darrell who already has his eyes trained on me, but says no more.

"Well…" I say into what feels like a suddenly awkward space, "I guess we should get going. My legs aren't going to hold me all day either," I look at Honey as I say the last part. That earns me a laugh, and the sound of it for some reason tugs at me.

"Yeah, right. We probably should get to it too if I want dinner tonight." Darrell says.

I offer a tight lipped smile and nod, only he doesn't move yet.

"Getting to it would require going down an aisle, son." Honey taps him.

He chuckles awkwardly, gives a parting nod and they turn away to begin their shopping.

"So, that's your new partner, huh?" My dad asks as he loops his arm back through mine while we begin to walk.

"Yup, for the time being." I respond.

He hums and only offers a curt nod and thankfully says no more.

I know exactly what he's thinking, and I'd rather those thoughts remain unspoken.

# CHAPTER *FOURTEEN*

## *Darrell*

*It's* raining and nearing the end of my work day, all I can think about right now is going home and laying in my bed.

I put out two fires today.

One due to a client not liking the way Anthony communicated with one of their team members, saying he talked down to the young employee. I can't say I don't believe them, but I know he doesn't do it intentionally. His default communication style is asshole HR.

The second was between one of our newer staff members and Sy'Asia who felt the staff member was incapable of completing what she deemed to be simple tasks in their position.

Was she wrong? Maybe not. Did she need to call the girl an incompetent child and have her run out of her office crying? Also, maybe not.

I think emotions are just high on all ends this week, Rayana says it has something to do with the stars or some shit.

I'm in the last meeting of the day and thankfully it's just a check-in.

"Where are we at with Love Unbound?" Anthony points the question to me.

"They accepted our offer, finally. Moriah and I met not too long ago to discuss a new family she's come across that is in need of some urgent assistance," I answer as I impatiently tap my pen on my notepad.

"Ms. Jackson?" Anthony responds, with an arched eyebrow.

"Hm?"

"Ms. Jackson, you referred to her as Moriah but from what I've heard, she's very strict about professional regards."

"Yes, yeah," I clean it up, "I guess because I'm a bit more informal with her partner, I just naturally extended it to her. But yes, I'm referring to Ms. Jackson."

Skeptically, he says "Okay," as he jots something down, "So she's currently got her eye on a new family to assist with sponsorship?"

"Yes."

"I'll try to reach out to her first thing in the morning to set up a meeting and further discuss that," Sy'Asia chimes in, typing on her laptop.

"For what?" I ask almost too quickly.

She scrunches her face at me, "So that I can do my job? What do you mean?"

"I think I should continue working with her, actually. With them," I don't look either of my siblings in the eye.

"And why would you do that?" My sister turns her chair towards me.

"Because, we all know the reputation Jackson has of being tough to get through to and deal with as a client. I've already established that line of connection and trust with her and

Nolan, so instead of working from the ground up all over again, I think it makes more sense for me to just continue working closely with them."

We both look to Anthony who hasn't spoken but I know has something to say. His attention is set on me, it's weighty.

"I think Sy'Asia is just as capable as you of establishing trust with our clients, do you disagree?"

Sy'Asia looks to me for my response.

"No, I mean yes, I agree. But, would you not agree this case is a bit different, as the client is notoriously known for being hard to please or convince? I was able to convince her to give us a shot. Clearly I've already made some headway," I defend.

My brother adjusts in his seat.

We sit in silence for a few seconds before he decides to speak again.

"I don't need to remind you that any personal interest beyond that of the project at hand can and likely will create issues, right? I figure I shouldn't have to, since you're our most praised team member."

I hear exactly what he's saying without saying it.

"You don't need to remind me," I respond guardedly.

He stares at me for a few minutes more, "Good then,"

Sy'Asia and I both sit in silence as we await whatever he's to say next.

"I do agree that since you've made this much traction thus far, and are capable of handling a project yourself, that it may be a good idea to just continue on that path."

I hold my sigh of relief.

"But," He adds, "I do advise you still report anything of importance to Sy'Asia or major changes. You're to keep her closely updated."

"Will do," I click my pen a few times, not sure where else to release my nerves.

"And you do well to keep in the forefront of your mind the reputation that we uphold as an establishment. A very clean reputation, with no scandals or misconduct," He says as if I told him I'm going to fuck this woman at our next meeting.

"That never leaves my mind, brother," I respond to him calmly.

"Good."

I meant what I said, I think it makes sense that I'm the one that continues this project with Moriah and her team and for the reasons that I stated. I didn't pull that out of my ass.

But, what I refuse to mention is that I also don't want to lose access to her.

Why? I'm not sure.

And, I'm also not comfortable with trying to figure it out, in case that it's a reason I won't know what to do with.

# CHAPTER FIFTEEN

## Moriah

When Darrell reached out to have a secondary meeting about the Henderson's, I was surprised and admittedly excited.

I've met so many men associated with potential partnering companies who said they cared about the cause we stand for, only to find out they only cared about finding their way into my pants.

I've been putting together a catalog of resources for the Henderson's to make use of when the time comes to finally meet with them and get our ball rolling. I assume Mister Washington has been putting in similar work.

Instead of meeting at a restaurant or bistro as has become our pattern, he requested that we have the meeting at his office.

When I arrive at the address he included in the email, the building I'm led to is massive.

He included directions in his email of how to reach his company's floor. I check in with the building's secretary as directed, go through security, get scanned and have my belongings checked.

You'd think the president secretly uses this as an office space with the measures they go through.

When I reach the elevator, I press the button that'll take me to

the 13th floor, as directed.

When I step off, I walk on to black marble floors that are so shiny I can see my reflection in them.

There's a receptionist that sits not too far away at a large cockpit receptionist desk as black as the floors.

I approach the young woman.

"Hi, good morning," I offer a smile, "I'm scheduled for a meeting with Mr. Washington,"

She chuckles, "Which one?"

I forgot there was a brother. I assume he handles the backend of things while Darrell handles the front, sort of like Elijah and I.

"Darrell."

She types something into her computer, "One moment,"

She presses a few buttons on a contraption in front of her that looks like a keypad that should have a phone attached to it. She then taps at a tucked away ear piece that's covered by her hair.

"Good morning," She says seemingly to no one, "Yes, your 10:30 appointment has arrived," I assume she takes a moment to listen to his response, and ends her call with an "Okay,"

She types something else on her keyboard, "Please follow me," She says as she stands from her seat and exits her station.

She leads me down a hallway with walls that match the floor, occasionally turning into glass, as they serve as walls to offices.

After walking down what felt like a never ending path, we reach one of the glass offices, only this one, like two others, is frosted.

"Here you are," She offers a polite smile and opens the door, ushering me in.

As I walk in, Darrell immediately begins to track me from my place at the doorway as I make my way to his desk. I also notice that there is a third person in the room with us whose back is facing me as they sit opposite of him, next to the empty seat I'm walking toward.

I feel a pang in my chest that could almost be mistaken as disappointment, but that wouldn't make sense.

I don't give it my focus.

Darrell stands, "Ms. Jackson, I appreciate you joining us," He says a bit stiffly, smoothing out imaginary wrinkles in his tie. "You remember my sister and our project manager, Sy'Asia?" He gestures to her, I hadn't taken notice that she's stood to her feet by the time I reach the two of them.

She offers her hand to me, I shake it.

"Yes, of course. It's a pleasure to see you again," I offer what I try to make of a sincere smile.

"Please, have a seat," She says, as if we're in her space and not Darrell's. We all sit.

"Well, Ms. Jackson," He doesn't tend to address me by name, and despite the unspoken boundary I set during our first encounter, him addressing me so formally doesn't sound right to my ears. I hide my disdain for it.

"Ms. Washington and I wanted to call this meeting to discuss a few adjustments in our dealings moving forward."

I do my best to shake any side thoughts that are not relevant in this moment and focus, I shouldn't be having them anyway.

"Typically, after our initial coming together, Sy'Asia would become our client's point of contact, as she is our project manager," He gestures with his hands as he speaks, she nods as if to approve of what he's saying.

"However, after some discussion, we found it best that I remain your primary point of contact with assistance from Sy'Asia, as we thought since Mr. Nolan, you and myself have already begun to establish that line of professional trust, it would be no point to start at ground zero basically."

I nod and try to ignore whatever this lightness is that I feel in my stomach, maybe I ate something that isn't agreeing with me.

"I agree. Not that I don't think you're great, Ms. Washington," I give what I call a professional laugh, "I just am, like anyone I'm sure, a person who appreciates familiarity and constants. Mr. Washington has been a constant since our beginning our work journey together," I look at him as I finish my sentence.

I'm not sure why now, but I've never taken him in, truly.

There's a certain depth that hides right behind his dark brown eyes and it's always there.

There's something innocent there, but also something… that I can't give language to.

His skin is a rich brown, with a jawline too prominent to be hidden behind his slightly closed shaven beard. I also didn't realize until now how prominent his arms are even through his semi-loose fitting shirt.

It's not until Sy'Asia speaks that I remember she's in the room with us.

"However," She speaks into the previously silent space, "I will still be closely monitoring in a sense. Not that Darrell can't handle it, but well, it's actually my job to be doing this and for whatever reason our brother agreed with this familiarity spiel."

I can tell she in fact did not agree with her brothers. If I was her, I wouldn't agree either.

I nod again, "Understood, that's totally fine."

Silence falls over us again, this time the awkwardness is louder than I'm comfortable with.

"Well then," Darrell claps his hands, "Since we're already gathered here, maybe it's a good time to go over what we have so far for this family and get Sy'Asia's insight," He offers an anxious smile.

I agree and take my laptop out of my bag as the two of them set up their devices as well.

As they set up, I can't stop myself from sneaking glances of Darrell over my laptop. And if I were any less sane, I'd swear I'd seen him catch my eye a few times, glancing at me in return.

I'm not exactly sure of what's happening right now, this tension that's growing here in this space between the two of us but I doubt it's even close to a good idea.

# CHAPTER SIXTEEN

## Darrell

"I've been thinking about your grandfather's memorial celebration this year," Honey says from her seat at the head of the dining.table. It's not often all four of my siblings are present at once for dinner, but we try to make it happen as often as we can.

"What've you been thinking?" Rayana asks.

While Honey is my person, Gramps was hers. She'd always be at this hip even before she was tall enough to reach it.

"I want to have a barbecue this year & invite everyone, your aunts and cousins too. Instead of keeping it between us, I want to invite those who loved him and those he loved beyond us."

"Which was basically everyone," My sister Angeline laughs. She isn't around as often as the rest of us, she's the only one of us with kids and an entire household to maintain while working.

But, she makes sure to come around when it matters.

"A barbecue sounds good Honey," Ray gives her approval of the idea.

Honey smiles and nods at my sister. Though she wasn't asking us for our input, she knows what Gramps meant to Rayana, so her input holds some weight in Honey's heart.

A comfortable silence befalls our table.

"I can't hold onto this anymore," Sy'Asia says suddenly and captures all of our attention.

"It's been a few weeks now, and I tried to think nothing of it. I certainly didn't think it was a good idea to bring it up at work as of late," She takes a breath, "But it's just been replaying in my mind since it happened."

All focus in the room is on her for those few silent minutes, and suddenly I get the feeling that I know where this is going.

"We know that DJ would literally rather sweep up the ocean than ever acknowledge that anyone but Honey is our mother, or any of the things that happened prior to moving in with Honey and Gramps," She continues.

Eyes start to bounce from her to me and back to her.

"But, during our meeting a few weeks ago with that Jackson woman, he brought it up like it was nothing. He said that he understands and appreciates the cause she fights for because he was abandoned as a child."

I hear an audible gasp from Angie, and a "Seriously?" from Rayana. Anthony and Honey say nothing.

"My job is to get our prospective client to see why they should want to work with us. That's all that I was doing. I didn't go into any detail other than that it touches the heart of someone who can understand a struggle similar to the one of some of the families she helps," I say in defense.

"You barely wanted to answer questions about it in therapy, but suddenly it's a talking point in a meeting because of her work? Hers isn't the first foundation we've worked with, but you've never brought it up to them," Anthony responds in a calmer than expected tone.

"Because we didn't need those partnerships the way we do this one, you know that. We're aiming to have a specific clientele, and we're looking to branch out our network. Her foundation, though still young, has gained traction and notoriety. The people we want connections to are looking to invest into her foundation because it makes them look good. So yes, I pulled out some big guns to solidify the deal."

I say it all in one breath and every word has a bad taste.

I hate talking about any interaction I have with her as if it's strictly business, even though it is, it doesn't feel right.

Talking about her like she's just another client.

As if it's not hard to look away from her when I'm in her vicinity, or like I don't stumble over my words when I'm usually the smoothest talker in the room.

But none of that is their business, and I won't let anyone question me as a professional just because I shared one moment of transparency about something I tend to avoid.

I can't tell if Anthony believes my words or not, but it's not hard to see that Sy'Asia does not. But I can't care about too many things at once right now.

Anthony wipes his mouth of the invisible food particles around it and sips his glass of water.

"I don't know much of that is exactly true. But, what I do know is, we are also still considered a young company. One that is spoken highly of when it comes to our client care. I'm not sure what it is that's been going on with you lately, but I suggest you do well to not allow it to affect that reputation."

There was no inflection in his tone from start to finish, telling me all the more that it was a warning more than a professional concern.

"I don't need reminding. I've been good thus far, I'll be fine," I nearly growl.

Silence and tension fall between us, when finally someone speaks.

"I let that conversation happen, but know that is the last time I want to hear business matters discussed at this table," Honey tells the three of us, "Now, what's the name of this woman?" She looks at me, snapping me out of the glare I have casted on Anthony.

"Huh?" I respond to her inquisitive expression.

"This woman your siblings are talking about. What's her name?"

"Moriah," I answer shortly.

"Hm," She pushes some food around her plate, "Isn't that the name of the woman from the market the other day?"

I'd totally forgotten she was with me that day.

"Yes, yeah it is."

She smiles to herself and nods.

"What Honey?" Rayana asks her. For once, I'm not bothered by her nosiness.

"Nothing," She smiles into her glass of water, "Just wanted to know the name of my future granddaughter-in-law," She maintains her smirk as she takes a sip.

While Rayana furrows her brows in confusion, Anthony's scowl deepens and my own heart skips a beat. Not because I agree, but because Honey has always had this special gift of knowing and this is one time I don't have an argument.

---

I set aside time to spend with Rayana one on one as often as I can, so the following day that's exactly what I do.

She's been my shadow ever since we were kids and adulthood didn't change that. Because she's the youngest and because we don't encourage her to work, I don't have to ask if she gets lonely sometimes or feels like Rapunzel in a locked tower. So, I do what I can to curb that as best as possible.

Today, I made it all about her.

I took her out for breakfast, we went to the mall to splurge at some of her favorite shops along with one of her childhood friends.

I did all I can to keep the smile on her face that I love so much.

We didn't really know how to navigate her illness at first. Constant hospital visits, as many specialists as my grandparents could think to consult.

I can't imagine how many thousands of dollars went into getting her the best care they could. It took a long time for them to realize that no matter how many doctors you see, this wasn't something medicine or a procedure could fix.

But, despite that being her reality she was the most optimistic of us all. She always kept a smile on her face and tried to live her life to the fullest, still doing all she could to ward off any episodes, though there isn't much she can do except manage her diet and take care of her body as best she can.

I noticed that her energy is starting to wind down, so I suggest we go to her favorite restaurant for some lunch after dropping off her friend and heading home.

"Did you have fun?" I ask her as I open the passenger side door and escort her out of the car.

"I had so much fun DJ, thank you. I feel like we haven't had a chance to hang out in forever, I've missed you big brother." She smiles and nudges my arm.

Though she tries to make light of it, there's still a sad air around us.

It has been forever since I've taken out time for her, and I'm disappointed in myself for that. Work has really taken the driver seat in my life and while I haven't let it get in the way of caring for Honey, Rayana became a casualty.

"I've missed you too Ray, I really have. I'm sorry I've been so busy."

"Don't be. Someone's got to make the money for me to spend." She laughs

We reach the entrance of the restaurant and I open the door allowing her to walk in first.

"God, I'm so excited. I can smell the kitchen from here," She bounces from foot to foot like a giddy toddler as we await to be seen and seated by the host.

"Good afternoon! Are we seating for just the two of you today?" The host finally asks from behind her lectern as she gathers two menus in her hand.

Before I can answer, Rayana nearly squeals "Yes," With a grin that could light up the dining area all on its own.

She leaves her spot and begins to lead us towards our designated seats.

Rayana continues to talk to me about the places she plans to wear some of the new outfits she bought today and I mindlessly nod and throw in a *"Oh yeah?"* So she doesn't feel ignored, though I am a bit burnt out from her energy today.

We reach a table with two chairs at either side. I pull out her chair for her, waiting for her to sit and my body freezes as I go to push her closer to the table.

"DJ? What's wrong?" I hear my sister say to me from her seat, though I'm having trouble meeting her eyes when my own are locked on that mane of curls with streaks of gold and brown.

Moriah is here, just a few feet away, laughing at whatever the woman sitting across from her is saying. I'm sure she hasn't noticed me at all, so immersed in her own world.

"DJ!" Rayana says louder, breaking my trance.

"Yeah, yeah I'm sorry," I say, rounding the table to the chair opposite of her, my back now facing the only woman that's been too frequently and too easily causing me to lose my focus.

"What's the matter? You look like someone on the run who just saw the dirty cop that's been hunting him down," She watches entirely too much TV with Honey.

"Nothing's wrong," I quickly glance back and then to Rayana again who now has a pinch of concern between her brows, "Moriah, the woman Sy'Asia was talking about the other night at dinner, she's here."

Her eyes light up with mischief.

"Where?!" Her head begins darting in every which way, extending her neck at times to try and see past me.

"Ray, stop!" I quietly yell to her.

"Where is she?! I want to see!" She whispers back to me.

I sigh, knowing I'll regret giving her a face to the name.

"She's to my left in that small booth in the back. Curly hair," *And a yellow top that brings out the highlights that crown her, a slight redness on her cheeks that make her smile even more beautiful and lips smothered with gloss I secretly want to ruin with my own.*

But, she doesn't need all those details to find her, she's hard to miss.

"Oh…" I can sense immediately when she spots her, "She's actually kind of beautiful."

I huff out a laugh, *Tell me about it.*

I don't look back especially now with Rayana doing enough gawking for the both of us. But, the brief glimpse I caught of her in absolute bliss I fear will be etched into my memory for far longer than I care to admit aloud.

She's breathtaking when she's serious, furrowed brows and tight lips with a tiny wrinkle in her chin from how she twists her mouth.

But when she's laughing? My god.

The sky gets brighter just because of her smile. I thank god I wasn't close enough to hear whatever melodies form to create the sound of her laugh because I may have needed to make a fool of myself just to hear it again.

"You should go say hi," Ray breaks me from the rabbit hole I was on the brink of.

"Why would I do that?"

"Because, it's not like you guys are strangers. It would be weird if it came up in conversation later that you saw her and didn't say anything. I'm sure she's waiting for you to speak first."

"I doubt she even noticed that I came in Ray," I take a sip of the water our waitress sat on our table at some point.

My sister stares at me like I just asked her if the lemons in front of us were yellow.

"Of course she noticed, Darrell. What are you talking about?"

I take a quick look again, and I'm able to see her laugh is gone and whatever the topic of conversation is now really has her attention.

She leaned into the table more, her breasts resting on her forearm, pushing them up. Who the hell gave her the right to wear such a small tube top?

I feel disgusted ogling at her this way, but I can't help but look just for a few seconds more.

My stare overstayed its welcome because she finally felt its weight and looked at me.

The speed at which I turn back around makes me feel like a kid in elementary school caught by his crush.

"Well, either you absolutely have to say hi now or you suffer the embarrassment during your next meeting," Rayana says as she sips her water, her eyes daring me to get up.

I wish I could explain to my sister that I'd prefer to do absolutely anything other than what she's suggesting. That talking to or around this woman makes me feel like I need to learn English all over again as if it isn't my first language.

That when she makes eye contact with me, I feel like she sees directly into me, not through me, but into any secret thought or worry I try to keep to myself.

But, I can't explain that to her, not right now.

So instead, I sigh, bowing my head briefly in defeat.

I guess embarrassment is inevitable.

“Come on,” I say, quickly standing at my feet before I change my mind. Rayana needs no help standing at lightning speed to trail behind me towards Moriah’s table.

I silently take a deep breath as we approach, *get it together. you’re not a teenager approaching some cute girl at the mall, you’re a grown man.*

”We can’t keep meeting like this,” Is the only greeting I can form fast enough. *God you’re embarrassing. When did you get so bad at this?*

She looks up to me slowly never in a hurry. I may be standing here but I am quickly reduced to a puddle on this floor the moment her eyes reach mine and hold the gaze like she’s daring me to do… something.

“I’m beginning to think you may be stalking me, Washington,” She replies. I do not know what to say in response, I’m locked in a trance that feels like a spell casted just by her eyes alone. ”Ah, so you’re Mr. Washington,” Her friend speaks when words clearly fail me, “I’m Anastasia, Stasi for short,” She extends her hand to me, I shake it.

Her friend must have an antidote to whatever it is this woman does to me whenever she’s around because I’m able to find more words.

“It’s a pleasure to meet you, Stasi. My name is Darrell, your friend refuses to use it no matter how many times I correct her.”

”Ha, correct her. That was probably the first issue,” Stasi snickers, “She doesn’t do well with correction, that’s always been the problem.”

I glance at Moriah who smirks at her friend as she speaks, “It’s okay. I’m patient, she’ll get the hint in time,” I respond, earning back her gaze. Silence, charged with… something else, befalls us. I hear someone clearing their throat behind me and suddenly remember my sister is here.

I forgot about anyone but *her* being here.

"My apologies," I step aside so the ladies can all get a better view of each other, "This is my younger sister Rayana."

She smiles, "Ray, for short," She shakes both of their hands and they meet her smile with their own and again I'm held captive by the sight.

"You guys should sit with us, Mo has us sitting here in this huge booth with all of this space for no reason," Stasi suggests.

*Mo*.

I never thought of what her family and friends may call her. Knowing her in the capacity that I do, I wouldn't be surprised if they called her Ms. Jackson too.

"No, that's-"

"Sure!"

Both my sister and I respond at the same time, while Moriah's eyes have surely grown in size.

I give my sister a pointed look.

"No, it's fine. We'd hate to disturb your girl's day," I offer a tight smile to them both. Rayana thankfully fights her urge to add on.

"It's no disturbance at all, we've run out of things to talk about anyway, right Mo?" Anastasia looks to her friend. I'm sure if looks could kill, we'd be calling 911 right now.

"Sure," Moriah drags her gaze from her friend to my sister and I, "Pull up a seat."

I'm conflicted, not knowing if this is another silent test and my accepting the offer will result in my failure. Rayana, on the other hand, takes a seat beside Moriah without hesitation, she quickly scoots over to make for her.

It'll be fine, Rayana needs to be around people other than her family anyway, maybe this way she'll make some new friends.

At least, that's what I try to tell myself is my reason for taking a seat in the same booth as the woman who causes all of my alarms to sound off at once.

# CHAPTER *SEVENTEEN*

## *Moriah*

*"It* was really nice meeting you guys, it feels so good to have someone to talk to other than my siblings," Rayana laughs and so do I.

"I can only imagine how refreshing it must be. I've had to talk to one of them quite a bit, I think you're my favorite," I say playfully.

She giggles as she and her brother slide out of the booth we're all seated in.

"It was nice to meet you, Stasi," Darrell says, his eyes linger on me for a second too long before he speaks again, "It was good seeing you, Moriah," He looks at me now.

My insides set ablaze and freeze over all at once whenever his eyes are on me. I inhale deeply like I'm preparing to go underwater.

It's instinctive.

Hearing him say my name with such assurance in his tone, I nearly see stars.

I give him a nod and muster up a friendly smile. I feel so broken sometimes.

After they leave, I release my breath and fix my gaze on the drink I have in front of me, absentmindedly stirring it with the straw sitting in the cup.

I usually only order two drinks max. Since Darrell and his sister joined us, somehow I landed on my fourth one.

I feel the weight of someone's stare on me and find it to be Stasi. She says nothing but too much at the same time with the smirk that greets me.

"What, Anastasia?" I say exasperatedly.

I know exactly where this is headed and all the energy I'd usually have to defend was used trying to act normal in front of a man who I'm sure has plenty of women throwing themselves at him.

His siblings surely gave him the right position, the man knows how to be charming without barely uttering a word.

"There was a lot of tension at this table a few moments ago," It's almost like the smirk is permanently etched onto her face.

I sigh.

"The only tension that *may* have been present was due to us being two professionals that work together, knowing that we should not be mingling like two friends at happy hour. That's all."

"I hear you girl," She takes a slow sip of her drink, "I think it was a bit more than that. I'm pretty sure I never see you that avoidant of someone in your space."

I don't have a response. As much as I don't want her to be right, she is, but I refuse to admit that.

Men couldn't pay me to act moved by their presence, but something about Darrell gets me stuck. I get around him and I'm suddenly less than fully in control.

I hate it. It makes me feel fickle or beneath myself.

"Listen, girl, I don't blame you," Stasi speaks into the silence we sat in, "The man is fine as hell, and kind of funny. You'd be crazy to not be attracted to him, I'd actually be cornered,"

I snicker, "Well, since you like him so much, you should ask him out."

I may say it jokingly, but I can't ignore the thump in my chest at the thought.

My best friend is beautiful, guys drool as she walks by.

Plus, she knows how to act like a regularly functioning woman around them. No one has ever called her cold or broken.

I'm sure if she did ask Darrell out, he'd say yes in a heartbeat.

"I would never do that to you bestie, especially not seeing how much you like him," She tells me earnestly.

"How many times do I have to tell you this, Stasi?" I roll my eyes at my mostly empty plate in front of me.

"You know how I know you like him, Moriah?" She leans in like she's about to tell me a juicy secret.

I laugh.

"Please, enlighten me on how you know Anastasia," I sit back in the booth and cross my arms.

"Because your response about the tension had nothing to do with your disgust for him and only spoke of your remaining professional."

I straightened against the seat my back was resting on and I sober a little.

"So, because I didn't call him a hopeless imbecile, that means I like him? Okay, the guy is tolerable and he isn't horrible to look at. You act like that's impossible for me to say."

"No, you act like it's impossible for you to say," She retorts. "I can't remember the last time you gave a man more than five minutes of your time, Mo. You're the only one that sits in on meetings with him when you usually delegate that task to Elijah. You barely have anything to say when he's around that isn't unnecessarily snarky and it's only because you don't know what else to say. You're trying so hard to act like it isn't there, but it is."

"What is?" I lean onto my folded arms atop the table.

"A crush. It's okay to at least say you have a crush on him, no one said admitting that is going to cause some sort of global catastrophe. Give yourself a break to at least call the guy cute. Crushes are fun, trust me," She looks at me with sympathy in her eyes, not the kind entangled with pity either.

God knew I needed her when he sent her to me. She's always been the sweet to my sour, trying to lighten me up when I'm tightly wound but still cuts no corners with me.

It's just unfortunate that this time around the corners she's choosing not to cut, has the potential of cutting me. Deeply.

# CHAPTER *EIGHTEEN*

## Darrell

*"You clearly like her DJ, you acted like a dumbass when you saw her," Rayana says from her spot in the passenger seat, "Just ask her out, don't be a pussy."*

The conversation my sister and I had after leaving Moriah and Anastasia at the restaurant the other day replays in my head today when I should be focused on this meeting I have with a grantmakers representative.

But no.

Instead, I'm focused on the woman who would not bat an eyelash if I fell before her and professed my undying love. I don't think she'd be moved by any gesture made by me or any other man for that matter.

Not that it matters if she's interested in me or not.

Still, that doesn't stop me from thinking about how beautiful that yellow looked against her skin or how delicate her bare neck and collarbone looked, like it deserved to be kissed, personally asking for me to caress it.

Or the way she'd cover her mouth when she laughed, like she had to hide her joy from onlookers. As if the sight of her in bliss isn't exactly what they all needed to see, to witness a goddess in real life.

*She's not thinking about you man*, I keep reminding myself. I'm sure if she was she would've given some sort of signal by now.

Even if she did, it's a bad idea.

We work together, at least for the time being. She doesn't give me the impression that she's someone who mixes business and pleasure.

Rayana's suggestion is a horrible idea, she has a lot to learn about the world around her. I just let her dream.

A tap at my door takes me out of my thoughts.

"Hey, don't forget that meeting. They're in the virtual waiting room now," My assistant, Ellie, reminds me.

This is the other reason it's a bad idea. Distraction.

Love, or the idea of love, it warps your mind. Takes you away from what's most important, from the people and things that matter most.

I've witnessed it personally, and I won't make that a cycle.

I sit up in my chair and shake my head to rid myself of the thoughts that are trying to consume me. I have more important things to do.

I log into the virtual meeting and for the next hour I do my best to sell the story of The Henderson's, and why they deserve the support of this guy's company, by means of Love Unbound.

This is my territory, relating to someone enough to convince them we're the better choice. That we have a connection to something that they want.

Not women, and dating, and love.

The last time I gave dating a chance was in college.

I met a girl, she was beautiful, smart and the life of the party. And there were a lot of parties.

I hadn't sought her out, she came for me by way of my roommate. She asked him about me first, if I had a girlfriend or if I even liked girls because she never saw me talking to any.

Before you knew it, we were hooking up, often. And then hookups led to being each other dates to parties, then actual dates and soon we were a couple.

She was my second ever girlfriend, the most serious one I had, or so it felt.

Eventually, she got bored with the fact I was in college to actually study and not have fun, which is all she wanted to do despite all the potential she had.

But, I stayed with her.

Even after she told me I need to start going out with her more because other guys were trying to fuck her and it was getting hard to tell them no when I was no where around.

It was such a trap and I fell right for it.

I ended up so wrapped up in her, chasing her from party to party, damn near obsessing over where she was and who she was with because she made me feel like every second I was away, there was a new guy trying to get next to her.

"*You need to be more possessive,*" she said, "*Or someone is literally going to just take me right from under you and put me under them instead.*"

My grades started to fall flat, I was missing classes and assignments, the programs I was involved in, I nearly lost them all.

I was lucky to have the friends I did to help me realize something was clearly wrong. When I did realize it, I realized something else - I almost became the exact person I worked so hard to be the exact opposite of.

My mother.

From then on, I've been on a straight arrow.

I'm not saying I've lived like a monk, I'm a regular man with regular needs. But I never allow it to become more than fulfilling a need.

My rule is: I don't hook up with the same person more than twice, after that it becomes personal and that becomes a liability.

Eventually the meeting I was in, ended.

I couldn't tell you how it went, but I'm assuming it went well since the rep said he'd reach out with a follow up email. I've done this so many times, I can operate on autopilot, clearly I just did.

After closing out of the call, I sit at my desk for a moment with my thoughts.

*"You haven't been on a date in years, big brother. The worst that will happen is she'll say no and laugh in your face," My sister says, trying to make a convincing argument.*

*"Or break off our company's partnership," I add, keeping my eyes on the road before me as we pull up to Honey's house, where my sister also lives.*

*"Yeah, or that. But that won't happen." She waves her hand like it's nonsense.*

*I don't respond to her.*

I stare at the new email I received earlier from Nolan with the details that we're to go over during our next meeting together.

My sister and I are both wrong. Those scenarios are not the worst thing that can happen.

# CHAPTER *NINETEEN*

## *Moriah*

***It's*** been a long day and I can't wait to get to my bedroom and melt into my covers.

I pull into the driveway of my fathers home and nearly fly out of my seat to get to the front door, as much flying as one could do with being only half awake.

I see that no one else is home because my sister's car wasn't here when I arrived.

I walk through the front door and sigh in relief for making it alive, evading passing out behind the wheel from exhaustion.

I start to take off my shoes while leaning my back against the door for support. While doing so, I notice the mail on our living room table unopened.

I pick it up to see if there's anything that needs immediate attention.

*Bill. Bill. Advertisement. Jury Duty. A suspicious manilla envelope.*

I place everything but the large envelope back in its spot on the table and quickly get to work opening it.

It's a letter, which is weird because this could've, I'm sure, been delivered in a regular sized envelope but okay.

I realize there's something else inside.

I turn the small packaging upside down to empty its contents and out falls 3 photos onto the floor.

I take them and move towards the kitchen as I inspect them. They're of an older woman.

She's in motion in two of them, her face partially covered either by sunglasses or someone blocking the view of the lens. The other photo is of the back of her.

The letter that accompanied them reads as follows:

Dear Ms. Jackson,

I'm pleased to inform you that we finally have a solid lead on the person you're in search of.

At this point in our investigation, we ask that you advise us of what would you like the next steps to be regarding either continuing to maintain a close eye or immediately initiating contact in the event that is still what you seek.

If you're looking to independently seek out further information, we have attached the needed information below. She has changed her last name as well as having moved to a neighboring city, which may have played a larger part in your inability to find her on your own.

As always, I would like to express the pleasure it has been working with you thus far, Ms. Jackson, and we hope that the discovery of your mothers whereabouts will bring you the peace and closure you've been searching for.

Adeline Marie Scott (maternal family's name)
59 years of age
Baltimore, Maryland
COO of Little hands, Big hearts

That concluded the letter.

As I reached the end, I heard the front door open and my family entered through it.

"What is this?" I waste no time asking questions, shaking the letter in my hand.

My father is visibly startled by my greeting tone.

"I can't see what it is with you shaking it like that. I take it whatever it is, you aren't happy about," He says, taking the letter out of my grasp.

He briefly reads it and I see him freeze in place when he gets to the line identifying who the letter is about.

He looks to me and then slowly to my sister who has not said anything.

"AJ…" He takes his glasses off and rubs his eyes, "I think this letter is for you darlin'," He passes the letter off to her.

She cautiously removes her gaze from mine and on to the words on the paper that now rests in her hands. Without words, she completes the letter, folds it up and places it in her bag that still hangs from her shoulder.

"Well?!" I don't have the ability at the present moment to come across as calm, because I am not that.

"Well," She removes the bag and sits it on the couch she stands beside, "I guess the cats out of the bag."

"The cats out of the bag?" I exclaim into the small distance between us, "You're looking for our *mother* and your response to me is the cats out of the bag?! How could you?"

She nearly jumps back with genuine confusion on her face,

"How could I… look for my mother? I wasn't aware that was a crime, Mo."

"How could you do it without talking to me first? Talking to dad especially. How the hell do you think it could make him feel after he was the one that raised us after she abandoned him?! All the work he put in by himself and now you want to tell him, *hey dad, thanks for the hard work and sacrifices but I'd still like to get to know the woman who is behind you giving up your hopes and dreams?!*"

I don't think my father has ever heard my voice reach this volume.

"Mo, just wait a second-" He tries to intervene.

"No! I won't wait a second. All AJ has is a second to explain why in the hell she would want to bring this woman back into our lives," I say more sternly than I've ever spoken to him.

"Because she's my mother, Moriah. That's why, You may not remember her, but I do. And, I have talked to dad about it. Clearly I chose the more level headed out of the two of you to trust this with," She says, her voice edged with razors.

"Clearly not! You are the most selfless person I know, but this has to be the most selfish thing you've done."

I don't give either of them a chance to say anything more before I walk out to my car after slipping back into my shoes..

As if on cue, my phone chimes with a reminder.

**ALERT: Meeting with Nolan and Washington.**

I sigh into the empty space, lay my head on the steering wheel and hope the deep breaths I'm taking will cause the tears threatening to fall to retreat.

I start my car and back out of the driveway. Maybe this is what I need to calm my nerves, something else to focus on.

---

After about an hour into our meeting, I realize this is indeed not what I needed.

I know I'm usually not the most pleasurable person to work with, but I'm sure both men can agree tonight this is peak displeasure.

"You know Mo," Elijah takes a breath after I've snapped at him for at least the 10th time in the last 40 minutes, "How about you order yourself something to eat or a drink? It is happy hour after all. I'll pay. Darrell and I can handle these details for right now, but since you're already here, treat yourself to something. It seems like you've had a hard day."

That was the nicest way Elijah could say "*Stop being a bitch before I quit. Tonight.*"

I silently pick up the menu that sits on the table in front of us.

Darrell doesn't say anything, but I feel his eyes on me. Assessing me.

I'm embarrassed by how I've acted during this meeting. Being a hardass is one thing, but moody hell on heels is another.

Thankfully, after what felt like too long, the meeting ended and I ate and drank my way through it all.

Agitated or not, I'm not dumb enough to turn down a free meal and drink.

I say my goodbyes to Elijah and Darrell and head for the door. As I'm about to reach for the handle, I feel a hand on my shoulder, causing me to turn on my heels immediately.

"Hey," Darrell says with a lazy grin.

I do not grin back. I don't speak actually, I just wait for him to spit out whatever it is he stopped me for.

"Can I um," He looks around, "Can I walk you to your car?"

This isn't at all what I expected so I'm not able to mask my eyebrows shooting to my hairline.

"Uh…yeah, sure," I say with more of a question mark than a period.

He opens the door for me and allows me to walk out first.

For a few moments we walk side by side in silence with a short but big enough distance between us.

The silence was all but comfortable.

"So," He finally says, "Rough day?" He looks down at me as we walk. I don't think I've ever had the chance to notice how tall he is.

I don't respond to him and continue walking to my car in the parking lot of the restaurant.

"Right," He says to himself instead of me, "Okay, I'll just get to my point I guess," He says.

We're close to my car now, I take my key fob out and disarm the alarm.

"I know this is totally inappropriate, and that you'll probably say no which I wouldn't blame you."

I don't make direct eye contact with him, but I do peer at him from my peripheral. My view is good enough to see he's looking at his feet on the sidewalk instead of me.

"But, my sister really liked you and wouldn't shut up about you on the ride home. You would've thought she sent me to ask you out for her."

We reach my car.

Instead of getting in immediately, I lean against it while he finishes whatever this is right now.

"Well, did she?" I finally speak.

As if my voice alone startled him, he stops talking.

"Did who, what?"

A smirk tries to fight its way to the surface, but I win the battle.

"Did your sister send you to ask me out for her? I'm not really into women but she's cute. Maybe I could make an exception," I say, now giving the car my full weight as I lean back more.

He gives a breathy chuckle, "Uh, no, actually. She sent me to ask you out, for me."

Suddenly everything in my mind stops making noise and I'm sure my eyes are the size of golfballs.

"Excuse me?" I responded and hoped it didn't sound as insulting as I think it does.

He takes a deep inhale and fully embraces my glare for the first time since we begin to walk.

"I'm sure under different circumstances, I'd ask a bit smoother than this but, this is all I got right now. So, even though I assume you'll say no, I have to be able to say I at least tried," He looks down at his shoes again, then back at me, "Will you allow me to take you on a date, Ms. Jackson?"

My mind lights on fire with the way he says my name.

He eyes me lazily, it matches the grin that was once there but has now been replaced with an expression that I'm sure could be the last crack to break a dam.

For a moment, I'm stuck just soaking up his gaze until I remember, I have to respond.

I swallow as much oxygen as I can considering the look he's giving me takes all the air out of my lungs.

I square my shoulders, lift my chin and say, "It's entirely against my ethics and my better judgment," His mouth begins to form a tight line as he prepares to accept rejection, "But, one date wouldn't hurt anyone I guess. Especially if only we know about it."

For a moment, I thought I saw actual lights in his eyes. I almost laugh as I watch him try to calm his reaction to my acceptance, *almost*.

"Right, of course. No one would have to know about it except us. Plus, I'm sure we both deserve a little relaxation, right?" His lazy grin returns.

"Right."

After he tells me that he'll send me details, and we say our goodbyes, I get in my car and begin to drive off.

I know this is probably a terrible choice. But, if my sister can make horrible decisions that'll possibly ruin everything I've built over the years, why can't I too?

# CHAPTER *TWENTY*

### *Moriah*

Anastasia sits on the other side of my desk with her feet up as if she's home.

Today, we decided to have lunch in my office, I just don't have it in me to be among crowds of people unnecessarily.

"Okay, so what did you need to tell me? I gave you your time, now you need to spill," She sits with her legs folded under her in the comfy armchair she managed to pull over to my desk. That chair took two men to bring into this office, so I have no idea how her skinny ass pushed it all the way over here by herself.

"Okay," I sigh, "But, I beg that you remain as calm as you possibly can," I ask her, knowing she can be just as calm as a toddler on a sugar rush depending on the information divulged.

"Girl-scouts honor," She puts to the air two crossed fingers, as if that's supposed to give me reassurance.

"Well, let me start with the biggest issue at hand," I place down the chopsticks I use to eat the sushi we're having for lunch, "Adella has actually lost her fucking mind."

Stasi's eyes grow wide, I'm sure she didn't expect the *biggest issue at hand* to be led with my sister's name, of all people.

"AJ?! What in the hell did she do?" She leans a bit forward in her chair, ready to drink up whatever I have to pour out.

"I got home yesterday and saw this weird envelope. I opened it, thinking it's important, right?" I talk with my hands gesturing about, "Come to find out, she's looking for our damn mother, Stasi."

"Oh, shit."

"Oh shit is right. What the hell is she thinking? I can't imagine dad's face or feelings when she first told him this idea because apparently he already knew," I pause to take a piece of sushi in my mouth while I wait for Anastasia's reply.

Only, she doesn't really have one.

I look up from my dish at her, "Is that not insanely inconsiderate?" I try to jolt a response out of my best friend.

"Well…" She goes to say.

"Well?! Stasi, please don't make me mad," I drop my chopsticks, "What do you mean well? That woman had a chance at being a mother and having a family. With a great man at that! Instead, she decided to jump ship the minute she felt that she couldn't live her life the way she wanted with now being a parent to two children. There is no 'well' for that."

Anastasia casts her eyes down and quietly eats her sushi.

"What? You don't agree?" I ask, since a cat apparently has her tongue.

"It's not that I don't agree, Mo. I think it was definitely inconsiderate to do without clueing you in first, and I can absolutely understand your irritation and your concern for pops and how he feels."

There is a clear *but* that hangs in between us.

"I do also, though, think that it isn't far-fetched for a kid to want their mom. No matter how much time has passed or what happened to cause the separation. You don't know why she's looking for her either. You two are entirely different individuals with your own needs and own coping mechanisms. This may be something she genuinely needs. No one said you had to be apart, just… try to see it from her perspective. Especially considering she's older, she remembers a bit more than you do."

I lean on my desk and push around a piece of sushi with my chopsticks.

I admittedly have a tendency to only see my side of things at times and believe there's only one right way to view matters. There's no way I can truly disagree with or argue anything my best friend has just said, and she knows it. That's why neither of us speak for a moment, she allows me to sit with my thoughts and feelings.

I appreciate her for that.

"There was one more thing," I say after a few moments pass, "Darrell asked me on a date."

This time she audibly gasps.

I look up at her from where my sushi is being flipped and turned, take a breath and say, "And I think I'm a little excited."

---

## Darrell

My sister and I sit on the front porch of Honey's home on her swinging chair at opposite ends, enjoying the cooling breeze that you experience only when the seasons begin to change.

"I wonder what it'll be like when we all start to have kids," . Rayana says into the silence, "Like, if one of us will keep this house and it'll be the house that everyone makes their memories with. If it'll be our family home."

I hum in response.

"I think you'll end up being the one to keep it," I say to her, "Keeping it homey and inviting feels like a you-thing for sure."

She smiles, hard.

"Yeah, it does sound like a me-thing. Focusing on traditions and what not. Keeping you and Anthony in line when you try to tell me you can't make it for a sunday dinner because you're too tired from work," She giggles.

I smile at the thought of Rayana being the glue that keeps us strong.

"I did what you asked, by the way," I lean my head against the cushion of the seat.

She turns her gaze to me, "What did I ask, by the way?" Her look is inquisitive and genuinely confused.

"About Moriah," I keep my eyes forward. "I asked her out."

I don't look at her when I hear her gasp from the right of me.

"Okay, okay, keep calm," She says to only herself, "So?"

"So, what?" I play as if I don't know the question she's dying to get the answer to.

"DJ, do not play with me right now," She hits my arm, "What did she say?"

I do my best to bite back the smile trying to form on my face. "She said yes."

This time my sister squeals.

"I knew it! I knew it!"

"Hush, Ray. Before you wake up Honey from her nap," I laugh at my sister's excitement and try to act as if I don't share it.

"Why are you trying to act like you weren't jumping to the moon when she said yes?" She asks. My youngest sister knows me best of all my siblings, so to try and hide my excitement from her is virtually pointless.

"Because, Ray," I responded, "We agreed we're doing it just because we both deserve a little wind down time. We swore we wouldn't tell anyone about it and definitely agreed it isn't appropriate in the slightest sense of the word."

"Who cares about appropriateness! You are two consenting and sound of mind adults. You can make your own decisions and I'm sure you can juggle dating and working together without things getting weird," She has so much faith.

"You know how I feel about dating, Ray." She knows more than anyone my beliefs on the dating to disaster pipeline.

She sighs.

"Yes, mister Donny downer, I do know how you feel about it. But, I also know that you are very picky and the fact that you actually went through with asking her out, especially considering you two work together, it says something."

”Yeah.” I direct my focus back on the scenery around us, “It says I’m possibly an idiot and walking into my own demise.”

“God, DJ!” She exclaims with exasperation clear in her voice.

I laugh, my sister is the most optimistic person I know. To propose to her that something won’t work is like sitting her in front of a bunch of puppies and telling her she can’t pet any of them.

”At least promise me that you’ll try to have fun and not think about whatever gloomy shit your mind is trying to get you to focus on,” She says with a plea in her eyes.

I chuckle, “I promise I’ll do my best, just for you.”

# CHAPTER *TWENTY-ONE*

*Darrell*

"You should take her mini golfing, she looks like a mini golfer. Her and her friend seem like the type to wear tennis outfits but never pick up a racket in their lives," Rayana says from her spot on the sofa.

"I'm very sure her friend plays Tennis," I respond as I sit on the sofa opposing her.

"Well, dinner is a classic idea of course. But, it can't be a boring one. Go somewhere they cook the food in front of you or something with theatrics. Big flames, knife flipping, the works."

I shake my head, *this girl*.

As she shares more ideas that I did not ask her for, but honestly do need since it's been so long I've given some actual consideration to what to do for a date, Honey walks in.

"Who is going to see flames and knife throwing?" She asks as she takes a seat on the sofa Rayana is planted on.

"No one."

"DJ & his date."

We respond together, both looking at the other with glares when our answers don't match.

"You're going on a date with no one?" Honey smirks.

I exhale with a bit of force, knowing I can't lie to her.

"I am going on a date," I look to Rayana and then back to Honey, "with someone."

She hums.

"Is this someone that… Moriah girl, that we ran into not long ago with her father? And the one your sister mentioned at dinner?" Her expression stays leveled with a glint of humor.

I hesitate to respond before finally saying *yes*.

"Ah, you finally decided to man up, huh?" She responds.

Rayana snorts as she takes a sip of the soda she's drinking.

"Excuse me, lady?" I say in shock at her response.

"You were a puddle when we ran into that girl at the market. And according to what I've been hearing, you've been trying to mop yourself up ever since you met her. You finally decided to give in."

Her brow raises with a silent dare for me to rebut her words.

"First off, granny," I jokingly say to my know-it-all grandmother, "We both agree that it's hardly a date and more of two people who need some rest and relaxation from work and the crap that life has been throwing our way."

She upholds her dare as she sips some of her tea.

"That's what he tried to tell me too," Rayana loudly whispers to Honey.

"Furthermore," I continue, "We both agree that it's probably a terrible idea and also not mention to a soul that it's happening. It's not like we'll have anything to say anyway."

I try to convince her so that she can stand down. But, of course she doesn't.

"I understand, son. It's a terrible idea to mix business and pleasure. Very sticky business," She says and exchanges glances with my younger sister who is just soaking up this interaction between my snarky grandmother and I.

"Very sticky business indeed," Rayana echoes.

"The two of you individually are a headache, but together? Absolutely insufferable," I say to them both.

They giggle.

My two favorite women in the world. There isn't much I wouldn't do to see them like this in every possible waking moment. Even when they're bullying me about a date that isn't a date with a woman who isn't interested in me.

"Well, date or no date, do me one favor," Honey says after their fit of giggles.

"What's the favor, granny?" I jest.

"Wear Gramps silver watch."

My sister and I both freeze in stares.

That watch was my grandfather's favorite, one of his most prized possessions, though I never learned why it was so important to him, I just knew to never play with it, never to touch it, not to get as much as a fingerprint on its face.

"Why on earth would I do that?" I ask with sincerity.

She smiles in response to me, "Because he always wore it for important occasions."

"I just told you this isn't even a date, Honey. There's no way this is the level of importance he'd want me to wear it for."

Rayana looks between the two of us.

Me, with pinched brows and Honey with bliss and knowingness in her smile.

"He was my husband before he was your grandfather, DJ. I know him, and I know you. This is exactly the level of importance he'd deem appropriate for his watch."

Almost instantly, this shoots my already buzzing nerves to the moon.

# CHAPTER *TWENTY-TWO*

## *Moriah*

*Anastasia* lays across my bed as she watches me go through my closet.

"Okay, where are you guys going again?" She asks as she switches to her stomach to get a better view of the options.

"Some restaurant in the city. He said, 'I hope you enjoy live music.' So, I'm assuming it's somewhere with a band," I answer while I shuffle through hangers.

"Okay mood setter, we love," She says with a smile I can hear in her voice with my back turned to her.

"What about this?" I hold up a black, form fitting dress with a low neckline, "I don't want to give the impression I'm easy or trying too hard, but I'm not going to act like I don't know I'm fine as hell."

As Stasi goes to respond, my sister says "I'd wear something with a cutout instead of a low neckline," From her position at the doorway, "It gives more to the imagination. A low neckline leaves little room to fantasize," She adds quietly.

We haven't said more than a sentence to each other since the day I opened that letter.

It's been hard because my sister is just as much as my best friend as Stasi is, but I just couldn't wrap my mind around what she's doing and why.

After talking to Anastasia though, I tried to have a change of heart and perspective, I just haven't figured out how to break the ice.

So, I don't give her the cold shoulder when she includes herself, I'm thankful for it honestly.

"I agree," Stasi adds, trying to smooth over the awkward tension, "You want to leave him wondering, not with new information he didn't have before. How about that red dress?"

I pull out the one she's pointing to.

A strapless red dress with two triangular cuts on either side. It's ankle length.

"If he can get hard off of the sight of just your collarbone and your ankles, well, then that just may be your man," AJ jokes.

We all laugh together, it's always relaxing to have both of my sisters with me, both of the women who mean the absolute most to me.

Even when we bicker, because trust me, I'm an easy one to bicker with, they love me still, and always give me grace, allowing me to right my wrongs. They're always there with open arms waiting for me to get my mind together.

Even though sometimes it takes a little longer than it should.

AJ joins Stasi and sits at the top of my bed with her legs folded under her, "So, is this the guy you've been working with?"

"How do you know about him?" I snap my head towards her. I know for sure I've not mentioned him in this household.

She and Stasi exchange a glance.

"Anastasia!" I exclaim.

The girl can't hold water, I swear.

"It wasn't me! I simply confirmed what she asked," Stasi defends herself with both hands up.

"She's not lying, it wasn't her," AJ comes to her aid, "It was actually your father."

My shock is tripled, if that's possible. How the hell would my dad know… "The market," I finish my thought aloud.

"He said you guys ran into a man at the market and he's pretty sure you like him but are trying to play hard to get."

"Since when do you two gossip with each other?" I ask with my hands on either hip.

"Girl, since forever. Dad always has tea to spill about something, I don't know how he does it," She laughs.

"Well, he's wrong. I'm not playing hard to get. I am hard to get," I hold up the dress once more to get another look at it.

"Oh please," Stasi rolls her eyes, "This man already has you, whether you'd like to admit it or not."

"I agree. When's the last time you've put this much thought into an outfit for a date?" AJ chimes in.

"Scratch that," Stasi says, "When's the last time you've even accepted an offer for a date?"

"I will not be attacked by the two of you in my own room," I go to my wide collection of heels, "Do not make a big deal of this or I will absolutely call him right now and cancel this date."

"You won't," Anastasia responds, "You guys only communicate via email, which is odd by the way, and I doubt he's checking his email right now when he's busy getting ready to be your dream man on this date."

“I don’t dream of men,” I say flatly, “Now, pick a shoe,” I step aside so they both get a better view.

”That one,” They point in unison to a pair of orange strappy heels.

I remove them from my shoe rack and place them on top of the dress now laid out on my armchair.

Though we may all laugh about it now, AJ and Stasi are all too familiar with my reasons for paying men dust every time they attempt to pursue me, if that’s what they choose to call it.

Despite watching my parents have the experience they had with love, I did try to approach love with optimism still. That was until my ex, my last actual relationship.

He sold me dreams just to turn them into scenes of a movie I would never star in.

He solidified my determination to never be tricked by the idea of love again.

I stand and view the two together then hear a fit of whispered giggles behind me. I look at the two women on my bed acting like pre-teens.

“What?” I say irritatedly.

”Nothing,” Stasi responds in giggles.

”We’re just excited for you, Mo,” My sister adds, “Something feels different in the air tonight, I have a good feeling.”

I roll my eyes at their overly optimistic mindsets. I’ve always been the realist in our trio, though they’d call me a cynic.

While they were excited about the cutest boy in the neighborhood or school, I was focused on the fact his grades were piss poor and he was a benchwarmer instead of the starting five on his basketball team.

I don't have time to entertain fantasies and dreams. Just what's here and now, and not get sweeped up in the hopes and what ifs.

Though, I can't lie… I agree with Adella.

There is something different in the air tonight. I just hope that whatever it is, isn't a horrible decision wrapped in a pretty bow.

# CHAPTER *TWENTY-THREE*

*Darrell*

She's beautiful, and I'm fucked.

# CHAPTER *TWENTY-FOUR*

## *Darrell*

She didn't let me pick her up for our not-date, so instead I paid for her Uber… that she ordered herself.

I can't pretend my breath wasn't robbed from me as soon as I saw her step out of the car.

She has this ability to walk under a moonlit spotlight every time she appears into a space, as if the stars beamed her directly to that spot and are guiding her steps.

The way she looks is torturous.

A red dress that teases the imagination with bare skin exposed on either side, just enough to make you wonder how soft it is to the touch or how much the material could stretch if you pulled on it.

Her hair is brushed back into a low hanging ponytail of curls, leaving her neck exposed, only graced by a thin chain necklace that kisses the space between her collarbone. I fight the mental images of my hand being its replacement.

The heels she wears, sharp enough to be deemed as weapons, as if she isn't one already. I can only pray she doesn't use them to walk over the space in me that feels fragile as soon as I see her.

I greet her at the curb where the Uber lets her out, taking her by the hand as she steps on to the curb.

"Thank you," She says softly but firmly.

"Of course," I respond. "You look… beautiful."

I did my best to search for another word, but even beautiful doesn't feel like it does her the justice she deserves.

She offers me a small smile, "Thank you. You don't look so bad yourself."

"Thank you."

I release her hand once she's taken a few steps away from the curb and is further on to the walkway, "Have you been here before?" I ask as I open the door to the restaurant, allowing her to walk in first.

"I can't say that I have," She responds over her shoulder as I catch up to her.

"Good."

We enter the waiting area and I approach the host posted at the entrance.

"Reservation for Washington."

The host gives me a curt nod after confirming something on the screen in front of her and ushers us to a table in the middle of the floor in perfect view of the band to the front of the room who's playing soft jazz music.

I pull her seat out and wait for her to take it before gently pushing it towards the table. I then take the seat opposing her.

She silently takes in the space around her, assessing it, judging it I'm sure.

"So, what are you feeling tonight? Pasta or steak?" I say, trying my hand at conversation.

She looks at me and with a firm line of her mouth she picks up the menu in front of her, going over the options presented.

"Maybe…" She thinks aloud, "The wine bathed salmon?" She asks to the menu more than me.

I nod, though she isn't looking.

"Sounds good," I glance at the menu as well, though I already know what I'm ordering. This isn't my first time here but it has been a while. On the days Rayana wants a reason to dress up, we come here.

"What about drinks? Are you a white or dark kind of girl?"

She takes in a breath as if she'd rather do anything other than answer my questions, "I'm a sweet girl. Whatever is the sweetest is what I prefer," She answers.

"Perfect, I know exactly what to get for you."

She quirks her eyebrow, "Who said I needed you to order for me?"

"No one," I respond, "But, I'm going to," I offer a relaxed grin. I figure since we're in the business of taking risks today, I might as well see how far she'll let me push.

She doesn't respond.

Time passes and I do my best to make small talk. She indulges me but just for the sake of doing so and not because she seems to want to. After a while, I allow us to fall into complete silence.

I take this time to just watch her.

I'm not sure if she even notices how her body mindlessly sways to the soft music filling the room around us, or the low hums she attempts to keep to herself.

To watch her be in her own world is almost just as enjoyable as joining her in it.

After some time, our silence is interrupted by a cry in the distance.

We both look to find the source of the noise and discover it comes from a toddler.

The dining area is filled mainly with couples, some families here and there, but with older children.

The family that has our attention consist of a young couple and a cranky toddler, I assume they tried to have a date night and instead of canceling due to a lack of a babysitter, tried to make it a family night.

The little one seems to have different plans.

The noise doesn't bother me, I'm not often moved by things like that. However, I notice Moriah frequently glances back at them, only unlike the other people that are looking, hers isn't based in annoyance. I can almost see a tug of war happening behind her eyes.

Soon, she gives in to the silent battle and makes a beeline towards the couple. Her sudden movement takes me aback and I tense. I'm only just learning who Moriah is, so to say I'm not a tad nervous about her plans would be a lie, but I stay seated and just observe.

Of course I can't hear whatever she whispers to them from across the room, but whatever it is, the young mother smiles at her despite the baby in her arms being unhappy and then passes her daughter to Moriah.

I'm dumbfounded.

Moriah pulls up a chair from a neighboring empty table and takes a seat with the couple as she holds the still cranky toddler.

She bounces, rocks, and soothes the crier. Though it seems to have lessened the wails, she hasn't stopped it.

She says something to the mother and points to the bar that isn't far off from the space they sit.

She takes the toddler to the bar and asks the bartender something.

Confused at first, he then gives an affirmative nod, ducks under the bar for something and hands an object wrapped in a paper towel back to Moriah.

She takes the little girl back to the table with her parents, places her in the high chair and sits next to her as she hands her the wrapped item.

Suddenly, the howls stop.

Moriah doesn't leave immediately, but when she does, the gratitude on the mothers face is undeniable and so is the sympathy in Moriah's as she hugs the mom and begins to walk back towards our table.

She sits silently, allowing the smile she had to slowly take its course and fade away.

"I'm sorry," She says, "I didn't intend to be gone for so long."

I'm nearly speechless at the act I just witnessed from her.

As hardened as she comes across, it's obvious that there's warmth behind the walls she's built around her.

"No need to apologize," I say, "What was it that you gave to her to stop the crying?"

"An icicle. I saw that she had some teeth poking through her gums and they were a little swollen, something cold to soothe is all the poor thing needed," She smiles bashfully.

While she was gone our waiter came to take our orders and they're now being brought out.

"Ah," I nod, "So, is your side hustle being a baby whisperer?" I ask her before we fall back into the silence we were in.

She doesn't try to hide her giggle and it's the sweetest sound I've ever heard.

"No, it isn't," She responds as she places a napkin on her lap.

"You're just naturally good with kids?"

She looks at me before responding, then picks up her fork and knife to begin cutting her salmon, "I guess so. I used to babysit a lot in high school to make my own money, I guess it just comes naturally," I notice her mouth fidgets as she tries to bite back a smile, I assume at the memories that may be flashing in her mind.

I nod.

"Do you want kids of your own?" I ask after neither of us speaks for a moment.

She takes a thoughtful bite of her food and of course, takes her time to respond. Always making me wait on her and I've come to realize it's something I don't mind doing.

"Yeah, I do," She answers with her eyes casted downward, "But only with a man I can trust. I've seen the effects of having kids with someone who isn't ready. I'd need a formal binding contract written and signed as well as a psych evaluation conducted before I agree to bear any children with a man."

Her reply seems more loaded than what she intended and I can see the pause she takes when she realizes that she may have shared more than she wanted to.

I nod in response, "I get that," I cut into my steak, trying to choose my next words carefully, "I think you'd be a good mother. A nurturing one," I look up at her as I finish my sentiment.

She pauses as she takes another bite of her food, staring back at me. I assume this isn't something she's used to being told. I'm glad I could say something she needed to hear.

Though the rest of the date isn't filled with riveting conversation, it is filled with a change of perspective.

Seeing Moriah in this light confirms to me that this fierceness she leads with, is more defense mechanism than who she is at heart. I don't think this is something that would've been discovered without tonight happening.

I don't know much of her story, or what she's been through, but it doesn't take much now to see that behind the stoic face she presents to the world is a soft, kind heart.

One that doesn't fall at the feet of every man that offers her something.

You have to earn her.

Though I would probably never admit this to my sister, I'm glad Rayana put me up to this. And, I'm even more thankful that I'm meeting a different side of the woman that makes me question everything I've known within just a moment of looking at her.

Before we know it, our night is over and I walk her outside to wait for her uber.

"Did you enjoy yourself?" I ask her as we stand side by side at the curb.

She offers a grin so small one could question if it actually existed, "I did," She looks to her feet and then back to me, "I'm sorry that I wasn't much of a conversationalist, probably not the most entertaining date."

"No, no," I laugh, "You were fine. I enjoyed my time just observing and sharing the space with you, honestly," I smile,

"Plus, I'm sure your nighttime job as a baby magician takes a lot out of you."

To my delight, that earns me a laugh, one of the most genuine I've heard from her tonight.

"Yeah, being a part time superhero really takes a toll," She jokes, something else I don't assume she does often.

Her uber finally arrives after a few minutes pass us and I walk her to the door of the backseat.

"I really did have a time tonight," She says after I open the door for her.

She surprises me when she places a chaste kiss on my cheek. While she may have thought nothing of the interaction… I know the feeling of her lips in that exact spot will not fade any time soon.

I close the door after I see she's entirely inside the car, wait for it to pull off and look at my wrist to check the time.

My grandfather's watch looks back at me, and I suddenly feel like we weren't the only two people on this date tonight.

---

## *Moriah*

The date ended quicker than I hoped it would, though we were out until almost midnight.

I admit that I am attracted to Darrell, very attracted if I'm being honest. And after tonight, I worry it's only grown deeper.

He looked like a girl's dream and worst nightmare all wrapped in one and I fear he'll prove himself to be both.

His haircut was crisp, his beard freshly shaped and trimmed and he wore an all black attire. A tucked black shirt, black slacks and belt as well as shoes to match.

He sported a beautiful silver antique watch as well, the man has taste to be.

It was simple yet still felt like my absolute undoing.

His smile, even when barely there, is something hand crafted by a mythical god.

Being able to have a closer look at him, I realized he has the absolute nerve to have dimples. God did not play fair when he was created.

He didn't try to kiss me, he didn't hug me either. He was the picture perfect gentleman, something I did not expect of him at all, this is what moved me to give him a very, very quick peck on the cheek. Something I didn't even expect from myself.

I appreciated that he didn't force anything throughout the night, conversation or otherwise, he allowed me to flow at my natural pace.

Most men view me as a challenge and try to throw axes at the walls they see around me. Unbeknownst to them, causes me to just further fortify them.

He didn't do that.

He didn't get upset with me for helping someone, or label it as me trying to get brownie points and prove that I'm a selfless businesswoman who runs a foundation, something that other dates have done.

He didn't view it as a marketing tactic.

He saw it as nothing other than me acting in accord with my true nature. He even called me nurturing, an adjective not commonly used when describing me.

My thoughts about the date come to a halt as the Uber pulls up to my fathers home. I step out and walk to the door, opening it and immediately begin to take off my heels as soon as I close it behind me.

My sister startles me when she emerges from the kitchen, "So," She speaks, "How did it go?" I notice she plays with her hands in front of her. I know that means her nerves are in the room with us.

"It was really good, actually," I answer her kindly, "Please, don't tell your gossip buddy I said that," Referring to our clucking hen of a father.

She giggles, "It'll stay between us."

Silence falls between us and neither of us move from our positions.

"Listen, I-"

"Moriah,-"

We both speak at once.

AJ smiles, "You can go first."

I take in a breath. It's been quite some time since I've had to do this, "I'm sorry, AJ. I shouldn't have blown up at you the way I did. I'm sure I gave dad a heart attack too." I look down to my feet, "I should've given you a chance to express yourself and defend your choices. You would've done that for me. I was wrong."

She just smiles and walks to close the large gap between us.

"Thank you," She says, "I'm sorry for not talking to you about it beforehand. I'm not the only one affected here, I should've been more considerate of your perspective."

We smile at one another for a moment.

I hug my sister and sigh into her scent.

I hate being on the outs with her.

She's my truest partner in crime, I could never treat her anything less than she deserves when she absolutely deserves the world for all that she does and has always done for me and our dad.

I vow to myself to never allow this to happen again.

"Do you want me to tell you why I'm looking for her?" She asks as we break out embrace.

I nod.

She leads me to the sofa so we can have a seat.

She takes a deep breath and says, "I found out I have a defect in my uterus."

I look at her wide eyed, "What?"

She nods with a tight smile, "I have cervical stenosis. To make a long explanation short, because of it, I may not be able to ever have kids, Mo," She gives me one of the saddest smiles I've ever seen on my sister's face.

"So, I need to find her. I need to find her to ask her how it was so easy to abandon not one but two miracles, two blessings that some women will never experience, and not think to ever look back," She explains.

I'm not an easy crier, but a tear sheds for my sister.

"I'm not looking for her to have a family reunion, I'm looking for her because I need to see her eyes when she gives me an explanation."

"AJ… I'm so sorry. I don't know what to say."

My sister is basically the only mother I've ever known aside from my grandmother, it would only make sense that we've always imagined her life with a family of her own. And to know she now may never see that day, it makes my heart ache as if the news is about me.

She smiles and squeezes my hand.

"There's nothing to say, Mo. It's not uncommon, it's just unfortunate. I'll have my family when the time is right, it just may not happen the way I've dreamt of."

I hug my sister.

The one that has taught me nurture and love and selflessness and forgiveness. If I have to have all of her children for her, I'd happily and readily give myself up to the task if it meant it was closer to the dream she's always had.

"Now," She ends our hug, "Back to you. Would you go out with him again?" She asks with that childlike excitement in her voice. It reminds me of our teens.

I take in a deep breath, trying to push away the conversation that she clearly doesn't want to continue.

"I think I would, AJ," I nod with my words. "I'm going to be honest though, saying that out loud scares the absolute hell out of me."

# CHAPTER *TWENTY-FIVE*

## *Darrell*

*I* pull up to Honey's home after ending my work day.

I'm here so much it's easy to forget I have my own home that I pay rent and utilities for.

I use my copied key to enter Honey's home and I'm greeted with the warm aroma of something being conjured up in the kitchen. I follow the scent and find Honey in one of her favorite spots in her home.

"Hey there," I calmly greet her to avoid a startle since her back is towards me as I enter. I place a kiss on the crown of her head and she continues to shuffle around vegetables she has in the skillet in front of her.

"Hey DJ," She smiles without breaking her focus, but despite her smile, there's something in her voice that betrays her. "How was work baby?"

I walk over to the refrigerator to scout out something to drink, "It was okay. You know, it was work," I answer her while I take out a can of soda.

She hums in response.

"How was your day? Ang took you to the doctors today, right? How'd it go?"

She moves from the skillet to the pot of rice, stirring it around.

"It was okay. You know, it was the doctors," She grins at me over her shoulder.

I return her grin, though I can't shake the feeling that there's something heavy in this kitchen with us.

"You never told me about your date. How did it go?" She takes a break from checking on whatever she's prepping for dinner and joins me at the kitchen table.

"The date was good. Better than expected," I tell her honestly.

It was way better than I anticipated it to be.

Moriah may not be a chatterbox but I now think it's only because she's so hyper focused on protecting herself.

For some reason I don't quite understand, I want to do my best to make her comfortable enough to share whatever it is that's going on behind those doe eyes of hers, with me. To show her I'm not someone she needs protecting from.

My grandmother smiles.

"I'm glad to hear that son," She calls me affectionately, "You've been so focused on work and everyone around you that I can't remember the last time you actually enjoyed yourself."

The concern Honey has always had for my happiness is genuine. Ever since I was a child she's encouraged that I do what makes me happy.

For as long as I could remember, I thought taking care of her and my sisters in any way I could, devoting myself to them the way Gramps did to our entire family would accomplish that. That it would be fulfilling enough.

But, ever since my date with Moriah, I've been questioning that more and more.

"I don't want you to put your horses before your carriage there though, Granny," I grin, "This was a one time date. We aren't rushing to write any vows for our wedding day. You know how I feel about relationships and the whole notion of love anyway."

She smiles at me, the way a knowing grandmother does.

"What I know is that you went through a lot at a young age and you've allowed it to affect your view of something that can be so beautiful."

I look at her with sympathy. You can see where Rayana got her hopeless romantic trait from.

"What's beautiful about something that can cloud your judgment so much so that you put it before your own children, at any cost?" I ask her, and though we're the only two in this room, I know that question isn't for her.

She knows it too, so she holds my hand across the tabletop between us and gives it a firm hold. She returns the sympathetic look I gave to her a few moments ago.

It's funny sort of when you think about it.

She feels bad for me because I refuse to believe that 'love' is a remedy, and I feel bad for her because she believes it's the best medicine a heart can have.

"Your mom being young and love struck is no excuse for her not owning up to her responsibilities."

"Yeah, five times over," I huff.

"But DJ," She continues, "that wasn't the only example of love, or lack thereof, that you were shown. You act as if you never witnessed how good love could feel, the joy that it actually does bring."

I cast my eyes down to where our hands are still joint on the table.

"Your grandfather and I swam in love," She offers a sad smile, "From the day we met until the day he left us. I'll never for the life of me be able to understand why your mother didn't soak up the example she saw of what real love looked like and chased after men who dangled dreams in front of her. Maybe she was too busy with her own life to pay attention. And Gramps as my witness, I beat myself up everyday for not getting to Sy'Asia, Anthony and Angie sooner than I did. But you and Rayana, I know you saw love way more than you didn't. I know we got to you in time."

Something in her voice tightens, and whatever it is wraps around my heart as she continues to speak.

"We made sure to pour all we had into you and your siblings as much as possible, to show you that your mothers choices didn't define love, that it looked different. Your grandfather taught you so many things about growing up and maturing and how to lead. But I know for fact, he always taught you about love. Because it's him who taught it to me." I hear the tears in her voice before I see them escape from her eyes.

"Honey-"

"No, boy. You listen," She raises her finger to me.

"Your grandfather made sure that everyone under this roof knew what love was and what it could do even to those who felt love just didn't exist. Look at how he never gave up on Anthony. Your brother saw way more of the things your mother did than you and by the time he came to live with us, he was a shell of a person, running on autopilot and sheer survival. And your grandfather and his love, that's what healed that boy. Love is what moved him to not give up on your brother until he couldn't find against it anymore."

I listen to her as the memories I have flash before me.

I was 9 years old and Rayana was 4 when we came to live with Gramps and Honey.

My three older siblings, Sy'Asia 17, Anthony 15 and Angeline 12, stayed with our mom for some time after our leaving.

Because they were so much older, there was plenty they were able to shield Rayana and I from. They are the ones that truly saw the worst of our mothers activities.

I faintly remember times Sy'Asia would have to help our drunken mom into the house while Anthony would try to scare off a man she bought home from whatever bar she'd just have spent hours at. Angie would take us into the bedroom before we could see things we'd be scarred from.

They all had some understanding of a chain of responsibility.

Sy'Asia being the oldest made the more executive decisions. Anthony would reinforce them. They took care of the bigger things like groceries, keeping the house clean and appropriate so as not to draw attention to us while our mom would've been gone for a few days.

While they did that, Angie kept us bathed and helped me with my homework. My unspoken responsibility was playing with Rayana or soothing her when she cried.

No one asked me to, but even at that young age, I saw everyone else had a role and I naturally wanted to take one on too.

"You better stop walking around here like love gave you the short end of the stick when you are one of the more fortunate ones of your siblings because love found you early. It's time for you to knock off this imaginary monkey on your back," My grandmother scolds me.

And she's right.

I'm lucky I didn't see even half of the things my siblings did.

It's because of all of this that I feel that I owe them so much. That I feel like I owe my grandparents for saving me and my siblings from shielding me.

But when making both parties proud conflicts with each other, with one side wanting me to focus solely on responsibility and the other to focus on my heart, something I've kept on ice for so long, what am I supposed to do?

"I'm sorry, Honey," Is all I can manage to respond, because I am.

I talk so much about the hard work she and my grandfather did raising me and I'm not showing my appreciation for it, truly.

"Don't be sorry, DJ," She grins softly, "You want to make me proud? Let yourself feel something other than duty. You like this girl, don't you?"

I chuckle, more to myself than at her question. Grandmothers have such a way of seeing you better than you do yourself.

"Honey, I told you. She made it clear that it was a one time thing, it was hardly a date if you ask her."

"That isn't what I asked you. Do you like her?"

I sigh, "I guess I do."

She smiles, "Then like her, DJ. If you won't give yourself permission then I will. Matter of fact, I'm not giving you permission, I'm telling you to like her, as much as your heart can. That's an order," She says in a feigned serious tone.

A weight that I didn't know was on my chest lifts from off of me.

Maybe that's what was holding me back, worrying that this would distract me from showing how grateful I am. But, the only way that could happen is if I actually stop being grateful.

My grandfather led a life of love, from his family to his friends to strangers. That's what he taught me, and I was walking my path as if duty and love are synonyms when they aren't.

I think it's time I genuinely follow his example.

I give her a small nod and smile, returning the firm hold she has on my hand before she stands and returns to the stove and oven to finish what's being prepared.

"Oh, and one more thing, DJ," She says as I go to exit the kitchen, "Make sure you're here for dinner tomorrow night, I need to talk to you and your siblings."

"Is everything alright?" I ask immediately.

"I just need you here tomorrow night, DJ. I need to talk to you all at the same time. Everything will be alright, but yes, it is important."

I don't move from my spot in the doorway.

At this moment, my body tells me that whatever this heavy thing is I've felt since I've gotten here, is actually heavier than I thought.

# CHAPTER *TWENTY-SIX*

*Darrell*

I made sure I was early tonight.

My siblings and I do our best to have an entire family dinner at Honey's when we can, but she's never specifically requested our presence as a whole group, so it goes without saying that I'm a bit concerned.

My thoughts have been so occupied today with whatever this news could be that I couldn't even take any excitement in the fact that when Moriah sent me an email for the agenda of our next meeting, she added a note at the bottom thanking me again for the date.

I was glad to see her mention it, but as quickly as my smile came, it disappeared when I remembered the impending doom of tonight.

We're currently all gathered at the table and Rayana and Angeline just finished bringing out the dishes that Honey prepared.

The tension among us is high as we all sit around the table waiting in anticipation.

"Honey, come on, are we going to get to the elephant in the room yet or not?" Ang is the first to speak. I think it's middle child syndrome that causes her to have less tact than the rest of us when she talks.

We all look from her to Honey, who sits at the head of the table.

She returns our stares.

“Well, I figured you’d at least want to start eating first. We usually talk about our days before any heavy stuff is sitting in between our meals,” She tries to make light of the circumstance before her, only she’s met with silence and blank expressions.

I notice Anthony, who sits to her left, hasn’t attempted to pick up a utensil to begin his meal or even pretend to. He takes a sip of water and tries to quietly clear his throat, not meeting anyones eyes.

Sy’Asia also seems off.

I look to them, then to my sister Rayana who is already looking at me, and something in my stomach tells me that one of my biggest fears is about to become a reality.

“Well,” Our grandmother clears her throat, “You all know that I’m no young and tender thing any longer,” She laughs, still hoping to lighten the air around her, “And, with aging comes its own issues.”

Simultaneously, I see Anthony’s jaw harden and Sy’Asia’s eyes cast downard.

All alarms set off within my body at once.

“With that being said, you also know I don’t take thousands of medications for no reason,” She looks around at all of us, “I’ve been doing my best to put this off for as long as I can, however, I’ve been told that it’s time to make everyone aware.”

No.

She swallows a deep breath, "I have cancer."

"What?!" Both Angeline and Rayana exclaim in unison.

I remain silent.

"I have heart cancer. I've known for some years now, since a little while after your grandfather left us. There was no need to be too alarmed at the time," She inhales, "However, now… my doctor says there isn't anything left for them to do."

I hear the strain in her voice as she tries to remain calm among the chaos that now surrounds her.

To my left I hear the sobs of my two sisters, Rayana and Sy'Asia. Angeline sits across from me with eyes wide and mouth open.

"You knew, didn't you?" I speak finally to my older brother who has not moved a muscle in his body since our grandmother began talking.

He finally looks up to meet my gaze, but he remains silent, his face hard.

"Both Anthony and Sy'Asia, being the two oldest, were told first, yes," Honey confirms.

My focus doesn't leave my brother who holds on to my glare.

"Why didn't you tell me?" I ask him.

Still he remains silent.

"Is that what all that bullshit was about in my office some weeks back, when I was telling you that I was worried about her and you basically told me we all have to die one day? It was because you already knew?" My voice begins to raise and I don't bother adjusting it.

"DJ, it isn't Anthony's fau-"

"Angie, I'm not talking to you," I cut my sister off, "Why didn't you tell me?" I repeat.

"It wasn't my information to tell," He finally speaks, keeping his voice so low it almost sounds like a mumble.

"Wasn't your information to tell?!" I shout, "You don't think I should've known that our grandmother that I care for every day was fucking dying? That wasn't information you thought you should tell me?"

"DJ," I hear Honey speak, but I feel l an Ox ready for battle, I can't back down.

"You aren't the only one that cares for her, Darrell," He says my name like it has a sour taste, "If I tell you, what justification do I have to then not tell anyone else? Do you think I wanted to keep this from any of you?" Though still deceptively calm, he begins to sit up in his seat a little more.

"I don't know. With this idea that someone appointed you the head of the household, maybe you did need to keep it to yourself, so you could feel like you actually had some fucking purpose aside from being an asshole."

"Are you fucking dumb?" He leans into the table.

"Anthony!" Honey yells.

"Are you?!" I stand from my seat.

"DJ, calm down, this isn't the time for this," Rayana tugs at my arm.

"Get off of me, Ray!" I snatch away my arm.

"Maybe if you weren't so busy worrying about getting your dick wet with some woman that you're supposed to be working with, you would've known something sooner," He stands from his chair also.

"Anthony Washington, that is enough!" Honey slams her open palms into the table.

Everyone silences.

Shouting never had a place in this home. Not from the adults, nor the children and that wasn't just for the sake of what we came from but a rule that was formed before us.

We haven't broken this rule since our adolescence.

"Darrell and Anthony, I suggest you sit your behinds back in those chairs at this very moment," She demands of us with a low but dangerous tone.

Keeping our eyes on each other, we slowly return to our seats.

Honey eyes us both.

"Now," She begins, "It is no one's fault that those who knew first, knew. Anthony is acting as my Power of Attorney solely because of him not only being the oldest of you two," She looks to me, "But also due to the role he plays in his work. It made sense to me. I requested that both he and Sy'Asia not mention anything until I was ready."

My sister still has not spoken, silently allowing tears to freely fall from her eyes.

"Because they have been through the things they have and they've seen the things they've seen, I trust them both to handle what I've asked of them to handle." She continues.

"How did you not know? Didn't you take her to the doctors?" Rayana asks Angie.

"She wouldn't let me into the office with her. When she came out, she told me everything was fine."

I keep my eyes on the now cold food in front of me.

"Anthony," She turns her attention to my brother, "Your brother's dealings with whatever woman, not only isn't your business but also is not something to use against him when he could've been here day in and day out and I still would have only shared this information when I was ready to," She reprimands, “Quite frankly, I hope that you soon follow in his footsteps in that regard.”

“So…” Rayana says quietly, “Does that mean you’re dying?” She asks aloud the very thing none of us, including our grandmother, wanted to give a voice to.

She squares her shoulders but keeps the empathy in her face, “Yes, my sweet girl,” She replies, “It does mean that I won’t be with you for too much longer.”

“But, can’t it go into remission or whatever it’s called?” Angie asks, trying to mask her franticness.

Honey offers her a sad grin, “No, baby. We’re past the possibility of remission.”

A sob escapes Sy’Asia.

Though our mother raised her primarily, Honey was truly the only mother she’d known. The one that allowed her to be a teenager, that didn’t leave her with a family to raise. The one that treated her like a daughter she loved, and not a roommate to help her out on a late night.

Rayana pulls her in close and allows her to continue her cries into her shoulder.

“I don’t want this to lead you all to treating me like I’m any more fragile,” Honey speaks once the sound of the cries around the room quiets a little more, “I’m not tied down to a bed yet. We’re going to carry on as we normally would until I cannot do it any longer.”

“Will you tell us when that is?” I ask. Knowing my grandmother, she’ll move until her last, dying breath.

She knows we know this about her, and she laughs, “Yes. I’ll be honest about my limits as they come. I’m not trying to speed this process by overworking.”

I nod.

Anthony and I exchange silent glances briefly, and then break them.

Life has a cruel way of poking at you.

As soon as I meet someone that I'm willing to take a risk on, here comes the worst thing I could ever fathom, just to remind me not to allow the idea of love to distract me from what's important.

Impeccable timing and a crossroads that I don't have an inkling of direction on.

And the only two people I'd think to ask, well, one isn't here and the other one won't be for much longer.

A matter of head versus heart, a game I've never been good at.

# CHAPTER *TWENTY-SEVEN*

## *Moriah*

*It's* been days since I've spoken to Darrell.

For the meeting that we had scheduled earlier this week, he sent one of his representatives in his place, not even his sister attended.

I told Anastasia how good our date went and that I'd definitely take him up on the offer of a second but now, I'm worried that I'm the only one that felt that way.

This is why I don't bother.

There's always certain disappointment when you start to allow yourself to get wrapped up in matters of the heart.

Here I am, sad that a man hasn't spoken to me, since when does that sound like me?

Exactly, it doesn't.

I decided instead of sitting around, refreshing my inbox, to go to the market and buy some of my favorite sweets. I'm not often saddened by things, but when I am, the only remedy is to give myself a stomach ache from sugar.

I approach the freezers and search for an ice cream that looks like it'll soak up any unwanted feelings, when I nearly knock someone out cold with the door.

"I'm so sorry, oh my goodness-" I stop short upon noticing who it is.

Darrell's younger sister, Rayana, I think her name was.

"It's fine," She laughs, "What better place to be knocked out than surrounded by a bunch of ice cream pints."

I laugh, I wonder if their whole family is this easy going.

"Well," I grab my ice cream and put it in my cart, "I'm still sorry. I'm usually more mindful."

"It's fine, really," She assures me again.

I quickly peek at her cart and see that we may have shared the same mind today.

"Having a sweet tooth attack too?" I nod at the cart full of juices, small cakes and other sweets.

She looks down and laughs again, "This makes me look like such an irresponsible shopper. I swear I'm not."

"Hey, it isn't for my fridge, what do I care?" I shrug.

She smiles for a moment and then it fades, "It's just been a long week, ya'know?" Her humor escapes her.

"Yeah," I look to my feet and back at her, "Yeah, I do know unfortunately." I give her a small, empathetic smile.

We're silent for a beat.

"Well, I better get going before they send the hounds for me. I'm surprised they let me go for this long," She smiles and begins to push her cart. I'm assuming that the they she's referring to are her family.

"See ya," I say as she passes by.

I stand for a minute in my spot and I can't find the urge as hard as I try, I call after her before she exits the aisle.

"Hey, Rayana?"

She stops and turns to me, "Yeah?"

"How's um," I try to think of something to say that doesn't give the impression that I'm waiting around for a guy who clearly isn't thinking about me, "Your family?"

She tilts her head slightly and gives a sad half grin, "They've been better, for sure."

That wasn't the response I expected.

"Oh? Anything wrong?"

She turns her cart around and heads back towards me, stopping just a few feet away, "No, actually. We just found out that Honey has cancer, and not only that," She huffs a humorless chuckle, "She only told us because know she's too far along for treatments to actually do anything other than maybe keep her comfortable for however long she has left."

If my mouth had hinges, they surely would've broken.

"Oh my god, Rayana, I'm so, so sorry to hear that. I can't imagine what you all are going through right now."

My sympathy is genuine and I hope she knows that, and that it isn't based on attempts to find her brother.

"Yeah, we're sorry too, thank you," She looks down and then back to me, "If Darrell hasn't been saying anything, that's why."

It's as if she could hear my thoughts.

"I don't know if you know this about him yet, but he's very, very loyal to his family and duty oriented. To a fault, if you ask me. So, after the news, I don't even have to ask him to know he's probably retreated back into his corner and wants to give his all to his family right now. He worries so much about failing us somehow, our grandmother doesn't even know where he got that from, that's just always been how he is."

I nod, “I understand that. More than you know, honestly,” I say, “I just hadn’t heard from him so I wondered if he was alright.”

“He enjoyed the date, Moriah.”

She has to have superpowers.

I try to hide the breath of relief I took.

“A lot, actually. I was very happy to see him excited. It’s not something we often see from him or my other brother for that matter.”

I give her a small smile, “Well, I’m glad I could help out then.”

She returns my smile.

“I am, too,” She replies to me, “He’s a little awkward when it comes to the dating thing, it isn’t you, I promise.”

I maintain my smile at her reassurance, and also silently chastise myself for caring.

We’re silent for a moment again.

“Actually…” She says, “I’m headed back home now, I live with Honey. It’s just us there. Do you maybe want to come with?”

I’m sure I couldn’t have looked more taken aback.

She laughs..

“Honey loves company, trust me. It’ll be fine.”

After a few hesitant moments, I accepted the offer.

We both take our carts and head to the checkout line. After being rung up, we head to our cars and I wait for her to take the lead so I can follow her home.

This is not how I expected this day to turn out, but since I’m already in the thick of making questionable decisions, what's a few more?

---

I'm trailing Rayana as she leads me to her family's home.

I can only imagine how crazy they'll think I am from popping up at their house. "*After only one date, and no sex, you're already making house calls?*" God, I'm already embarrassed.

When we arrive at the house she pulls into the driveway and I park on the street. I take a breath as I watch her getting out of the car, knowing that I can't back out now.

The walk from where my car is parked to the driveway is not a short one.

The home looks straight out of an old country movie.

The movies of the big families that have kids running around the huge area of land, swinging on tire swings that hang from a tree, which they do have.

There's a porch that wraps all the way around with outdoor furniture that you can tell isn't new, but I'm sure is filled with so many memories.

"Here," I say as I approach Rayana at the trunk of her car, "Let me carry something," I offer. To be so young, she seems to have tuckered the hell out. I figure the least I could do was lighten the load.

She thanks me and we walk up the long pathway, into the house.

"Honey!" She calls out as she opens the door, "I'm back, and I bought a random woman I found at the market."

I laugh, because she actually seems like the type to do something like that.

"Girl, you better not have bought no-" The older woman stops her fussing when she sees me as she walks out of the kitchen.

"Oh, this is no stranger!" She smiles, I can't help but to smile back, "Come on now, bring those bags back here and sit them down." We follow her footsteps into the kitchen.

"Ray baby, you okay?" Her grandmother calls over her shoulder to her.

With a few huffs of breath, "Yeah," she responds, "I'm good, I'm good," She plops down onto a chair at the kitchen table, "I'm glad Moriah is here though, there's no way I was going to be able to make a double trip."

"Yes, so good you ran into her," She looks at me again with a hand resting on her hip, "How are you, Moriah? How's your dad doing?" She asks me as if we've met on more occasions than just that random day in the grocery store.

Something about her energy sucks me in.

"I'm good, and he's good too. Thank you for asking," I smile, "How are you doing?" I ask before I can stop myself and I feel like an idiot.

I'm guessing the expression on my face reflects my inner thoughts. She smiles at me, "I woke up today, Moriah. So, I'm great."

"That's beautiful," I tell her, honestly.

"Mo, I hope I can call you that," Rayana looks at me, not exactly asking for permission but more so giving me a moment to adjust to her using the nickname.

I laugh, she has this glow about her that you can't help but smile at, "Yeah, you can,"

"Great. Mo, can you grab a water out of the fridge? I'd get it myself, honestly. I just am pretty sure that if I get up right now, I'm going to fall back into my seat."

Though I'm curious about her being tired, I readily grab a cold water from the refrigerator and hand it to her.

"Now, when you've gathered yourself," Honey says, "Y'all need to help put away these groceries. I don't eat all this stuff alone," She turns back to what I assume is the lunch she's preparing.

"You want a sandwich too, Moriah?" She asks me from her spot at the counter.

"Yes, she does," Rayana answers before I can open my mouth, she then looks at me, "Trust me, her sandwiches are better than the ones you get straight from a deli," She says confidently.

I just laugh.

To be virtually strangers, it feels like I'm in the home of a family I've known for years. It's the oddest, yet most comfortable thing I've experienced in my life. Almost like being around the family of my best friend, only with better food.

After a while, Rayana is ready to put away groceries and I'm at my feet prepared to help her.

The two women and I fill the kitchen with footsteps, clankings of dishes and laughter as we all move around the kitchen completing our respective tasks.

We were so wrapped in our own world that we didn't hear the guys come into the house at all.

"Well," A deep voice startles us all from the doorway, "What's going on in here?"

I assume the man asking this question is Anthony. A sibling I've had yet to be introduced to.

His face is serious, it looks like his brows are permanently furrowed and jaw constantly set hard. His eyes are filled with scrutiny, and he doesn't try to hide it.

He asks the question to the room, but his eyes are only focused on me and I don't know how to respond.

Darrell appears from behind him with a few other bags filled with what I'm assuming are more groceries.

His eyes find me immediately, only I can't read them as easily as his brothers.

I don't know if he's happy or sad to see me. I'm sure he's confused above all, which is understandable.

What if Honey's circumstance isn't the real or only reason why he's been avoiding me? And now I look like a crazed woman who has found a way to infiltrate his family's home.

He found me, not parked outside, across the street like a normal crazy person, no.

He found me laughing and talking with his baby sister and grandmother, in her kitchen of all places.

If I were him, I'd immediately call the police and curse him out from A to Z while we wait for them to arrive.

I prepare myself for him to ask me to leave. Instead, he walks past his brother and sits the bags he held onto the kitchen table.

He then finds both his sister and grandmother and greets them with hugs and kisses.

He stops a foot or two away from me and I hold my breath.

He softly grins, only it doesn't reach his eyes.

"Hey," He quietly says.

"Hey."

We don't say anything else, and the air feels thin around me.

"May I ask, Ms. Jackson, I assume, what are you doing in my grandmother's home?" Anthony asks from his place at the doorway.

I open my mouth to respond but my voice doesn't find its way out.

Instead, Honey answers for me.

"She was invited, Anthony," She says a little less warm than I'm sure she usually is.

I look between the two of them and I think there's a silent understanding that he isn't to respond any further.

"Now that's out of the way," Honey claps her hands together and smiles, "I'm making sandwiches for lunch. Tell me now what you want on yours before I just make it the way I like it," She returns to busying herself with the contents.

Anthony damn near breathes fire out his nose and walks away from the kitchen.

Rayana finishes putting the last of the groceries away.

"Hey," Darrell touches my arm, "Come out back with me?"

I nod and follow him to the other half of the wrap-around porch.

I brace myself for him to unleash what he may have been trying to contain in front of his family, and square my shoulders to face what I feel is impending rejection sure to come.

# CHAPTER *TWENTY-EIGHT*

## *Darrell*

*Confused* and surprised would be an understatement if someone asked me to give language to what I felt seeing Moriah in my grandmother's kitchen.

Then after confusion started to fade, anxiety took its place.

I haven't exactly been avoiding her, but I haven't been seeking her out either. I know I have to give her an explanation, she deserves that, I just haven't had a chance to think of one that makes sense.

The words still haven't come to me even now with her in front of me in my grandmother's backyard. She always looks too beautiful for me to collect my thoughts, even with nerves painted on her face.

Her hair sits on top of her head, ringlets spilling in every direction. She wears no makeup, clothed in a baby blue tank top that doesn't exactly meet the top of the matching sweatpants she's wearing, and a hoodie she keeps pulling around herself.

Her eyes haven't exactly met mine yet.

And her lips, they aren't covered in lip gloss but they look moisturized still. Soft and plump, just begging me to skip the words and let my actions do the talking instead.

"So…" She speaks into the silence around us, "This is where you grew up?"

I nod, kicking an imaginary rock at my feet, "Yup, this is the place," I chuckle.

"It's nice," She observes, "Very homey."

I nod again, not too sure about what to say.

"I'm sorry for popping up," She continues when words are failing me, "I ran into Rayana at the market, we got to talking, one thing led to another and she invited me back here. I figured it was a bad idea after I'd already said yes."

I just watch her as she spits out an apology that isn't deserving.

"What?" She asks.

I smirk, "Nothing," Shaking my head, trying to get rid of the thoughts I'm having of silencing her with my own mouth, "Nothing. You have nothing to be sorry for. I told you, my sister likes you. She has good taste in people."

If I didn't know any better, I would've thought she blushed.

"I should be the one apologizing, honestly," I turn my body to face her fully, as she leans on the railing, "I didn't mean to go radio silent on you. A lot happened after our date, but that doesn't give me an excuse to not communicate with you properly."

"You're right," She keeps her eyes on her hands, "It doesn't give you an excuse. But, I understand why it happened, and I'm not upset with you for it," She looks up at me.

"You're not?" The surprise in my voice betrayed my attempt to appear calm.

"No," She stands upright but keeps her eyes out on the grassy land I grew up playing on, "Rayana told me about Honey."

My breath catches in my throat.

I wasn't prepared to discuss that yet, not with anyone.

"I see," I keep my eyes casted on my feet, bracing myself for the unwanted emotions that come up when I think of my grandmother lately.

She grabs my hand that rests on the banister. I try to stop my body from immediately reacting to the contact firstly, because I'm too thrown off mentally to even know how to react and secondly, because I'm almost certain she'd take her hand away and this is not a moment I want to cut short.

I didn't realize until this moment that closeness was something I've needed, not isolation. "I'm sorry you guys are going through this, Darrell," She tries to catch my eye, "I know this is tough anyway, but especially because the loss of your grandfather is so recent."

I laugh, though there is no humor in it.

"Yeah," I scratch at my eyebrow with my thumb, "Yeah, it's hard. She's really the only mom I know. She is for all of us, in different ways."

We don't speak for a moment, and I appreciate that she doesn't look for filler words to get rid of the silence.

"She's a snarky one for sure," She laughs, "She wasted no time giving me chores and it's my first time here."

I laugh, this time it's for real.

"Yeah, that's her for sure. If you come to her house, you're one of her kids just by association and you absolutely will be put to work," I laugh again.

"I know it may be a little forward, and don't feel bad if you want to tell me no but," She hesitates, "I'd like to help around here, with Honey, if that's okay."

My eyebrows meet my hairline quickly, "Are you serious?"

Any trace of humor in her expression dissipates, "Absolutely, if it's okay with you guys."

"Why would you want to do that? I don't have to see your schedule to already know it's tightly packed," I ask.

"Because I know how it feels to lose the most important woman in your life, and I know the effects it can have on a family. I've seen it up close. I'll make the time." She answers with a firm line of her lips. Her face reads determination and dedication to the task, fully aware of what she's saying.

I don't know if it's appropriate but this makes me want to kiss her even more. This woman is full of surprises. First, she's a baby whisperer and now she wants to care for the infirm in her free time? What the hell?

"I'm not going to deny help, the more hands the better. Especially now that we know the truth about what's going on with her, we all plan on rotating the schedule more with her appointments and things."

My brother and I still haven't addressed our moment at dinner, but we've fallen into this unspoken agreement that it's not time to focus on our own issues with one another and to put whatever energy we can spare into Honey while we still can.

"I can jump in, come and clean up, cook dinner, maybe even just keep her company."

"She's probably not going to let you cook," I laugh, "That's the one forbidden thing in this household. All cooking is done by Honey, so long as she's able to do so," I smile, "But, I'm sure she'd have no qualms about the other things."

Moriah smiles, "Great. I'll check my schedule when I get home, and then we can compare to see where I can fit in."

I stare at her for a moment.

"That sounds good."

"Yeah," her voice falters, "I really like her," She smiles.

I nod at the ground, "Yeah," I pick at something on the railing and take my turn to lean on it, "I think she likes you too."

"Can I be honest with you about something?" From the eye contact she gives me I can see the shift in energy.

"Of course."

"I wasn't upset when I didn't hear from you," She looks at her feet now, "I was a little… I don't know, nervous?"

"Nervous?" I repeated back to her, confused, "What for?"

"Well, the reputation I have in the work field isn't limited to just the work field. Guys have been on dates with me and because I didn't talk from entrance to exit or wasn't inviting them back home," She looks back at me now, "They just don't bother calling back," She laughs.

"You thought I didn't enjoy your company?"

She maintains the grin to herself, "Don't get me wrong, I know I'm a catch. I'm beautiful, I have a lot to offer, I get that. But, you know, life and its experiences, the burdens we hold ourselves down with, they can affect you sometimes and in ways you don't expect or ways you don't have the tools to combat. I wouldn't have been surprised, you wouldn't have been the first."

And just like that, another layer is peeled. I want to say it happened effortlessly, but I don't want to get too ahead of myself.

The fact that anyone made her feel like something was wrong with her for taking her time, trying to hold her to the standard of women who readily hand themselves over after the offer of a free meal turns my stomach.

"I told you, Moriah, I enjoyed just observing you in the moments we had nothing to say. I like my silence too sometimes, it's underrated in my opinion."

That earns me a giggle.

"I'm sorry that I didn't give you the reassurance you deserved, I dropped the ball trying to deal with my own things. I should've reached out to you sooner."

"It's fine, life happens," She shrugs.

"It's not fine, especially when someone of your caliber is the subject matter. I'm a communicator. I promise you that unless I say so, you'd never have to doubt what I'm feeling. I'll tell you out of my own mouth," I try to give her the reassurance I should have given her days ago.

"Yeah? Okay, mister communicative, how are you feeling then?" She grins.

I don't return the expression. I'm silent until she looks me in the eye.

"I'm feeling like I'd love to take you on another date, Moriah. That's if you'll let me."

She smiles, this one reaching her eyes and my heart trips over its own beat at the sight of it.

"I feel like…" She feigns a moment of deep thought, "I'd like that very much."

This time, I smile, "Great, I'm happy to hear that."

# CHAPTER
# *TWENTY-NINE*

## *Moriah*

*I'm* normally an open book with those close to me, but when it relates to my recent closeness with Darrell and his family, I've wanted to keep that sacred.

Lord only knows how much Stasi and my sister would overreact.

I've technically been there for working purposes only, but I've still enjoyed getting to know the Washington's. I've missed having a grandmother around, there's nothing like the feel they bring you and Honey easily makes you feel like you're a part of her little village. It may take a little while for those outside of Darrell and Rayana to get on board, but they're coming around slowly. Most of them.

While Sy'Asia is starting to warm up and Angeline is beginning to talk to me more, Anthony still does not hide his not wanting me around.

I'm not sure if it's just about his brother and I, if it's about my offering my help with his family, or both. Either way, he does his best to make me question my own existence whenever we're in the same room.

The daggers Anthony shoots me have been worth it though. Having a front row seat to witnessing Darrell in his natural habitat, seeing him caring for his family… It can make a girl melt, and drip.

Watching him be so attentive to his grandmother, showing her extra patience on the days she's a little more crabby than usual, being at her beck and call is sexy in a way I don't quite understand.

His siblings say this was him before the news came out and it's only increased since. I noticed he shows Rayana the same care. He keeps a close eye on her while she's moving about and is stern about telling her when she's done enough, and taking care of her the rest of the way.

No one has mentioned anything to me directly, but I believe she's ill in some way because his other siblings, even Honey, as sick as she is, treat her the same way.

I've accepted that I've started to like him, and that even while I try to ignore it, it deepens each time I walk in the door and see him helping out in the kitchen or cleaning around the house.

Today we have a meeting scheduled, but because of some conflicting appointments Honey had, he sent a representative instead. It's unfortunate he wasn't able to be here, today is the day we finally meet with the Henderson family.

"I'm so happy to finally meet with you all," I say to the family of three, "I came across your story a while ago but I wanted to have something worth discussing with you once we did finally reach out."

Mister Henderson smiles at both myself, Elijah who sits to the side of me and Tucker, the representative sent by Darrell.

"We thank you for even wanting to reach out, Miss Jackson," He gives a polite nod of thanks, "I've heard about your work in neighboring communities, even with some families that once stayed at the shelter we're at right now. The work you do is selfless and appreciated."

"Thank you, so much, that means a lot," I reply, "I want to assure you that the work we do at Love Unbound is solely from our hearts, it's not to land a spot on a media page or on the news or anything like that."

He gives me a tight smile and nod.

I maintain my smile as I prepare to discuss with him all that we've been working on leading up to this moment.

"As I mentioned a little earlier, joining us today is Mister Tucker, in the place of Mister Washington who typically joins us. They're affiliated with The Middle Men network, an intermediary that assists organizations and foundations like ours to gain access to grants, funds and sponsorships that help families that have found themselves in unfortunate situations such as yourself."

Mister Henderson just listens as I speak.

"Before we reached out, we did work on the back end. The Middle Men team have worked very hard presenting your story to grantmakers and sponsors, showing from the details we were able to glean about you all, not only how deserving you are but also how imperative it is that you have means to care for your two young daughters," I look to the girls who have remained clung to each other since their arrival.

"May I ask the two of you your names, by the way?" I say to them directly.

"Makyla and Everest," The older one, Makyla, answers for them both.

"It's nice to meet the two of you," I smile and return my attention to their father whom I can see appreciates my including them in the conversation.

I go on to explain to him the possibility of receiving funding for housing, direct assistance with finding a new and stable job, as well as tutoring and new clothing for his growing girls.

After I run down all of the options that he was not previously privy to, Tucker then explains what he and his team will need from Mister Henderson and his daughters to further increase his chances of sponsorship, after his team have done their part.

We assure him that we will minimize the need for in person meetings, interviews and any sort of press related things as well as avoid any exploitation of his girls. He needs his free time to prepare himself to find a new job, and we don't want to drag his girls through unnecessary additional stress.

By the end of our meeting, Mister Henderson shared that he had a new found hope. He knew that things would eventually work out, but he didn't see a means for it to happen in his new future and now he does.

I'm beyond grateful that I'm able to provide him with that peace of mind.

As they begin to leave, I notice the girls don't speak during everyone's exchange of goodbyes.

"Hey girls," I call them quietly. Everest turns to me first, Makayla follows immediately after, "Come here."

They cautiously walk to me, Everest wide-eyed, Makyla defensive.

I crouch down so that I can be eye level with Everest and look up to her sister.

"I know that there is a lot going on, stuff that you didn't expect and stuff that you also don't understand. I'm sorry that you're being put through all of this, I can't imagine how stressed you must be," I look at Makyla, "Especially you. I can only imagine the role you must be playing for both your father and your little sister."

She lifts her chin slightly, not in defiance, but almost as if to make me believe she's too strong to be fazed.

"I have a big sister too and she took care of me for a while just like you're doing for Everest. I wouldn't be who I am today if it wasn't for her. So, in case you haven't heard it lately, I speak for all the little sisters around the world when I say, thank you for being you."

I see the resolve in her crumble just a little, but not too much that it's noticeable.

"You guys better get going. I'll see you again soon," I stand, turning them both back to join their father.

Before they walk away, Everest turns around and gives me a hug so quickly I almost don't believe it happened. She says nothing and rejoins her sister and father, leaving me standing with a wealth of emotions.

Moments like that are a part of why when I think about striving to carry out this work. It may seem thankless, it may seem like it isn't a big deal or that it isn't real work, but nothing will ever beat the rewarding moment a child thanks you for helping their family.

I suddenly feel a certain tightness in my chest. Not because of the sweet sentiment, but because the person I would've wanted to share that moment with isn't here.

# CHAPTER *THIRTY*

## *Darrell*

*I've* been looking forward to this date ever since I asked her days ago.

Having her around my family suddenly and so often has definitely required some adjusting to, but it hasn't been a hard thing to do.

As soon as she walks through the doors she's looking for the first task to mark off the to-do list. Honey said she's had to force her to sit down and rest at times, reminding her that she isn't bedridden yet.

It isn't a funny thought, to imagine my grandmother incapable of doing the things I've seen her do all my life, but it is funny to imagine two such strong personalities in that dynamic.

One ready to help and the other fighting to hold on to their independence for as long as she can.

For our second date, I decided to take her to a new adult-only arcade that just opened up in town. I figure we both could use a night to let our hair down, if that's something she does.

"Games, okay," She nods as she takes in the scenery, "This is different," She says more to herself than me. I laugh as she at least tries to sound a little enthusiastic.

"I loved when Gramps would bring me and my sister here. It's the best way to clear your mind in my opinion," We approach the kiosk to purchase our game card, "Instead of worrying about how to be memorable during your next presentation, you can worry about whooping some random, cocky kids ass in air hockey."

I earn a laugh, hopefully just the first of many tonight.

Walking further into the game area, I'm able to get a better look at her under the flashing neon lights around us.

I told her to dress casual, and I realize by her attire that our definitions of casual differ.

She wears a pair of light blue jeans that do wonders for her slightly curvy figure, a tightly tucked white shirt, an oversized black blazer, and low heeled open toed shoes.

Her hair is in cornrows that are pulled back in a bun with curls here and there, and she has that barely there makeup look thing going.

For her, this is simple. But, compared to my black graphic T shirt and wash jeans, she looks like she's fresh out of a conference.

"Okay, so, what do we do first?" She asks with a cadence that tells me she's trying to commit to the idea of clearing her mind, assuming it's not something she does often.

"Whatever you want," I shrug, "What's your favorite?" I scan the various noisy machinery with couples and friend groups filling the room from wall to wall.

"Um…" She hesitates.

"What? You've never been in an arcade before?" I jest.

She doesn’t respond but continues to pretend to scan the room looking for her first target.

“Wait,” I place myself in front of her, filling her vision with only myself, “Have you actually never been to an arcade?”

She bites her lip, trying to avoid my eye contact.

I wish she’d chosen a different time to do that, because that small action has me fighting my inclinations to take her by the hand and beeline for my Range Rover.

I shake my head of the now inappropriate images I have floating through my mind of all the things those lips may be capable of and focus on the bigger issue currently at hand.

“My father was a lawyer. And when left the courtroom, he taught law instead. Arcades weren’t exactly our version of recreation,” She answers me. Now I understand why she looked so out of her element when we arrived.

I assumed it was just a matter of another adult losing their inner child, but her inner child doesn’t even know the freedom an arcade provides.

I take a breath and square my shoulders, accepting the challenge I've been given, “Okay then,” I lower my chin to meet her eyes better, “We have some very serious work to do here tonight.”

I see a ghost of a smile fight its way onto her face as I take her by the hand and lead her towards the bar area.

We start with drinks, I don’t trust her to loosen up enough without assistance. Especially not when relaxing is the main objective, she’ll be too focused on trying to do it rather than just doing it.

I remember that she likes sweet drinks, so I order her the sweetest sounding one on the menu and order myself a whiskey sour.

The bartender places the drinks in front of us where we sit.

"So, here's what we're going to do," I take a sip of my drink then swivel myself towards her, placing my knees between her own, "We're going to start with the age old classic Skee-ball," I point to its location.

She follows my finger and looks to the left of us.

"Then, after that loosens you up a bit, gets your shoulders lubricated, we'll go to the Whack-A-Mole table, just over there," I point over her shoulder.

I didn't realize my arm was so close to her face until she turns to look behind her and her mouth just barely grazes my arm.

Every hair on my body stands at attention. At this rate, I hope that's the only thing on my body that stands up tonight.

If she was fazed at all by the brief contact, I can't tell.

"Then," I try regaining my composure, "We'll see how you're doing and start to move to the big boys."

She takes her straw lazily in between her lips and raises an eyebrow at me, "The big boys? There's tiers?" She huffs a chuckle.

I don't return her laugh, remaining as serious as I can be.

She sobers.

"Right," I empty my glass and stand to my feet, "Let's go rookie," I offer my hand to help her step down from the raised barstool.

She sucks down the rest of her drink through her straw without taking a breath and takes my hand.

"You're a little fish, huh?" I chuckle.

"Weekly brunch dates with Stasi will do that to you."

After walking for a few moments, I feel her eyes on me. I look at her, "What?"

"Um," She laughs and looks down, "I'm off the stool, you know. You gonna let go?"

I didn't notice I never released her hand after helping her down, nor did I notice that she didn't immediately pull away.

Either way, after she brings it to my attention, I let her go.

She smiles, "A pretty corny move for a guy that seems as smooth as you, Washington."

The grin I offer is faint, "Sometimes, corny is best," I reply, "When I *do* intentionally hold your hand, it won't be because of some playbook move. It'll be because you wanted me to."

We reach the Skee-ball machines with a few more silent steps. I glance up at her to take in her non-verbal reaction to the game.

"So…" She eyes it, "You, what? Just throw the balls in the holes?" She places her hands on her hips, not taking her eyes off of the machine.

"If you throw those heavy ass balls, someone will for sure be injured," I correct her, "You take the ball and roll it up the ramp. The goal is to get it in that middle hole as many times as you can."

"That gets the tickets?"

"The most, yeah," I swipe the game card in the two machines in front of us and wait for the games to come to life.

The balls descend and I grab the first one in my machine. She doesn't move, "Have at it, Jackson," I smirk as I prepare to take my first shot.

She watches me for two turns, and then follows suit.

Holding the ball firmly, she eyes it and then her target. The determination in her face is clear and funny as hell. Her brows are pinched closely and that wrinkle in her chin makes its appearance as she twists her mouth in concentration.

As if it's the opening pitch in a baseball game, she lines up the ball to the intended hole, swings her arm a few times to gain momentum and releases it up the ramp.

Determination is met with frustration and damn near vengeance when the ball lands nowhere near the middle hole and instead flies into the top right.

I try to keep my laughter to myself but it's hard.

"You're laughing like you're doing so much better," She gestures to my machine and slaps her hand on her leg.

"Well firstly, I am," I point to my score in comparison to hers, "And secondly, it's not about who's doing better. No one ever really gets the middle one, it's just fun to try. In the meantime, you get some tension out of your body while doing it," I continue to take my turns.

Her hands planted firmly on her hips, she grabs the next ball and watches me again, I can tell she's studying.

After a moment, she drops her arm at her side, letting it hang loosely and swings it two times before releasing the ball up the ramp again.

She still didn't hit her intended target but she scored right below it, that was enough for her.

She tries to contain her excitement of the 'victory' but I catch it anyway.

I'm amazed at how someone can go 27 years without once stepping foot into an arcade, it's as normal as going to the park. If I find out she hasn't been to a playground, I may have a heart attack.

After a few tries she finds a steady flow. She never hits the target she hoped to, but with every score she makes you can see the pride of making it at all.

"Okay," She takes a deep breath, "What's next?" She adjusts her jacket and sticks out her chin as if she's ready for a battle.

I shake my head and retrieve the Skee-ball champions tickets that spill on to the floor.

"Whack-A-Mole, follow me champ," She giggles and trails behind me.

"The fact that you wore heels to an arcade is truly behind me, I must be honest," I tell her as we make our way to the next game.

"It's not like I knew where we were going, you said casual, not athletic," She defends.

I laugh, because who differentiates the two?

We reach the game table.

"Do you need me to explain this one or do you get the gist?" I ask her as she sizes up the machine in front of her, she eyes it like her freedom depends on conquering it.

"No, no I got it. Just fire it up," She picks up the mallet and plants her feet apart, taking a firm stance against the little robotic creatures that prepare to taunt her.

"Just imagine every person that's pissed you off, or every memory you want to forget and fire away," That's the last piece of advice I gave before she attacked the table like there were small fires popping up everywhere.

I knew the girl had some anger in her, but the way she beats at the table, you'd think every single Mole that pops its head through a hole was an ex boyfriend that cheated on her with her best friend.

"Geez, don't break the table Rocky," I laugh at her zeal.

Soon, the game ends and the machine spits out her long line of tickets. Maybe contact sports are more her thing,

"What's next, my arcade connoisseur?" She giggles.

I look at her with a lazy grin, "That drink kicked in, huh?"

"I totally forgot I drank anything. And I had a taste of yours too didn't I?"

"You did," I smile, "Okay, let's try…" I look around, "Basketball," I spot the electrical hoops a few spaces from where we stand.

"I can't play basketball," She says walking next to me.

"You will tonight."

We reach the various basketball games, "I'll give you a choice," I begin, as we face them all, "Little, moving hoop or big and far hoop?"

She takes a thoughtful look at both options.

"The big one. If we're gonna do it, it might as well be close to the real thing."

We approach the large twin hoops and I swipe the card in both machines, releasing the basketballs.

As the balls are being released, I immediately begin to shoot. For a moment I lose myself in it, remembering the way Gramps would pick up to give me a better chance of making a basket.

I could never make it, no matter how high he held me, but he still held me up every time, letting me try. Until one day, I made it and he celebrated with me like I'd won my first championship.

It wasn't until I heard a frustrated gruff that I'm taken out of my memories. I look to the right of me to see an irritated Moriah, not getting anywhere close to the hoop with the shots she takes.

For a moment, I just watch out of the corner of my eye, her irritation growing with every throw but she keeps trying. It isn't until I see she's about to call it quits that I stop shooting.

"You have to bend your knees a little," I throw my basketball back into the pen and turn my attention to her fully.

"What? That doesn't make sense," She contorts her face at me.

I leave my own machine and join her, "Yes, it does. It helps the ball propel when you throw it. And," I stand a foot behind her, "Your not bending your wrist when you throw."

I can see the tension in her body appear as I stand behind her. She looks over her shoulder to me, "Try it. Even just bending a little will get you closer" I say, still keeping space between us.

She stands with her feet shoulder length apart, bends knees and shoots. The ball goes higher, but not closer to the hoop.

"Ball-related games don't seem to be my thing," She laughs to herself, but I hear the disappointment. Just meeting Moriah, it isn't hard to tell that she's been an overachiever most of her life, or at least isn't used to failing, at anything.

"It just takes practice, like with anything else," I respond even though she wasn't talking to me.

She doesn't respond and the game times out.

She turns to face me, I assume waiting for me to lead her to the next game. The excitement she had a little earlier is now gone.

I stepped to the side of her and swiped the game card again,

"Come on, let's try again."

"Let's just do the next game, it's fine," She begins to walk around me.

I catch her by her wrist, "You can't advance to the next tier of the arcade leagues if you don't try again, little miss."

She doesn't move, but looks down at where we're connected, "Okay, fine," She concedes and takes her place back in front of the machine.

I grab a basketball and step behind her again, but this time her back is flush against my chest. From this angle I can see her inhale deeply at the proximity.

"Relax your body," I direct her, "You can't have the wrong sort of tension and make a basket."

She takes another deep breath, no tension leaves. Her body feels ridgid against mine, "Loosen your shoulders and neck, you're fine."

She takes a third breath, rolls her neck and shoulders and takes another breath, "Okay," She says quieter than the tone she's used this entire evening so far.

"Hold the ball, whatever way feels comfortable to you," She takes the ball from where I hold it in front of her.

"Okay, now," I view her body from behind, what I can see of it being this close and notice her feet are too far apart. Without thinking, I place my hands lightly on her hips to steady her, "Widen the gap between your feet."

She moves them apart.

"More."

She moves them a bit more.

"Can you get them the same distance as your shoulders? My foot shouldnt be hugged by them," I say tapping both of her feet with one of my shoes, giving her an idea of how wide the space is.

She spreads them.

"Okay, now," My grip on her hips firm, I faintly hear her breath hitch. I lean in closer to her, so I can help guide her form, “Bend your knees,” I tell her quietly enough for her to hear.

She bends onto me almost as if she’s sitting on my lap.

“Just a tiny more,” I guide her hips down.

I wait for her to regulate her breathing, and she says “Now what?” Almost too quietly for me to hear.

“Now, you shoot.”

She does and to my surprise, she makes the basket and squeals.

“Ah!” She turns and throws her arms around my neck quickly without thinking about it first because when she realizes she pulls back just as fast.

“Um, sorry,” She nervously chuckles, “I just didn’t expect to make it,” She tucks some curls behind her ear, “I guess you’re not that bad of a trainer.”

I hum in response.

Though the moment happened so quickly I almost question if I imagined it, I want to pull her back to me immediately after she’s pulled away.

I don’t know when it happened, but being around this woman, so close to her, it fills up all of my senses. My thoughts get consumed with fantasies of us being as close as we just were, closer even.

“No need to apologize, feel free to throw your arms around me anytime,” I hope I successfully cover the heaviness in my tone with a chuckle.

She smiles and tucks a loose curl behind her ear.

“Okay boss, where to next?” She asks.

I lead her from game to game for the rest of the night, most of which she did terribly at, but we were able to share laughs despite it.

Every moment we spend together, I see another side to her, a side that makes me care less about how we got here and focus more on the fact we made it here at all.

I've learned that she's as nurturing as she is a force to be reckoned with in the workplace, that she's not selfless just for show, and that she, despite prior belief, does know how to laugh at herself.

Moriah reminds me of an onion with many layers to peel back, but I wouldn't mind the time it takes to peel until there is nothing left.

Hours have escaped us and our evening comes to an end. We concluded with an order of wings, fries and a few more drinks.

We walk in a comfortable silence back to my car.

"So," I push my hands into my pockets, "Did you have fun?"

She smiles at the ground that her heels pound on.

"Yeah, actually, I did," She answers to my relief.

"Good, good."

"Well…" We stop at the passenger door of my car, "Did you?"

I place my hand on the door handle and allow myself to be consumed by her under the moonlight. This look that she gives me, peering up at me through her eyelashes, it makes me feel like a fifthteen year old boy again around his crush.

"Yeah, I did," I open the door for her and she gets in.

I round the front of the car, entering the drivers side and take off towards her home.

The ride was comfortably silent, with a few casual conversations and debates about the music that came on my playlist.

After some time passes, we arrive at her family's home. Seeing her home in comparison to the one I was raised in adds context to why we differ the way we do.

I park the car, get out and open her door for her. She takes the hand I offer as she steps out of my SUV, and we begin to approach the single townhome.

I walk her up the few steps that lead to a walkway to her front door.

"You didn't have to walk me," She laughs, "Trying to get some extra brownie points for chivalry?"

I offer a half grin, "Of course I have to walk you to the door, Moriah. What sort of men do you date?"

She offers a tight smile but doesn't respond.

I take that to mean she dated the sort of men who unlocked the door from their side panel and said goodnight, pulling off before ensuring she got inside the door.

"Well, I was raised to be a gentleman," I say in her silence.

"I've noticed," She says with a hint of humor in her voice.

"Are you surprised?"

"A little," She answers honestly, "All I'd heard about D. Washington from peers was that you lead with your charm, that's how you've brought in so many clients. I figured that charm was used for evil," She giggles.

"Ah," I chuckle, "Well, no. I'm sorry to disappoint you, but there's no evil here. Just a guy with southern manners, unfortunately."

Her face reads of confusion, "Unfortunate? Why unfortunate?"

My smile fades as I take exactly two steps closer to her, using up a sporadic boost of courage. She doesn't retreat.

"Because, if I wasn't such a gentleman, I'd be willing to take more risks."

She looks into my eyes, briefly to my lips and back.

"What sort of risks are you wanting to take, Darrell?"

I take another step closer to her, nearly pressing her back into the door.

I instinctively lick my lips as I search her face for any sign that she wants me to stop.

"Plenty. For instance," My voice is not far off from a whisper, only loud enough for the two of us to hear, "Every time you say my name, or try to steal a quick glance at my mouth like I don't notice, or bite your lip because you're unsure of something…"

I see her take in a breath, stealing the oxygen that I need for myself.

"Yeah? What about those moments?" She blinks up at me slowly.

"If I wasn't such a gentleman, I would have grabbed you by now and kissed you the exact way I've been picturing it in my mind."

She steps into my chest, though there isn't much space between us at this point anyway.

"So, let's pretend for a moment you aren't a gentleman then," She whispers, "Show me how you see it in your mind,"

For a moment, I'm stunned at the permission she's just given me. But the shock doesn't last long before I place one hand on her waist and the other on her jaw so that while I caress her cheek with my thumb, my other fingers can feel the silky skin of her neck.

I bend slightly to meet her as she reaches up to me, standing on the tips of her toes, and kiss her.

I could've easily mistaken the day for the fourth of July with the fireworks that go off in my mind's eye.

The kiss we share is patient and starving all at once while I pull her bottom lip into mine, devouring what I can of her.

To hear her breath escape in the brief moments we break our embrace makes me animalistic, primal.

She keeps her head tilted, giving me more access, making room for my tongue inside.

With a final tug of my lip between her teeth, she breaks the kiss.

She stares up at me, wordlessly and this is one time I don't have anything to offer to makeup for the silence.

"That was…" She speaks first, "actually very gentlemanly."

I squint only slightly, unsure of how to take the comment.

"Is that a bad thing?"

I hardened my jaw, prepared for some ruthless reply that'll lead me to never kiss another woman in my life.

She smirks.

"I think it's my new favorite style."

I release the breath I was holding on too and return her smirk.

"Goodnight, Miss Jackson."

"Goodnight, Darrell."

She smiles, turns to unlock her front door and enters her home.

As I walk back to my car, I can't help but lick my lips, grasping at the taste she left with me.

I'm not one to be dramatic, but that kiss….

It felt like the last first kiss I may ever have.

# CHAPTER *THIRTY-ONE*

## *Moriah*

*I'm* still on a high.

When I accepted my first date with him, I figured it was just hormone driven, given I've been in a drought for who knows how long, I just needed some male company.

I thought if I went on the date, I'd want to leave it at that. That I wouldn't have even enjoyed being in his company for more than forty-five minutes, and even that was being generous.

I did not anticipate being where I am now.

Enjoying taking care of his grandmother, looking for his name to pop up on any of my devices, liking him as much as I do and definitely not kissing him.

That kiss, my god.

I've never felt safe with someone's lips, if that's even a thing. It was like he took me to an entirely other world with just a touch.

His lips, they were dominant and gentle at once. They are perfect in size and soft. I wouldn't be surprised to find out he exfoliates them at night or something.

The way he gripped onto me while we were at the arcade sent me soaring inside. I can still feel all the places he's made contact with my body.

I've kept so much from Anastasia and my family about what's been going on with us so that they didn't make it a big deal, I wouldn't even know where to start if I were to tell them right now.

I can hardly make heads or tails of it in my own head.

It's been a very, very long time since I've even entertained the idea of liking someone, being so focused on building my career and pouring into my work what I should've been pouring into therapy that I didn't have time to really notice anyone.

But with Darrell, he didn't try to get me to notice him. I just did and now, I can't stop.

It's my day to visit Honey and see what she needs while her grandchildren handle whatever else needs to be handled.

I stop home first to change my clothes so that I can move around more efficiently and to check on my father even though I know he's in the best hands he could be in.

Neither he or my sister are home and they don't arrive between my arriving or departing.

On my way out, I see our mail laid on the coffee table, unopened. I hesitate to go through them considering what happened the last time, but my curiosity gets the best of me.

I shuffle through the stack containing bills, advertisements and other things until I see an envelope with a handwritten backing, my heart thumps right through my chest at the sight of it.

It's addressed to myself and Adella.

I sit down the rest of the mail, take a deep breath, open it, and extract the paper that's folded inside. The letter reads:

Dear Adella and Moriah,

I don't exactly know what to write, but I know I'm to write something. I'm sorry that it took for you to look for me to prompt me to reach out to you, this is added to the list of things I am not proud of.

I thank you, though, for seeking me still, after all these years and the trauma I'm sure I've placed on you by my choices.

I know that the objective was to meet together in person, and I hope that even after receiving this, that is something that you still want. I know I don't deserve to want that, but I still do.

Hope to hear from you soon and I hope that you and your father are doing well.

All my love,
Mom

Even though I know now what AJ is up to and why, holding this paper in my hands, knowing that my mother also held it makes my body feel unseasonably cold.

I stare at the paper for a while, frozen in place. I don't know if I'm trying to will more words, trying to make her physically appear before me, or trying to erase this reality altogether, but eventually, I'm able to sit the letter down, face up and opened on the table.

I take my purse, my keys, my phone and head towards the door.

My mind that was full just moments ago with only a to-do list of things to tackle, is now clouded. Filled with all the things I imagined a letter from my mother would say, the things I'd hoped it would and all the things I'd say back.

I support my sister with her search, especially knowing the reason, but I don't know if I can stomach standing by her side when the time comes to meet the woman that abandoned us.

---

I arrive at Honey's home.

I'm not sure when I'll adjust to the long walk from the street to her front door but I don't think it'll be anytime soon. I've learned the hard way that wearing anything other than sneakers when I come here is just a senseless act of violence on myself.

You do appreciate the trek, though.

Each time I walk it I move just a little slower, taking in how green the grass is, the random little daisies that pop up throughout it, the single tree that has seen more than even Honey has.

There's love on this land and more memories than I'm sure a single person could recount. I can almost be fooled into thinking I have some of my own memories here, that's how nostalgic it feels.

I reach her front door and the screen door is unlocked with her main door wide open, welcoming me in.

"Hello?" I shout before I enter so that I don't cause anyone alarm, even though I'm expected.

"I'm in here, Mo!" The older voice calls to me from the back of the house. I follow the sound to the back porch, where I find Honey vigorously sweeping.

"Hey, here let me do that for you," I reach to grab the broom only for my hand to be smacked away like a child reaching to touch a stove.

"Girl, I can do a little sweeping," She says through a frown and continues to make a forward and backward motion with the broom, "You really want to do something, since you can't sit still? Go get a wet rag and wipe down this railing. When the winds get heavy it blows dirt everywhere, making it look like this home is without a keeper."

She directs me without breaking focus from the task in front of her..

I retreat back inside to the kitchen and wet a cleaning rag that I find stored under the sink. I fill up a small pan with water and a pinch of a random concoction of cleaning liquid I find and join her again on the porch.

Seeing her face, I can see that right now isn't a time for pointless questions and conversation, not that I have much to say at this moment anyway.

I begin on the nearest part of the railing.

After about ten minutes pass us, she finally breaks the silence.

"I'm a sucker for a quiet home just as much as the next old geezer but this is a lot even for me. What's wrong with you girl?"

She takes a break from her workout and takes a seat on the swinging chair that matches the one out front.

"Nothing's wrong with me, Honey. I'm just working," I reply halfheartedly while I get the posts of her railing,

"Now," She takes a deep breath that I'm sure her lungs are begging for, there's no telling how long she was at it before I'd gotten here, "I may not be your grandmother, but that doesn't mean my grandma powers don't work on you too. I know you ain't telling the truth and it's unlike you to lie from what I know of you so far. So, you might as well say it."

I take a deep breath myself as I weigh my options.

I may be an open book with my loved ones, but when it comes to matters like my mother, you'd have to hypnotize to get something out of me.

So the fact that I'm preparing myself to tell anything to this old woman who is still basically a stranger to me, is a lot.

She offers me patience while I work up to this moment of vulnerability with her.

"It's my family," I say flatley.

"Oh," I hear the change in her facial expression without having to look at her, "Are they alright? Hopefully no one's ill?"

This would be my final chance to give her a vague answer and try to deflect the attention off of me, but Honey has that effect on you.

Even if she didn't start out as your grandmother, after a while you forget that she isn't, she just assumes the role.

I decide this is as close to therapy as I'm going to get, so I continue.

"My mother, she left my sister and I and our father when we were really young, she left us with our dad and never considered looking back, not once. My dad did an amazing job on his own with what he had, my sister and I never really wanted for anything. But all he knew was his career and he'd lost his own mother not too long after ours left, so he was entirely out of his element with two young girls."

I'll never accept ignorance as an excuse from a man when it comes to caring for his family, not after watching my father do it all on his own for years.

While our grandmother was alive, she helped as much as she could. Though she didn't have any girls of her own, her maternal instincts never missed a beat, guiding him in what to do and when.

She passed when I was 8, and it took a toll on us.

She watched us every day until my dad got home from work, made sure dinner was prepared and laundry was put away.

I think that's when Adella'a nurturing instincts kicked in. She'd watch my grandmother so closely, right by her side when she'd cook, asking her questions, and was the first to help her clean.

No one made her, she was free to just be a kid. It's like she knew that someone else was going to have to step up soon, so when it was time, at the age of 13 that's what she did.

She tried to fill the shoes of the woman of the house when she could or if dad had to work late which was more often than not.

You could tell he hated it.

He wanted so bad for our lives to be the way he pictured it. When he'd met my mom and they had AJ, he thought this was the reward he'd gotten for being so focused in his career early on in life and that now he could finally start the family he'd dreamed of having.

Our mom had other plans.

She'd taken a gap year from schooling, wanting some time off before she finished and planned on opening up a children's psychiatric practice.

When my mom met my father, she saw an opportunity. A man with money that could fund her dreams.

Starting a family, at least before she got to live out her own dreams, wasn't a part of her plan.

She tried to go with it for a while, and one day she just couldn't anymore. She packed up, waited for him to come home and told him that she needed to focus on herself before she could focus on being a wife and mother.

Honey remains quiet and waits for me to finish.

"We haven't seen her since that day, and I recently found out that my sister has been looking for her and my dad was fine with it," I stare at the pail of water at my feet, "I found out why after I blew up at her. Today I found a letter from our mother asking to see us both."

I look at Honey who hasn't spoken a word since I began.

"I support my sister with all my heart and if this is what she needs to do for herself, then I'm fine with that. I just don't know if I can show up for her in the way that she may be expecting."

"I see," She says finally, "I won't ask your sister's business, but I'm assuming this is a personal, important reason she's needing to find her, one that's a bit bigger than you?"

I nod.

"And, I take it you and your sister are close?"

"She's one of my best friends."

"Well, if you didn't like your best friend's mom, but she needed your support to confront her, would you be there for her?" She asks me.

"I would, without a doubt."

She nods now.

"Okay. Well, don't walk into this as if it's your sister and your mother. Walk into this with the idea that you're just here to support your best friend. You don't even have to speak if you don't wanna, but sometimes just the presence of someone we love near us in a time of trial is enough to get us through something."

I soak in her advice.

After a beat of silence she speaks again, "I don't know how much you and my son have gotten to know each other so far, all the secret sharing and what have you. But, you'd be surprised to know how similar your paths are."

"Yeah?" I ask.

"Yeah. You know, his grandfather and I were the same way. Two sides of the same coin before we'd even known it. You may even find that to be true of your mother and you, though that may not be something you'd like to hear right now, if you do take the time to hear her out, you may see that you end up understanding her more than you expected to," She says while gently rocking herself on the swing.

I take in the possibility of my mother and I having anything in common outside of the one person we're both related to.

"We're back!"

# CHAPTER THIRTY-TWO

## Darrell

Seeing Moriah and Honey on the back porch together when Rayana and I arrived was a sight I think I can get used to seeing for a long time.

We all exchanged our greetings, Honey asked Rayana to get out the ingredients for dinner this evening and for me to move around a few pieces of furniture in the living room.

After a little while, Honey kicks us all out of the kitchen while she begins to prepare.

While Rayana sits in the living room watching TV, I find myself making my way to the front porch where Moriah sits on the swinging chair.

"Hey, you. Not feeling social today?" I ask her while I walk to the railing and sit against it.

She grins, "Not particularly."

"Oh. Well, I can leave you with your thoughts then," I begin to stand and head back towards the door, "No," She stops me, "I don't mind the company."

I'm glad, but I try to keep that to myself.

"Listen," I take a seat on the chair at the opposite end, giving her space between us, "I wanted to apologize about the other night."

She looks at me, confused.

"The kiss. If it was too much, if it was too forward at all, I'm sorry. I just got really… caught up, I guess."

She smirks, "I told you to kiss me, Darrell."

"I know, but you know, maybe you were a bit caught up to and-"

"Darrell," she cuts me off, "I don't say or do anything I don't mean. I wanted to kiss you as much as you wanted to kiss me."

"Well hold on," I reply, "Let's not say it like I was just dying to kiss you."

She laughs, "Let's not act like you don't have to talk yourself down at any physical contact we share."

I go to rebut and come up short of a reply.

"I was okay with the kiss, more than okay with it," She smiles.

I smile back and we fall into a comfortable silence.

"So um," She looks down at her lap where her fingers flip around each other, I don't often see her nervous and while I don't wish her to feel that, it's one of the most precious sights I think I've ever seen, "Honey invited me to the barbeque you guys are having for your grandfather."

My head whips in her direction, "She what?"

I see my reaction startles her, "She said for me and either my sister or Anastasia to come by… is that not okay?" she answers.

"No. I mean, no it's fine, it's okay. I'm just surprised. This is usually a very… specified guest list thing. Usually only close family and friends."

"Well," She looks to her hands again and back to me, "If you don't want me to come, I understand that, I don't have to."

"Moriah," I stop myself from grabbing her hand and it lands in the space between us, "I want you there."

She gives me a tight smile.

Soon, the aroma from the kitchen drifts to where we are.

"Mmmm… I do love a woman that knows her way in the kitchen," She hums in delight.

"Yeah?" I raise my eyebrow to her, "Well, I'll have you know, she learned how to make her gumbo so well because of me."

She looks at me with humor in her eyes, "Is that so?"

"It is so," I smile back at her, "Maybe I could make it for you sometime,"

Her smile is faint but genuine, "Yeah? I think I'd like that."

"Yeah… I'd like it too."

# CHAPTER THIRTY-THREE

## *Moriah*

I remember saying before that the heart leads to dumb decisions.

As I drive to Darrell's apartment, I know all the more that I'm right because there is no way this is a good decision.

The concern of proper work etiquette has been long gone, clearly right along with my better judgment.

Now, this is simply a matter of what I've tried so hard to protect myself from for years. The inevitable doom that comes with hope in someone, there's always disappointment.

But even though this goes against everything I stand for, as I pull up to his building, more like a tower, I realize I'd prefer to deal with the consequences of my actions later.

He lives downtown, a sight entirely unlike the country-side home he was raised in.

A tall, sleek building that screams money, even though looking at Darrell, you wouldn't assume he was more than a casual businessman, not a bachelor sitting on duckets.

I enter the lobby of the building and head straight to the elevator after checking in with the receptionist at the front.

Once inside, I press the button for the 9th floor as he instructed me.

When the doors open, I step out and am greeted with a short hallway and another door. I knock a few times and wait for a response.

After some moments pass by, the door swings open and I'm met with a casually dressed Darrell.

White shirt, blue jeans and barefeet.

"Hey," He greets me with an excited smile.

"Hey four eyes," I playfully refer to the glasses I've never seen him wear, "Since when do you need those?"

He moves aside so that I can enter.

"Since I was about 12," He closes the door behind me and follows me further into the apartment.

"Then why have I never seen them?"

"I'm usually wearing contacts, they're not my favorite accessory," He chuckles.

"Aw, my blind chef," I poke.

"Yeah, yeah," He walks past me, "Come in, have a seat," He leads me to his common area, "The food just finished," He says, making his way back towards his open kitchen.

Though I won't give him kudos yet, I must admit it smells delicious.

His place is very modern but still homey.

His sectional faces a small fireplace that sits below a wide screen mounted television. A small glass coffee table sits in front of me atop a very large, soft gray area rug.

The only thing that separates the living area from the kitchen in the transition from dark hardwood floors to dark kitchen tiles.

It isn't until he goes to speak that I realize he's been humming to the soft music that's filling the room, "Hey," he calls from the kitchen, "I do want to impress you and all but, I don't eat on my couch."

I laugh as I stand from my seat and go to the dining table that sits a few feet away, near a wall length window overviewing the busy city streets.

He sits the dishes filled with gumbo on the table first before pulling out a seat, "My apologies, pop-pop," I laugh again.

"Hey," He rounds the table and sits opposite of me, "You see how grandparents have furniture older than us? That's because they don't eat in the living room," He grins.

I hum, "I see."

"So, ready to dig in?" He asks.

"You mean, ready to see how your claim to gumbo fame was bullshit? Absolutely," I smile.

He returns it and waits for me to pick up my spoon first before he begins his own meal.

I take my first bite and cannot hold back my moan at the taste.

"Oh yeah?" He says with humor painted across his face, "If just my food can make you sound that way then…"

"Then, what?" I challenge.

He stares at me, debating if he'll lean into the dare of elaboration.

"Then, I'd say we're off to a good start," He replies in a low tone. He doesn't need to say much else for the air to thicken.

I smirk and continue enjoying my meal. Sometime passes and the only sound that fills our space is the clanking of silverware to dish.

"So, Moriah," He breaks the silence we sat in. The sound of my name on his tongue does horrible things to my mind, I have to inhale to regain my focus, "We've spent plenty of time together by now and yet, I feel like there's a lot more to your story than I know."

I sip the wine he poured at the beginning of dinner.

"I figured that I just hadn't been deemed worthy enough to know more about the mystery that is Miss Jackson," He sips his own drink.

"I don't think I'm that much of a mystery," I smile.

"Maybe not a mystery. More of… a jigsaw puzzle, with pieces you've hidden pretty strategically," He sips more.

"I'll take a puzzle. It helps me weed out the time wasters more efficiently, not everyone has the tolerance or attention span for a jigsaw puzzle."

"Yeah, I'm sure."

"Why don't you tell me some of your story?" I counter, "Tell me some of your favorite memories from childhood."

He clears his throat, takes the last gulp of his wine and sits his glass down as he shuffles through his memory bank.

"Moving in with my grandparents takes first place for sure," He begins, "Um, playing outside with the neighborhood kids, doing some of my favorite activities with Gramps in the living room after I'd finished my homework and dinner. Having Rayana follow me around like a puppy because she thought I was cool, she's cooler than me now," He chuckles to himself.

I smile, seeing the happiness on his face while he recounts the memories.

"Do you mind me asking why you moved in with your grandparents in the first place? I've been around you guys a lot now and haven't ever asked," I continue finishing the last of my food.

He rolls an imaginary kink out of his neck and clear his throat again, "Well," He looks down at the table as if he's searching for his next words in his dinner, "To make a long story short, my mother didn't really care to be a mother more than she cared to chase men and have fun. Sy'Asia and Anthony were basically our parents before our grandparents stepped in."

"Oh," I didn't know what to expect of his response but I know it wasn't that, "I'm so sorry, that's terrible," I don't know what else to say.

"Yeah," He shrugs, "It was pretty shitty to see some of the things I saw. I always tried to do my part in taking care of Rayana while Ang took care of me, just so I had a load to carry too and show them that I could be responsible like they were."

"I guess some habits don't die, huh?" I chuckle.

He returns the chuckle, though his lacks humor, "Yeah, I guess so."

"What are the activities you'd do with your Grandfather? I know you guys were really close."

With elbows resenting on the table and hands clasped beside his face, his jaw tightens for a moment and responds, "Jigsaw puzzles, they were my favorite."

My breath catches in my throat and I'm now out of conversation topics.

After some time passes, we finish what's left of our dinner in a tension filled silence.

I wipe my mouth with the napkin.

"I unfortunately have to admit," I sit my spoon inside of my now empty bowl, "I haven't had gumbo this good in… probably ever."

"So, you're saying it was the best gumbo of your life?" He asks as he goes to stand.

"I'm saying, take the compliment for what it is before it's gone."

He snickers.

"Fair enough, little miss, fair enough."

# CHAPTER THIRTY-FOUR

## *Darrell*

*I* can't call to mind the last time I've had a woman, especially such a dangerously beautiful woman, in my home.

Cooking for her, trying to woo her, being worried about saying something wrong and embarrassing myself.

I don't know how we let it get this far but I don't think I'd be capable of going back now.

Not after having been so close to her, seeing her with my baby sister, with my grandmother, the people I love the most in this world.

I watch Moriah as she gathers our wine glasses and brings them to me in the kitchen.

Even the way she walks feels like my undoing.

She moves like she knows her touch could poison you, and even though I've already been compromised, I can't resist the urge to touch her again.

"You know, you're supposed to be a guest," I say as she approaches me, "You should be sitting down with another glass of wine."

She giggles, taking her place at the sink and playfully bumping me away with a throw of her hips.

"The last thing I need is another glass of wine, I assure you," She giggles again, "Plus, I offered to do this. If it makes it better, how about I wash and you dry?" She turns on the faucet.

I think that was more of an order than a suggestion, so I fall in line.

"Can I ask you something?" I ask after a few moments pass.

"I feel like you're going to anyway," She laughs.

"Not if you say no, I'd respect your boundaries," I answer her seriously.

Her smile fades slowly, "Yeah Darrell, you can ask me something."

"I don't know if you know, but, Rayana is my best friend and because she isn't around too many people other than myself and one or two friends, she can't hold water," I shrug.

"Mhm," She responds.

"Your name came up a time or two and she told me you've mentioned, on more than one occasion, that you don't date. That you've surprised yourself for accepting even one date with me, let alone two."

She finishes the last dish and passes it to me to dry,

"I won't say I wasn't surprised also," I chuckle, "but it did cause me to wonder, why is that? Why don't you date? Why did you say yes to one with me?"

She takes a while to respond, even after she's turned off the water.

She starts with a thoughtful deep breath, "I don't think anyone is worth the sacrifice," She says thoughtfully.

"Sacrifice?"

"Yeah. Of me, of my heart, my life," She turns around, leaning back on the countertop but looking at nothing, "I watched my father give his everything to what he thought was love, just to end up getting the short end of the stick, uprooting the plan and the life he had for himself entirely."

I don't speak, allowing her the space to say what I'm sure isn't something she easily shares.

"I still gave it an honest shot though, love and dating, I thought I'd met the person I was going to marry. We were young and in college but you couldn't tell me that every promise he made to me about life after graduation wasn't going to come true. For the longest, he treated me like I hung the sun in the sky with my own hands. Then, graduation season rolled around, and the week before the big day, he told me that he'd rather focus on more important things like his career. Love would come for him later but now wasn't the time."

She laughs at her feet while I wish I could find whatever dickhead did this to her.

"He said all the promises he made me sounded right in the moment but he realizes he just said them all because he thought it was the right thing to do," She pauses for a moment, "I'd been so scared to live the same reality my father did that I basically manifested it for myself. Did he make it work? For sure, and then some. But, I don't know if I could persevere the way he did, being told by the person most important to you that you just aren't important enough."

I do my best not to linger on what she just revealed to me, for fear that she'll just retreat behind the shield she's created herself, "So… what changed?" I ask.

She looks at me, her face telling me she's having a thousand thoughts at once.

"I'm not sure just yet," She smiles softly to herself, "But, you're not the worst guy to take a chance on so far. Our first date, when you didn't… force anything, you didn't treat me like a challenge to conquer and you didn't try to feed me the things you thought I'd want to hear. When you let me just be there, moving at my own speed…"

I lose her to her thoughts again, but I don't mind as long as she keeps allowing me to know them.

"I just appreciated it, that's all," She smiles, at me this time, and I return it.

"Yeah… the country-boy manners, what can I say?" That earns me a giggle, a sound I can hear every day and never tire of.

I find myself lost in her.

The indent her bottom lip has, the depth of her cupid's bow, the way the spaces beside her eyes crinkle when she smiles. If you look close enough, you'll see the faintest dimple on her chin.

I don't have a chance to stop the impulse of my hand from tucking the few hairs that escaped her bun behind her ear, and her laughing stops.

It feels like all the air has been sucked out of the room.

I think carefully about my next words, but I figure there's no point in acting like the tension that I know we both feel isn't engulfing us at this moment.

"Remember," I begin quietly, "when you told me how much you didn't mind that kiss on the night of our date?" I ask, moving close enough to her that we can speak in whispers.

"Yeah, I remember," She absentmindedly licks her lips. As if my body is responding, I copy the subtle movement.

"What about right now?" I lower my face to hers, "how much would you mind if I did it again?" I offer her my own oxygen with the nonexistent distance between us.

"I wouldn't."

It feels like I'm signing over the last bit of my willpower.

She invades my almost every waking thought.

All I can picture is her, all I continue to feel on my lips is the ghost of hers.

I know that after this line is crossed, I'll have nothing left in my line of defenses against what she does to me.

So I decide that I'll stop fighting it at all.

When I kiss her, I'm immersing myself into the deepest parts of the ocean.

I feel the pressure building, but there's no part of me that wants to swim to the surface. She makes me forget where I am, where I've been or anything that isn't her with just her lips.

I sit her on the island of my kitchen, we haven't broken our kiss since we've begun. The difference between our first embrace and this one is hunger, the submission to our desires.

Her arms wrap around my neck while my fingers dance on her back along the hem of her shirt, grazing the bare skin that's exposed.

I hold onto her lips with my own like they're the last ones I'll ever touch.

She grabs at my hair like she's trying to find anything to pull me in closer to her, though it's impossible.

I have her legs spread wide enough to hold space just for me and they wrap around my waist like they were made for my body only.

"Take me to your bed," Is the only thing she breaks the kiss to say.

Panting, I respond, "If I take you in that bedroom, I can't promise I'll remain the gentleman you've been getting acquainted with."

Breathing into my open mouth like she knows I need her air to survive, she whispers back to me, "That's exactly what I was hoping for."

Without a further thought I pull her off of the counter, holding her with both hands firmly planted on her ass and carry her down the hall to my bedroom.

I'm thankful that I know the layout of my apartment like the back of my hand because it prevents me from having to let her lips go, the last thing I want to do.

We reach my bed and I lay her down as gently as I can despite the ravenous feeling building inside me.

I abandon her lips and place kisses slowly down the side of her neck. She arches into me like it's the first time she's been touched this way.

The quiet room is filled with her pants and the sound of my lips sucking her skin.

I move toward her collarbone, then the space between her breasts, and slowly down to her navel. Her skin tastes like the sweetest thing to ever touch my lips.

"God, stop playing with me Darrell," She groans in frustration.

I smirk at her desperation, "Unfortunately beautiful," I kiss the slither of the exposed skin above her pants, "That's exactly what I intended on doing."

I position myself back over her to taste her lips again, "Do you mind," I slide my hand slightly underneath the loose white cropped tee she wears, "If I take this off of you?"

"No, no," She says in hurried breaths, reaching for the hem.

I stop her.

"That isn't your job," She freezes with my hand over hers, "All you need to focus on is speaking when you're spoken to, do you understand that?"

She looks at me, wide eyed.

"Do you understand that, Moriah?"

She nods slowly, "Yes."

"Yes…"

"Yes, I understand."

"Good girl. Sit up and raise your arms."

She obeys, and I pull her shirt over her head and reach behind her to unclasp her bra.

"Lay back."

She does as she's told.

"I'm not a man that moves in a hurry, Moriah. If you learn that in no other instance, I'll make sure you learn that tonight."

I kiss her lips considerately once more before I down her neck again and slowly to her collar bone. I kiss the bare skin between her breasts, keeping a steady pace as I move towards her navel.

I tease her with kisses above the waist of her pants and I could explode right now at just the sight of her reacting to me.

I move back towards her breast.

"I know you don't want me to tease you," A gentle lick to her left nipple as I flick and rub the other with my hand, "But you need to learn how to be patient, baby," Suck, "Let me appreciate you," Tug.

I move the attention of my mouth to the jealous breast, repeating my actions on her right nipple while I curl my fingers into the top of her jeans.

Watching her as she wriggles beneath me, desperate to create friction to relieve her ache. It drives me crazy. The whimpers she makes with each move of her hips against me, it's enough to make a man fall to his knees.

"Do you know how good these jeans look on you?" Lick, "Hm?" Bite, "That was a question, Moriah," Suck.

She releases a moan into the air, "Yes, yes."

"Oh, you knew?" Bite, "You wore them so I wouldn't be able to think straight, huh?" I suck on her nipple to soothe the sting of my bite.

She hums at the relief.

"I bet though," I move my fingers to the button of her jeans, running them down in between her legs and back up, "That whatever is underneath them, looks a million times better," I repeat the motion a few more times until she struggles to keep her legs open.

"Can I take these off of you?" I ask, slowing down my movement at her core, slightly pressing into her with my fingers.

"Oh my-" She doesn't finish her sentence.

"I need you to answer me, Moriah. Can I take these off of you?" I repeat my question.

"Yes, yes please," She pleads.

"Please?" I repeat, "I don't think I've ever heard manners that sound so good. I'm going to make sure you use them more often," I unbutton her pants and wiggle them down her legs, exposing her burnt orange lace underwear.

"God," I sit back on my heels and take in the sight of her bare body, "Orange must have been made especially for you."

She looks at me through heavy lids, lips puffy from the biting she's been doing.

"Tell me, Moriah," I bend to kiss along the line of her panties, "How do you like to be pleased?" I ask, kissing gingerly along both hips, "I don't want to assume, I want you to guide me."

I take her hand and slide it into her panties, "Show me what to do to make you feel good."

I watch as the print of her fingers begin to move. I watch them glide up and down the length of her pussy, wetting them with her own juices that I'm watering at the mouth to taste. Then, I watch them dance upward towards her clit, and perform delicate figure eights.

I lay on my stomach, and position myself so that I have the perfect view of the lesson she's teaching me. I kiss just below her fingers, on the outside of her underwear that are becoming soaked before my eyes.

"That's it, teach me how to get you that wet."

Her back begins to arch, "Good job, baby. Let me take notes as I watch," I kiss at her lips again, and she lets out a loud moan.

"Fuck," She groans.

"Are you almost there, baby?" I ask excitedly, "Tell me if you're almost there."

"I'm so close," She pants, "I'm so close."

"Yeah?" I grin into the kisses I plant, "Take your fingers out."

She continues her circular motions, "Moriah," I call her name, but she's too lost in her rise.

"No, no, no, baby," I place my hand firmly on her fingers so that she can no longer move them.

She looks at me with confusion riddled across her face.

"That's for me," I pull her hand out, "Let me show you how well I paid attention in class," I place her hands above her head and slowly remove her underwear that are not drenched in her juices.

I see her chest rise and fall rapidly.

"I need you to relax, Moriah. Take deep breaths for me," I pause a second, allowing her time to regulate,

"I want you relaxed so you can feel everything my tongue is about to do to you, okay?"

She nods.

"There's one rule. No matter what, do not close these legs, do you hear me?"

"Yes," She barely makes out.

I position myself again at the lips between her thighs and spread them apart.

I begin with light, chaste kisses just above and below her clit. I touch everything except it, and still I feel it harden under the pad of my thumb as I rub it softly.

I place a kiss to her left thigh, "I understand you're used to making men cower," I place a kiss to her right thigh, "But I need you to know, the only shuddering that will be done tonight is from you, because I'm going to drain you of every ounce of come your body has to offer me."

Almost instantly I feel her shudder.

"You like that motion with my fingers, right? You like small little circles?" She barely answers yes, but I can make it out.

"How about this?" I touch my lips to the aching bud, her back lifts from the mattress, "Yes" She hisses.

"Yeah?" I kiss a few times more, making sure she's nearly at her wits end before I give her what her body is begging me for.

"Darrell, please," She whispers.

"Ah, there's those manners," I kiss once more before allowing the flat of my tongue to lay against her.

"Fuuuck," She cries.

I continue to mimic the shapes and rhythms I watched her make on herself with the tip of my tongue while one hand keeps her spread open as wide as I can manage.

"Oh my god," She laughs out.

The taste of her, the exotic nectar that spills from her on my tongue, I wouldn't mind if this were my last meal. If I were to die, right here between her thighs, I'd surely die a happy man.

"Do you like that, Moriah?" I continue.

"Yes, yes," She struggles to say.

"Tell me if you like this as well, okay?" I resume my motion on her clit as I slowly slide two fingers into her and curl them.

"Ugh!" She exclaims, "Fucking, hell," She says as I pump into her while continuing to massage her with my tongue.

"Oh I can tell that you like that, you got so wet," I laugh into her.

I continue this combination until she's unraveling in front of me, clawing at my head and threatening to close her legs.

"No, remember what I told you baby, there's one rule," I remove my hand from her lips and push down on one thigh, "Keep these open for me."

She's no longer speaking proper words, just pleas intertwined with moans.

To see her, my powerful lioness, the woman you couldn't pay to give a man on the street the time of day, the one who has fought to present herself so stoically to the world, come undone at my hand, at my doing, is a sight I could watch for hours on end.

"Are you going to come for me, beautiful? Give it to me," I maintain my pace, "I worked so hard for it, give it to me Moriah, let me taste you."

I continue to lap at her and pump into her until she can't hold on any longer and she's run out of defenses against the sensation at her core.

I make sure not to miss a drop.

She lays there, a mess of pants and stray hairs glued to her face with sweat.

"I hope you don't have any troubles with breathing," I say as I place myself on top of her once more, "Because, I'm not finished with you yet."

I smile as I kiss her open mouth.

I knew I wouldn't want to stop once I got a taste of her, but this… this is worse than I could've anticipated.

# CHAPTER THIRTY-FIVE

### *Moriah*

I'm barely able to catch my breath or place my soul back into my body before Darrell warns me that his performance was just the opening act.

He stands at the end of the bed as he undresses himself, never taking his eyes off of me.

He first reaches behind his head and pulls his white T shirt over it, revealing a body that must have been prayed over and handcrafted. You can see easily that he takes care of himself in all the ways that matter.

His abs lead down to the subtly defined V line that leads into his jeans and does horrible things to the imagination.

With his jaw hardened and gaze locked on me, he undoes his belt, removing it with a swift pull.

I hope that it's just due to my already heightened state that the simple action sent my body soaring higher than I thought possible.

Next, he removes his jeans and stands for a moment in just his black boxer briefs.

I appreciate the view more than I could express.

He stands there as if he wants me to take him in entirely, he wants me to recognize that he knows he looks like he could destroy what's left of me, and that he will.

I try not to focus on the bulge in his briefs but finally my curiosity betrays me and I give in.

He smirks, taking that as a greenlight to remove them, freeing the monster they contained.

I do my best to fight the gasp that is fighting its way out of my throat but I know my eyes betray my silent battle.

"Moriah," He says low and deep, bringing my attention back to his eyes, "Relax, I won't break you. Not in a way you wouldn't enjoy at least."

I don't have time to think of a response before he mounts himself on top of me.

To think this is the behavior of the man who looks like he forgets his own name most of the time we speak is not something I at all expected.

He kisses me out of my thoughts and I lose myself in the feel of his body pressed so closely against mine.

"Mmm," He says into our embrace, "I'm not even inside you yet and you already feel too good," He bites and pulls at my bottom lip.

"Remember when I said I may not be a gentleman once we entered this room?" He hovers over my lips.

I nod my head.

"This is the part I was talking about," He whispers before kissing me again, then leaning to his nightstand and grabbing a condom.

After a few strokes of his dick, he slides on the measure of protection and hovers me again. He kisses me, thoughtfully and deeply.

"If I hurt you, tell me to stop, do you understand?"

"Yes," I whisper.

As if he knows the danger of his own body he uses his tip to gently tap me, asking permission.

He rubs it up and down the full length of my slit and slowly introduces himself inside of me.

Before my eyes close, I see him physically brace himself with a deep breath and his teeth clenched.

He doesn't make it too far past the tip before he holds both of my hands above my head, and he leans down to kiss me. I'm too lost in the kiss to realize it was to distract me from him entering the full length of himself inside of me.

It's a shock to my body and we both groan.

"Oh my fucking god, Moriah," He growls into my ear, "Fuck."

His doesn't move immediately, allowing our bodies the chance to adjust to one another.

Slowly and considerately he begins to pump in and out and I could finish right here and now.

"Are you okay?" He whispers with his forehead pressed to mine, gently moving his hips.

"I'm okay," I answer.

"Good, because this pace is going to kill me," He responds as he slowly builds his momentum. Before long he's pounding himself into me.

"Fuck, Darrell, yes."

The change in stroke was one quick enough to leave me breathless. I've never experienced someone that felt so right, fitting like my missing puzzle piece.

He groans, "You can't say my name like that, princess."

"Yeah?" I make out between breaths being stolen from me.

"Don't play with me, Moriah," He says in puffs, "I'm trying to be gentle."

"Don't be, Darrell," I say panting, "I can take it I promise."

I can see the last straw break behind his eyes and he slams himself into me.

It's a delicious pain and I quickly feel myself climbing a mountain that I can't see the top of.

"God, you feel like heaven, you feel so good baby," He says in between grunts. The heat of his breath in my ear feels like the very thing that will take me over the edge.

"I can feel you, Moriah. Don't hold back, let it go," He continues his punishing pace, "Let it go for me, princess. It's mine isn't it? Give it to me."

I can't stop the shrieking moan that I release into the air.

The demand in his tone awakens something in me and he does indeed break me, whatever power I had left to hold on entirely dissipates and I pour on to him.

"God," He says, blanketing my face with hot breaths, "You look so fucking beautiful this way," He gently grips my jaw, rubbing his thumb across my bottom lip before he kisses me.

# CHAPTER THIRTY-SIX

## *Darrell*

Oh my god.

---

## *Moriah*

Oh my god.

# CHAPTER *THIRTY-SEVEN*

### *Moriah*

*It's* been a week since I saw heaven's gates- I mean, since I've had sex with Darrell.

I may not have been actively dating prior to this journey I'm on with him, but that doesn't mean I haven't had my fair share of men in my life. I'm an experienced girl.

But, out of all of my experiences, none of them could have prepared me for the whirlwind that is Darrell James Washington.

He was willing to accept rejection and move on from me and move on. he asks me questions about myself, he wants to learn me, not just rip me open.

I walk into my home after work. I took a half day so I'm back early.

As I take off my shoes at the door, I hear rustling in the kitchen.

I follow the noise and find my father, I assume he didn't hear me come in because I catch him red handed with a can of soda, something that is no longer allowed in his diet.

"Damnit, Mo!" He jumps when he closes the fridge and sees me standing with arms folded.

"Yeah you little sneak, living on the edge isn't good for your nerves at all," I walk over to the island and lean back on it as he opens his chilled can and takes a seat beside me.

"I'm a grown man, Moriah, I'm not sneaking anything," He takes a sip.

"So you're telling me if it was AJ that walked in here instead, you wouldn't have tried to play it off like you were reaching for a water bottle that was allegedly behind the soda?" I raise my brow.

He makes a pfft sound and waves me off with a hand.

"You're lucky I'm not the strict daughter, old man," I pat his back and make my way to the fridge to get a soda for myself as well.

"Actually," He sits down his can, "You both are usually about the same level of pain in my ass. You're slacking… why is that?" I feel him eyeing my back.

"I figure she's doing a good enough job for the both of us," I pop the top and release a hissing noise from my can, "Someone has to play good cop."

"Yeah, but you're never the one I'd assume to take that role," He chuckles, "You've actually seemed a little lighter for the past few days now. Is there something I don't know?"

Here goes my gossip king, waiting for some hot tea to spill.

"There's nothing going on, father," I answer exaggeratingly.

"I may not have that maternal instinct, but I still know my daughter, Mo. I know when something's changed," He gives me the impression that this isn't going to be easily dropped.

"It's that boy we met all them weeks ago in the grocery store, isn't it?"

I fiddle with the tab of my soda can before I respond, "Yeah," I answer quietly.

He hums, "I knew that was going to happen," He laughs and takes a sip of the soda that I'm debating snatching from his hand right now.

A frown forms on my face before I can even register it, "Knew what was going to happen?"

"That he was going to get to you, doll, that's what."

"Get to me?" My tone immediately becomes defensive, "No one's gotten to me. We're simply two adults who just so happen to not  mind each other for right now."

Saying that aloud feels like betrayal, like disrespect to the connection we've formed, but I sweep that feeling aside.

My dad chuckles, "Baby, love is nothing to be upset about or ashamed of. It's beautiful."

"Love? Dad, please," I let out a breathy sounding laugh, "I'll admit I enjoy him, sure, but love is a bit much."

The very word coming out of my mouth causes goosebumps to erupt through my skin, it feels right and wrong at the same time.

It's the thing I've been able to avoid from miles away, and while the topic now is at hand, I realize that the way I feel about Darrell is for sure something I've never felt for anyone else before, of that much I'm certain.

And, I'm just as certain that this isn't something I can stomach right now.

He is kinder than any man I've known, aside from my father. He's patient, not just with me but with others. Watching him interact with people, people he may not even know, is touching to say the least.

He deserves someone who doesn't get nauseous at the possibility of liking someone beyond a few dates and good sex.

A gentle man is a rare thing in this world and I'm lucky enough to have met one of the gentlest men left. But at this very moment I feel that there's no doubt he deserves someone better.

"I hear you, daughter. But, I see what you don't see. The smile that hasn't left your face, the softness your tone has taken on, the lightness in your step. You may not feel it, but it's obvious. And, it's okay. Love changed my life, it's just what it does."

I huff, "It changed your life alright, it left you with two kids to raise on your own while you balance a new life and a drastic career change you never wanted."

"It gave me the two brightest lights of my life and gave me meaning and purpose," He corrects me, "Without you girls, yes it's true that I would've been active in the career I've always wanted but that excitement wouldn't have lasted my whole life. You girls gave me drive, something to live for. That's what love does."

I listen to him, taking in his words.

I'd be lying to myself, which apparently isn't new for me, if I said I didn't feel the difference that Darrell has made in me. I feel… hopeful. In people, in men and in love and I know that the minute you feel hopeful, is exactly when everything comes crashing down around you. I can't afford that right now.

I don't get a chance to reply to him before my sister joins us in the kitchen. The look on her face tells me that something's not right.

She stands in the doorway without a word.

"AJ?" I call to her, "What's wrong?"

She fiddles with her fingers in front of her before looking back to me and our father, “It’s… mom. We set a date to meet.”

# CHAPTER THIRTY-EIGHT

## *Darrell*

*I've* never done drugs, but I imagine this is what being high feels like.

I didn't walk into work this morning, I floated in sitting on top of a bubble that the devil himself couldn't pop.

Moriah hit me like a freight train, and like a fool, after being hit I ran after it until I found a cart with enough space for me. Because she didn't make room for me, I had to find it on my own and do what I could to show her that I fit.

It's something I've come to love about her.

From the beginning, she's made me wait, she's made me show and prove. She didn't readily give herself to me, and even when she did begin to feel something for me, she wasn't quick to show me.

So many women I've come across in my past, not even the ones that I've actually dealt with, they hand themselves over to me. Not because of some sweet nothings I tell them, or charm that I lay on, but just because I've opened a door or held general conversation.

My mother, I think of her when I think of women like that. Any man that made eye contact with her for too long, she became a trackstar for, chasing them no matter how long they ran. Even if they never stopped running, she trailed after them until her legs gave out.

Moriah didn't care about my attention, hell, I don't think she wanted it at all at first. She didn't even address me by name for the longest. I had to give her something worth turning her attention to.

While I sit in my office, lost in my daydream about the woman I least expected to crash into my life, my brother comes in.

"Back in my day, one knocks before they enter," I jest.

He doesn't smile, he only uses his eyes to assess me.

"What's up with you today?"

"I don't know what you mean, big bro. If you're talking about the three meetings I just knocked out, securing a sponsor and two grants for Love Unbound, I don't know," I shrug, "I'm just on a roll."

"No," He replies, "You're acting… giddy. I know you're the friendlier one out of the two of us, but this," He gestures to me, "Is a little more than usual."

I do my best to act like I don't know there's a bit more pep in my step than usual.

"I know there's obviously a bit more than business happening between you and… Moriah, is her name?" He shoves both hands in his pockets, squinting his eyes.

My smile drops at the sound of her name leaving his mouth.

"There's no way she's found her way into our grandmother's home just on the strength of goodwill."

"You know absolutely nothing about her. That's actually the exact sort of thing she'd do."

"And I assume you know way more about her than me, right?" He tilts his head.

"Enough to know that she didn't and wouldn't offer to help out with Honey just off of the strength of me, yes."

He huffs a chuckle that lacks true humor.

"Listen, I don't care what it is you do with your dick in your spare time Darrell. But the two things I do care about are those sparetime affairs affecting our business and infiltrating our family. You know better than that," He chastises me.

"What I know is," I sit straighter in my chair, "I'm a grown man and you aren't my father. Mine died four years ago."

"And do you think he'd be proud of you right now?"

He asks the one thing that could ever make me reevaluate my every life choice.

"Yeah, I don't think so either."

My teeth could break with the pressure I'm using to clench my jaw to refrain myself from reacting.

"That isn't for you to worry about brother," I say, as calmly as I have the ability to, "What you should be focused on is why you're so worried about my personal affairs but have literally none of your own. When's the last time you've even looked a woman in the eye?"

He swallows.

"I know that there are bigger priorities at hand, something I thought we both saw eye to eye on," He walks closer to my desk, "I know that if whatever the hell you have going on fucks up anything we care about and everything we've worked for, that's your ass. And I'll cash that check personally."

A grimace creeps onto my face, "I haven't felt threatened by you in a long time Anthony," I say to my older brother who once trumped me in size. I stand from my desk so I can see him eye to eye, “So, whatever check you want to cash, I encourage you not to hesitate.”

Something hardens in his eyes, and he begins to retreat after holding my glare.

“I warned you of what happens when business and pleasure mixes, little brother,” He reaches to my doorway, looks to his feet and then back at me, “Gramp’s barbeque is set for this sunday. Honey asked that I let you know.”

He holds my eye contact for a moment longer before exiting completely.

I sit back down at my desk, reprimanding myself for giving any of his words space to reside in my head.

The devil may not have been able to pop my bubble, so he sent my brother instead.

# CHAPTER *THIRTY-NINE*

## *Moriah*

*I'm* sitting with Anastasia in my bedroom, she sits in a lounger on the floor while I hang over the edge of my bed.

The last few weeks I'd felt like nothing could take me from the euphoria I'd been engulfed in, it was the most blissful I'd ever felt.

Until I talked to my father.

Since our conversation in the kitchen that day, I've not been able to enjoy Darrell's presence without guilt slipping her way into the space we share.

Guilt because I know I've let this get too far. I knew it was a bad idea from the beginning and I ignored the warning signs, now I've swam too deep into uncharted waters and I've forgotten how to swim.

Darrell and I talked every day, but lately I've been too busy with work to answer his calls.

The peace that came with his presence has been ripped away faster than it came to be. I can barely look him in the eye in his own family's home, doing what I volunteered to do.

"Aside from your marriage," Stasi laughs, "What else has been going on with you?"

I push around the food in my container, “AJ spoke to our mom.”

“Oh,” She drops her fork, “How did that go?”

“I don’t know, I didn’t ask for details. I just know that they’ve set a time for us to meet.”

“You too? I thought this was an AJ thing?”

“Yeah, well, she wants me to go with her for moral support,” I take a forkful of food into my mouth.

“How do you think that’ll go? I hope she doesn’t think that just because you don’t directly remember anything that you’re coming in with open arms,” My best friend scoffs.

“I hope not too.”

She looks at me suspiciously, “But?”

I sigh, “But, I talked to Honey about it.”

“To who?” The confusion in her face makes me chuckle. I’m around her so much that I just assume that those I know will know who I’m talking about.

“Darrell’s grandmother, that’s what they call her.”

She nods.

“Anyway, I talked to her about it and she gave me some really good advice. I’m going there to support my sister, not to pass judgment or air my own grievance, this isn’t about me. It’s about what my sister needs,” Because the three of us are so close, Adella told Stasi on her own what this was all really about.

She hums, “I see.”

I roll my eyes, “What, Stasi?”

“It’s just, you guys must have gotten pretty close for you to talk to her about not only your family but your mother of all things. The FBI can’t even get that conversation out of you, but all it took was a grandmother and her home cooked meals to get you singing," She smiles.

The image of Honey popping up in my mind restricts my airways a little.

"She's just really comforting, you know? She reminds me of my Mom-Mom. I haven't had that maternal connection in… well, you know."

She looks at me with sympathy, "I know, Mo. I'm just kidding. I absolutely love that you've found your place in an extended family and that they've made you feel this comfortable."

"Well, most of them," I huff, "His brother might as well hang a 'No Moriah's Allowed' sign with the way he clearly doesn't want me around. I'm sure he's made up a handwritten one and is just waiting to bust it out."

"That's the only other brother right? The older one?"

"Yeah, he walks around like he's at war with the world around him."

She chews a bit more of her food.

"People like that just need a hug, whether they want one or not. They just don't know it."

"Yeah," My voice trails off.

"What else?" She knows me better than herself, "Miss I hate all men found a man she actually likes. I hope you don't think his moody ass brother's opinion is holding any weight with him," Stasi says as we eat our take out dinner. She notices when I don't laugh in response, "Unless… it is?"

"Maybe his brother is right to have his defenses up with me."

"Girl, what the hell are you talking about? Why would he be right to do that?" She asks in a tone that says she's sure I've lost my mind.

"God," I drop my head into my arms that support me, "I don't know what to do. I'm such a horrible person and I don't know what to do."

"What are you talking about? What happened?" She sits up a bit straighter.

I look at her, my vision blurring slowly, "I can't do this Stasi. What was I thinking? Why did I let this happen? And now, he's going to hate me and I don't blame him," I sniffle.

"Moriah, slow down, why is he going to hate you? What can't you do?"

"This, Anastasia!" I sit upright, "I can't do this. This wasn't supposed to go beyond a first date and now I have my father saying that he sees love is changing me?" My frantic fingers run through my loose curls, "What do I know about love other than it does no favors for you in the end? I've avoided that shit strictly so I didn't ever fall victim to the damage it brings again and now it's changing me?"

She joins me at the foot of my bed, "It's not a bad thing Mo, it's making you happier, that's what it's supposed to do. He makes you happy."

"And that's the danger of it all, Stasi," Sniffle, "He's made me hopeful. He's changed my mind on so many things I thought were true at first but now feel silly for believing. That's how it starts, that's how you get trapped and you end up a single parent struggling to be in too many places at once and you forget yourself, or how you end up crying for days on end in your lonely apartment that you were meant to be living in with the man who promised you the world but gave it to his new girlfriend he'd gotten just four months after telling you that he didn't want love to distract him. I don't want that for me, Stasi."

"Oh, girl…" She rubs my back, "That was your dads reality. One that he ended up feeling blessed for, might I add. And that asshole Rhysen, never deserved you. I know it doesn't feel like it, but he did you a favor when he left. You're so much better off without someone to make you compare yourself to people who couldn't see you even on your worst day."

"Love has too many variables Stasi, ones that I can't afford to give myself to."

"Well, Mo… I really think all this only matters if you think you're falling in love with him."

"That's the other problem, Stasi, I can't tell you that I'm not," I trap my bottom lip between my teeth, "His family has welcomed me into theirs, I've built bonds with them. I've had fucking sunday dinner with them and one on one lunches with his grandmother."

"Yeah," She agrees, "You have. And he's wanted you there, it's obvious."

"Exactly and now I'm going to be the certain disaster that love brings. I was worried all along about it being me having to face it, and look how funny life is," I laugh, "Moving me to commit an act of my biggest fear."

"I don't think you have to do that Moriah, just tell him that you want to take a step back or something."

"You don't see the way he looks at me, Anastasia," I shake my head, "You don't know the way he holds on to me when we touch. A step back won't register to him, it's better that I do it fully."

"Is it better for him, or is it better for you?" She says quietly.

"I don't know," My fingers trip over one another in my lap, "But I know it has to be done before this goes any further and someone says things that shouldn't be said."

# CHAPTER *FORTY*

## *Darrell*

*We're* all buzzing around the kitchen as we prepare food, snacks and beverages for all the family visiting us at my childhood home today.

Rayana helps Honey monitor the food that's finishing, Honey finishes last minute additions to what is already made and I'm just taking orders from either of them.

Honey moves slower than either myself or she is used to, but she's trying not to make too much mention of it.

While we're floating around each other, we hear more voices enter through the front of the house.

"Hey, I have the soda and wine!" Moriah's voice rings through and my heart does an extra thump at the sound, then plummets to my stomach when she reaches the kitchen's doorway.

"Okay," She sits the beverages on the kitchen table, "Where's my station?" She asks as she assesses the room to look for a task she can assign to herself.

"You can start with carrying these to the tables outside," Honey gestures to the dishes that have already been completed and sat on the countertop.

"Yes ma'am. Oh, by the way," She stops mid-walk to the kitchen sink, "Honey, this is my best friend Anastasia."

Her friend that I've only met one time before greets Honey, then the rest of us and proceeds to assist Moriah in the task she was given.

I don't get a chance to say hello to her before she's already jumping into action so I'm stuck in place, only able to admire her from my space in the kitchen.

Her readiness and willingness to be wherever she's needed is something that I think adds to the attraction I have to her.

She's a busy bee, and won't sit around when she knows there's work that could be done.

I watch her enter and exit, enter and exit the door that leads to the backyard where our family and close friends reside. She smiles with them as she fulfills the duty she was given, not lingering too much in one place.

She's focused.

"Your eyes just may fall out of your socket's son, trying to keep up so closely with her movements," Honey sneaks up to me.

I jump.

"I'm just making sure she doesn't need any help or doesn't… trip or something."

She chuckles, "If that's the story you're going to stick to when she asks you why you're standing there and not moving around then you're going to need to work on it."

I shake my head at my grandmother who looks up to me from her place beside me.

"I don't think I've seen hearts that big in a man's eyes since I met your grandfather," She adds on.

I look to her and back to Moriah, as if I'll lose her if I take my gaze away for too long.

"Well, I'll leave you to your dreaming then son," My grandmother pats me on my shoulder and walks past me to get to her large wicker chair that sits on the grass.

After more time passes of everyone mingling with one another, the chatters quiet down and everyone is asked to give Honey their attention.

"On behalf of my grandchildren and I, we wanted to thank all of you for coming to celebrate the life of Regine Washington," She begins her speech, "Some of you knew him as Reggie, Uncle, or Gramps. I knew him as the man that saved me."

Her mouth tightens as I imagine she tries to hold back the emotion that comes to her as memories of him flood her mind.

"I was 17 when the two of us met. I was the oldest of 9 children that I myself had to care for, due to an abusive father and a mother who didn't want the job. When Regine found me one night out with friends, he somehow knew that he'd eventually wear me down and get me to be his wife," She laughs to herself, "He knew it would take a lot to get me to leave home and my family. But, he taught me that I can't continue to take away someone's responsibility from them, that I didn't need to save everyone."

As she speaks, everyone gives her their undivided attention.

I look at the faces whose eyes are trained on my grandmother while she recalls the times she and her husband shared and I see emotion overcome some, understandably so.

My eyes soon find Moriah, who is crouched down in the grass with my niece and nephew, Angie's children, and they lay on her like she's been their means for comfort all their lives.

I struggle to take my eyes away from the sight of her. How much she blends in with my family as if she's known them for years, like she belongs there.

After some time my siblings and I give speeches of our own about what Gramps meant to us, and we're surrounded by red eyes and stained cheeks who haven't had a chance to recover from the sentiments Honey shared.

Angie tells her audience how safe he made her feel after coming from such a volatile environment.

Sy'Asia tells stories of how he made her feel heard after feeling that she only served a purpose for others.

Anthony, though a man of few words, says that he wouldn't by a long shot be the man he is today without the love our grandfather continued to give him, how he showed him patience until he learned that the love offered was safe to fall into.

I share the teachings he imparted on me for as long as I can remember about love being the true foundation of a good and real man.

Rayana goes last.

Her struggle to form sentences through tears is evident enough that everyone begins to console her from their space on the grass as she stands on the steps.

She talks about the way Gramps felt like her personal gift from God after so many things had been taken from her such as her health and by association her childhood. Gramps did all he could to make sure she felt no lack, he treated her the way she asked him to and saw her for her and not her plague.

He was her person.

My older siblings and I gather around our baby sister, pouring into her all the love we have to offer.

After the speeches are completed and some others share their brief stories of Gramps, I find my way into the kitchen. I've had my share of reminiscing and there isn't much more I'll be able to handle without crying.

I grab a can of soda that was left back on the kitchen table, pop up the tab and have a sip.

Moriah joins me.

"There she is," I greet her.

"Hey," She responds but her voice comes out too low.

"I'm glad you were able to make it still," I tell her, "I've barely been able to get a hold of you, didn't know if you'd still come. Thought maybe all the possibilities of tears were a little too much to handle," I laugh lightly.

She only offers a barely there grin in response, "I wouldn't let Honey down, I told her I'd be here and help."

I watch her for a moment, leaned against the kitchen counter with arms wrapped around herself like she needs consoling.

"Hey," I walk over to her, "What's up?"

She sighs.

"Too much," She answers me with a lifeless chuckle, "We're getting closer to the date of having to meet with my mother and I just… I don't know," She hangs her head, "I want to support my sister, of course. But, the more I think of it, the angrier I get it. The less I can clear my head enough to go into the meeting with open ears and a receptive heart."

She talked to me briefly about her feelings regarding her biological mother and how mixed they are. I don't know what I'd do if I ever saw my own mother again, none of us know where she's been for the last 8 years.

I remain silent and give her the space she needs to speak.

"There's just no part of my mind that can swallow the idea of starting a family with a man that could've been any woman's dream and just… walk away. The problem isn't that she wanted to follow her dreams, it's that she didn't even try to figure something out. Like, we just weren't enough."

The last part comes out in a whisper and I know she's still trying to hold back all she wants to let out.

She gets silent, trying to hold back the feelings that come up but a single tear betrays her.

I don't wait for permission before I pull her into me. She doesn't unleash a round of heart wrenching sobs, but she allows me to console her, and that's enough for me.

"I don't think it was about you being enough for her or not, Mo," I lean back just enough to see her face, "Sometimes our selfishness just means more to us than anything else and we don't think about the after."

She sniffles and tucks an imaginary curl behind her ear.

Seeing her this way makes me want to hide her away from the world, to nurture this version of her that she rarely allows anyone to see and hold it just for myself, as selfish as it sounds. I want to be her person at this moment.

"Follow me," I grab her hand and head further into the house, up the stairs leading to my childhood bedroom.

We enter a time machine.

The room hasn't changed since my adolescence, right before I left for college.

Dark blue walls with a few basketball posters here and there.

The same cotton sheets and red comforter.

My dresser collects dust now, as well as the pictures that sit on top of it.

Moriah takes her time scanning the framed photos of me and the people I love most.

"So," She talks to the frames more than me, "This is the infamous Gramps, huh?" She picks up a photo that was taken of us after a little league basketball game, "Honey's got good taste, he wasn't bad on the eyes," She smiles softly.

"I'd like to think I take after him," I joke and it earns me a chuckle.

"Maybe you'll grow into it," Another chuckle. I'm just glad they're here in the place of tears, so if it takes poking fun at me to make that happen, I'll accept it happily.

"I don't think you ever gave me the long version of how you ended up with them," She turns her attention to me partly.

"Looking for a storytime?" I grin at her, I'd tell her whatever she wanted to know.

"Yeah, why not?" She walks to my old bed and plops down, making herself comfortable with legs folded in front of her like a pretzel, "Lay it on me,"

I take a seat on the right side of the bed, kicking my feet up. "I can only tell you what I remember. Therapists have told me my mind decided to forget some parts that it doesn't want to hold on to, or something like that."

She nods.

"So, my mom was young when she started having kids, about 17, way too young," I begin, "But, she kept having them. Because she was so young, she sort of grew up with us in a sense. More so with Sy'Asia and Anthony than the rest of us. By the time she'd turned 20, grandparents got her a house. A whole house for her and her growing family with the promise that she'd firstly stop having kids especially unmarried and that she'd also handle her responsibilities. It lasted for a little while, then Angeline came, then me and then Rayana."

She doesn't interrupt me while I speak.

"My grandparents being who they are continued to do what they could to financially support her, but they soon realized anything they put in her hand, she'd blow on herself in one way or another. Her problem wasn't just the sex, it was men and whatever promises they dangled in front of her. She'd run after it like a horse does a carrot, no matter how much they ran ahead of her, she'd trek behind them. Random ones, ones that'd stick around for a few weeks, ones that would move in."

I shake my head at the memories of coming home from school to see a man I don't know sitting on our couch, eating our food.

"She'd always swear it was love and that this one was different. After a while, one of my siblings, I think it was Angie, told my grandparents how bad it'd gotten no matter how much my mom would lie to them and say she had everything under control. They tried to shield Rayana and I from what they could, whatever the worst of my mothers doing was, I never saw."

She stares at me while I stare ahead, looking at the memories my mind plays for me like I'm watching a movie of my own life.

"But they did, the three of them, front row seats. When my grandparents came to get us, they only packed for Rayana and me. They said they needed to stay back because someone had to look out for our mom. After a while they realized that wasn't a job they could handle, but they were thankful that they were allowed to move on their own time."

"God," She says only after seeing I'm done, "And I was complaining about my mom leaving, meanwhile, your mom should have to do you a favor."

I laugh, she says whatever comes to her mind.

"That doesn't invalidate what you went through. Absence is damaging no matter what, rather they physically left you or they're still there but don't see you."

She nods, looking at her hands that lay on her lap.

"It's nice to have someone to talk about it with though, someone that gets it to some degree," I say in the silence.

"Yeah," She nods again, "It is."

"And I'm glad it's you, not just anyone," I add.

She just offers a smile that doesn't reach her eyes.

I lay my hand over hers where her fingers are attacking one another, she stops and looks at me.

Like a moth to a flame I can't stop myself from leaning in to kiss her, so she stops me instead.

I'm not able to mask my confusion.

She shakes her head gently, "Darrell, I don't think we should keep doing this."

Out of the many possibilities of the things she could've said in the moment, this was not one I anticipated. It doesn't register properly.

"What?" Is all I can say back.

"I'm sorry, I've been thinking about it for days now. I just... I enjoy being around you, I do. I just don't think that we're a good idea for each other."

I hear her speaking but she might as well speak a different language.

"Did I do something? I didn't mean to-"

"No," She stops me, "You did nothing wrong. It's me, honestly, as much of a bullshit response as it is. It's true."

"I thought everything was going good between us, how did we get to not being a good idea for each other?" I can't wrap my head around the change in air around us.

"We just let this get too far and too fast. And, it's my fault, I'll take full accountability. But, I just think before we get too deep into something we aren't ready for, we should stop here."

I create space between us on the bed, "Before things get too deep? Moriah, you're taking care of my fucking grandmother nearly every day, I think we've gotten there already. Plus, who are you to tell me if I'm ready for something or not?"

"I know, and I'm sorry. I met her, got to spend just a few hours with her and fell in love. And after finding out about her circumstances, I just wanted to help."

"That wasn't the only reason why," I reply to her.

"What?"

"That wasn't the only reason why you wanted to be here, around my family Moriah and you know that. Yes, it played a big part because you have a kind heart but that wasn't just it. It was because you wanted to be near me too."

"Darrell," Her eyes squint like she's trying to dissect my words, "I like you yeah, but-"

"But you knew that I was pulling back because of Honey, and you knew that helping out with her would allow us to see each other more. I'm not mad about it, I don't fault you for it, but I won't let you act as if that isn't true."

"I-..." She searches for a line of defense and falls short, "Even if that were true, that further proves my point of this getting too far."

"What is it that you're so scared of, Mo? Because this is bullshit and you know it."

"I'm not scared of anything except for wasting both of our time just for it to end up badly."

"And who's to say it will?" I retort.

"Who's to say it won't, Darrell?" She all but yells.

I'm taken aback by the change in her volume but it confirms exactly what I thought.

"But, who's to say it will, Moriah?" Searching her eyes, I turn to her while we still sit on the bed, allowing my legs to support me from underneath, "Listen, I get it. You saw your dad pour into someone and it didn't work out the way he hoped, and you feel that your experience with ole' boy in college was too similar to that experience than you're comfortable with. That's fucked up, it is. But you can't let that dictate the rest of your life. Your story doesn't have to be that way. It won't be that way, not with me."

"I'm sure everyone thinks that at first Darrell, but things happen that we don't have control over."

"Yeah, like us," I gesture between the space that separates us, "We happened and neither of us saw it coming," I reason.

Nothing could be truer.

The day I met Moriah I knew there was something about her that pulled me in, but never did I predict I'd feel for her the way I do.

I never thought that she would consume me the way she does the moment she walks into a room, like a magnet is pulling me towards her and I haven't the strength to fight it.

I don't want to.

She shakes her head.

"We aren't equipped for this," She laughs, "You've had all of what, two relationships in your life? One being in highschool. Me? I've had one that shattered my heart and after that I've had men come and go, taking the promises they never cashed in on with them. I'm not going to find myself one day sitting in my room crying and heartbroken again, because you decided something else is more important to you than what you've promised me."

And there it is, the tears that she tried to keep away with a brave face. It's not just about pouring love into someone and not getting a bang for your buck, it's the fear that she won't be enough to keep someone around.

"I'm not your mother, Moriah and you aren't a child. Nor am I the dick from college. This isn't what you're trying to make it out to be. That wasn't love, Mo," I try to wipe away a tear but she swats away my hand.

"What do we know about love really, Darrell?" She says through broken sobs, "You're okay with needing me around and I'd rather not need anyone. Love is too dangerous, especially for people like us who come from two different versions of broken homes. You want to act like you don't see that, but I can't live life blindly that way."

"Moriah, I understand that you're scared and I know you have your reasons. I'm not a begging man, but if you need me to get on my knees right now I will if it'll convince you to give this a chance. Let me show you that you're safe with me."

She starts to shake her head. She opens her mouth to speak, but I don't give her the chance to utter a word before my mouth lands onto hers.

"I never believed my grandfather when he tried to convince me that I'll know when I meet my person. I told him that was just his story and he was lucky, but it wouldn't be mine and he swore that it would be. Now I know that he was right."

I hold her face in my hands even though she tries to avoid my gaze.

"You may not have felt it, but I knew there was something here the first day we met. The first day you made me question my own name, I knew, even if I didn't want to accept it."

"I'm sorry, Darrell, that I toyed with your feelings knowing that mine had a weight capacity. You deserve better than that," She looks at me with empathy and lays her hand on my cheek for consolation.

But all I get from her touch is a fire inside of me.

I've never met a woman like Moriah.

One that doesn't settle, that doesn't bend or break for anyone no matter what value you may hold. She doesn't hurry just because you're waiting, if anything she'll go slower.

"I deserve you," I whisper, "I deserve the woman who puts everyone before herself just because it makes her happy. The woman who can't let a stranger's baby cry too long without being moved to help. The woman who wants to take care of a stranger's grandmother because she knows the family is still mourning."

I brush away a tear she didn't mean to let escape.

"I deserve the woman who won't rush for anyone, not even for the man who would wait ions for her to move and would stop the world to make it do the same."

Her heart is so much bigger than her body and it makes me want her even more.

I hold on to the hand she uses to touch me with my own and kiss her palm, she tries to pull it away but I tighten my grasp.

"Darrell," Her voice comes out in a whisper.

I continue to kiss up her arm, needing to touch her, have something to hold on to before she tries to slip away from me.

"I'll take care of you Moriah, I swear it," My lips make their way to her shoulder. "Let me show you how safe you are with me."

"Darrell," She says again in a plea, "We shouldn't."

I make my way to her ear, "My heart is on the line right now for you Moriah… even if you don't feel the same way I do yet, lie to me, just for tonight."

She hisses and it sends my body into a frenzy.

I breathe in her scent, "You smell so good," I whisper into her ear. I make my way to her face and for a moment I hold it, soaking in the rawness of her state.

If I thought she was beautiful before, she's mesmerizing right now.

Her words may tell me no but her lips part for me while her eyes are closed. I accept the invitation she gives me and kiss her like she's the last lips I'll ever touch.

She latches on to me with her arms around my neck and I guide her to lay down with me on top of her.

"I can make you happy, Moriah," I whisper while I kiss down the side of her neck and make my way to her collarbone, "Let me, please," I beg, making my way between her breast and onto her stomach.

I raise her shirt to her neck to see what hides underneath, and begin unfastening her pants as I continue to grace her skin with my lips anywhere I can reach from this position.

"God, Darrell," A moan escapes her and pours into me like fuel to an engine.

I free her of her pants and underwear, and remove my clothes after.

"Keep saying my name that way and you'll never leave this bed Moriah," I tell her in pants as I position myself back over her.

I rub my fingers on her core and release a growl that I couldn't hold back, "You're so wet for me, and still you want to leave me baby?" I align my length with her.

She groans at the contact.

I enter her and release a sound that is nothing short of animalistic. Being inside of her makes me feel primal, there's no higher feeling

I pump in and out of her, grunting with every movement, allowing her moans to encourage me.

"I love the way you sound for me, I know that it's just for me," I connect my forehead to hers and begin to increase my pace causing her melody of moans to fill up the room.

She claws at my back, "Fuck," she cries out and I feel something snap inside of me.

My thrusts become punishing and she takes me perfectly. "God," I pant, "I feel you. I feel you Moriah, let it go,"

As if she needed my permission, the insides of her become too slippery for me to handle and I feel the pressure building inside of me.

"Oh, fuck!" She yells, and I've ever been more thankful that all my loved ones are outside so they can't hear the destruction I'm inflicting on the women beneath me.

In only a few thrusts more, the pressure becomes too much and the both of us explode in unison.

It feels almost spiritual.

We lay in the sweaty messes on my bed, trying to catch our breath.

"Darrell…" She begins to speak.

"No, Moriah, please not yet," I stop her and so we continue to lay beside each other in silence.

After a while, still in silence, we gather our clothes and make ourselves appropriate again. I watch her as she dresses herself and she avoids my eyes. I can't help but feel a weight on my chest.

After we are both presentable, we go to exit my room and run into Angeline whose eyes are as wide as saucers.

"Angie, what's wrong?" I see the panic on her face.

"It's Honey," she says quickly and my heart drops, "We've been looking all over for you. She's been rushed to the hospital, she's unconscious."

# CHAPTER *FORTY-ONE*

## *Moriah*

*After* dropping off Stasi at her house I raced to the hospital to meet Darrell. When I find him, he is a ping ponging mess as he walks from one side of the waiting room to the other and then back again.

"Hey," I approach him with shortened breaths since I all but sprinted to the ER, "Any news on her, is she awake?"

He shakes his head with eyes that tell me while his body may be here, his mind is far away, "No," He answers without looking at me, "Nothing yet, she's still unconscious."

"Okay," I run my fingers through my chaotic curls, they reflect my current state of mind, "Okay. It's going to be fine, she'll be fine," I say to the both of us, trying to catch him by the shoulder on his wall to wall sprint.

He shakes his head at something with his chin trapped in his fingers, "No," He says, "No, no," He repeats to himself.

I almost want to grab him before he goes on the spiral that I see pending behind his eyes, at least whenever I can see them.

"I should've been down there."

"Rell, you couldn't have stopped her from collapsing if something was wrong anyways. You could've stood right next to her and it could've still happened."

"No," Firmly he nearly shouts at me, I jump back just a hair but not enough for more than us to notice, "No, I should've been down there, paying attention to her, not w-" He catches the rest of his sentence on his tongue and it stays there, but we know what he was going to say.

"Excuse me," An angrier male voice says loudly from behind me, causing me to immediately spin in its direction.

It's Anthony.

"This doesn't concern you, I think you've played a big enough role tonight," He growls at me.

"Chill out, Anthony," Darrell says to him from behind me.

"Chill out?" He huffs out a laugh, "I'm not chilling shit. This is her fault as much as it is yours."

"And how is that, may I ask?" I square my shoulders and fold my arms, he may be used to intimidating people in his place of work with his stature and his deep voice, but I've encountered many beasts of men, he's no different than the ones I've been able to send away with their tails between their own legs.

"If you weren't so busy fucking my brother in my grandmothers fucking home, because I know that's exactly what the hell you were doing, maybe this wouldn't have happened," The vibrato of his voice could shake the room, "That's how."

"That's not even remotely fai-"

"Anthony, fucking relax," Darrell cuts off my reply, "She couldn't have known just like I couldn't and just like you couldn't. Weren't you actually down there? Why didn't you stop it, since that was so simple?" He yells at his brother.

Their three sisters joined us during their exchange.

"Because I was tending to other things at the time but what I wasn't doing was being so distracted by pussy that I was nowhere near my sickly grandmother in case she needed me."

"Antony," Sy'Asia says quietly behind him.

"That's not fair and you know that shit. And what the hell is your fixation with what I'm doing with my dick? You've become more concerned with it than I am," Darrell gives up his attempt to control his tone with his brother.

"My concern is, your little obstruction right there," He points to me, "needs to get the hell out of here and away from what doesn't involve her. It was cute she tried to do the whole "I care about your dying grandmother act, but look where it got us."

"You're so-"

"He might be right," Darrell and I speak at the same time but to different people.

I avert my attention to him.

"What?"

He looks at me with something in his eyes that I can't distinguish, but I know it's not something I like.

"You should go, Moriah, not for the reason he's saying… but still, you should," He sounds defeated, I just don't know what by.

I'm speechless. I look at him, then to his siblings who all have their eyes on me.

Rayana who can't even look at me.

"Oh," I finally respond, grabbing my bag from a nearby chair that I sat it in when I arrived, "Yeah, okay. I'm sorry if I overstepped coming here."

He doesn't respond, he just looks at his feet.

I begin to walk towards the exit, "Will you keep me updated with Honey, at least?"

She's become so much more to me than a kind older woman who welcomed me into her home, she's become like a grandmother to me as well.

Before Darrell has a chance to allow the words to leave from his mouth, Anthony answers for him.

"I don't think that'll be necessary. We thank you for what you've done for our grandmother leading up to now, but it's best we keep everything moving forward between just family."

I look from him to Darrell, who finds something else fascinating with the floor beneath him. I form my lips into a straight line and offer them one last curt nod before I exit the automatic sliding doors I entered through.

I knew something about tonight would be rough, I understood things may not go smoothly.

But this wasn't what I anticipated, and what's worse is not only do I not know if Darrell does impart some blame on me, but I know above all he's blaming himself.

And that, I know, is entirely my fault.

# CHAPTER *FORTY-TWO*

## *Moriah*

*I* haven't heard anything about Honey, not even from Rayana.

I haven't spoken to Darrell since that day and though it hurts, I'm sure it's for the best.

Eventually, something would've happened to pull us away from each other anyway, better now than later, at least these are the things I've convinced myself of.

It's hard not to miss him though.

I often picture him doing work around Honey's house or singing around his apartment while he cleans. The memories are invasive and I try to rid them almost as soon as they pop up.

I say almost because sometimes, I can't help but allow them to linger in my mind's eye for a few moments.

But, I know in the long run we would've hurt each other, that's just how that goes. Someone would've come up disappointed.

I can't focus on reminiscing right now though and what would've been, I have work to do.

I'm at an event hosted by a foundation that does similar work to Love Unbound.

Many founders of nonprofits are here, as well as silent investors, grantmakers and sponsors. We've invited the Henderson family to be our company's plus one.

"I wanted to thank you for all the dedication you've poured into my family," Mister Henderson says to both Elijah and myself, "There had been so many people that reached out but hardly wanted to get to know us. They just wanted to put us on a poster and use some sob story that was barely our own to get money. It was easy to see that you guys really cared about who we were, that matters so much to the three of us."

Makyla and Everest stand just behind him as he speaks, the both of them looking from him to us as he shares with us his gratitude.

In the time we initially met with them until now, Mister Henderson has gotten a handful of promising job offers with more secure establishments. The girls have begun their tutoring and barely missed a beat with their schoolwork and will be ready to go once school starts.

"The pleasure was entirely ours," Elijah places a hand over his heart, "We of course care about all the families we work with, but I think I speak for the both of us when I say we truly enjoyed working with your family."

I smile and nod in agreement with his words.

When we met the Hendersons, Mister Henderson was so nervous about being a provider for his two girls and giving them a proper place to lay their heads as well as making sure their needs were taken care of.

Makyla and Everest were attached at the hip, clearly worried and nervous from their lives being turned upside down so suddenly.

Now, even Makyla smiles instead of trying to appear bigger than she is.

Some time passes and the event is fully underway. I've done the mingling that's expected of me and found my way to the hors d'oeuvres table hoping that I can take a break from forced interactions for a moment.

That hope fades when I feel a tap on my arm. I turn to see the person who isn't good at taking hints, only to look down to see a wide eyed Everest.

"Hey, Everest. What's up?"

Her eyes hold an emotion that I don't think I've ever seen in a child her size, concern.

"You aren't talking that much… Are you okay?"

The observations of a child, man.

"Um," I let multiple answers weigh on my tongue to figure out which I'll choose, "Honestly Everest, I'm not sure."

"Well, what's wrong?" She quirks her head at me.

"There's just… a lot going on you know? Probably too much to lay on you at once," I smile softly, trying to give the kid an escape.

She crosses her arms instead, "Lay it on me, I help my sister with her problems all the time."

I laugh, because I totally believe she has decent advice to be a half sized human.

I sigh, realizing she probably won't go away easily, so I indulge.

"Well," I take in a breath, "I have to meet my mom tomorrow."

"Oh," She says, "That's all? What's so bad about that?"

"I haven't seen her since I was two years old. It'd sorta be like we're meeting for the first time."

"Oh…" Her tone changes with realization, "I get that. I don't remember my mom too much either," Her voice fills with empathy and understanding.

"Do you mind if I ask you what happened to her? Where is she, if you know?" There was never a proper time to pose the question in prior meetings, and while this may still be improper, my curiosity gets the best of me.

"She died when I was 4. It was unexpected apparently, she'd gotten really sick out of nowhere and the doctors had no idea where it was coming from. They couldn't save her before it was too late."

I'm at a loss for words.

"I'm so sorry Everest, I can't imagine how hard that must've been for you guys."

Talking to her, it's easy to forget she's only 8 years old, still such a little kid. It's this moment that brought me back to that reality.

"It's fine," She shrugs, "I think it affected my sister and dad more than me. I was still really little."

"Still, I'm just as sorry to you," I rub her arm.

She shrugs again and smiles after a moment, "Back to you though," Everest changes the subject, "I get why you'd be nervous, it would be weird meeting your mom for the first time ever and she's… your mom, you know? But, try not to think of her as your mom. Just, i don't know, maybe think of her as one of the people you meet with to help them. Figure out her story and go from there."

I'm shocked, that isn't a bad approach.

"That's not a bad idea, kid," I chuckle.

"I told you I'm the problem solver in my family," She shamelessly says, "Just remember that not everything people do that hurts us is on purpose. Makyla hurts my feelings sometimes, but it's just because she's trying to look out for me. I just have to remember it wasn't on purpose even though she could've said it better. Second chances are important, or else we would never like each other."

---

The day has finally come and nothing has prepared me for this moment at all.

Adella has tried to present as a picture perfect example of calmness but with her being my sister, I see how she hasn't stopped fiddling with her fingers in her lap.

She's bitten the skin around her finger nails and it's finally starting to show just how much their day has been weighing on her.

She says that our mother has no clue about her reason for wanting to meet her, or what set her out to search for her in the first place.

I know that I'm here for support, but I truly wish I had someone outside of just my sister to be supporting me while I try to show up for her.

We arrive in Baltimore and visit the small cafe where we agreed to meet. Adella and I take a seat next to each other, showing ourselves as a united front against the empty seat across from us.

We haven't spoken much since we left our home an hour ago, the hands that are joint together under the table right now on Adella's lap is the most communication we've shared.

After all those years of being the one that gets protected, it feels like it's finally my turn to be the big sister.

Our heads snap up in unison at the sound of the front door opening.

We don't see her face at first, only a blanket of dark, graying hair. When she turns to face us, the air is sucked out of the room. She smiles softly and makes her way to us, as if she just knows even though it's been over twenty years since she's laid eyes on us.

She takes a seat across from us and it feels like a rod has taken the place of my spine.

She meets our clearly hesitant faces with a smile, "Hi."

I don't speak.

"Hi," Adella says a bit quieter than I'm used to her being, she squeezes my hand under the table and I'm not sure if she's trying to pull strength from me or if she's trying to prompt me.

Either way, I'm frozen.

No one speaks for a moment and the space around us is rapidly filling with tension.

"I have to admit," Adeline, my mother, begins to speak, "I never thought I'd see the day that you all would seek me out."

"We did not," I correct her, "And trust me, I don't think either of us saw the day coming either."

Her smile drops. The knock of AJ's knee against my own tells me that maybe my approach was too heavy.

"We didn't really anticipate having to reach out first, no," AJ tries to dull the edges of my sword for a tongue, "But, I figured the day would come one way or another at some point."

Adeline nods.

"So, what-" Adeline is interrupted by a waitress coming to take our orders. We all ask for coffees, I don't think anyones stomach can bear anything more than a beverage this morning.

"What caused you to reach out?" She continues her original question.

AJ visibly takes in a deep breath beside me, I firm my grip on her hand to remind her that I'm here for her.

"I went to the doctors recently due to some pains I was having in my neck that were chronic, and some challenging period" She clears her throat, "When I went to the doctor with my concerns, it led to them wanting to do some tests. I found out that I have a condition called cervical stenosis and that I may not be able to ever have children of my own."

Because she's my sister, I hear the break in her voice that may not be easily detectable by others, like a woman who hasn't been a mother to her since she was a child.

"Adella," Adeline leans forward a bit with her hand on the table, I noticed the twitch as she stopped herself from reaching out, "I'm so, so sorry to hear that. I can't imagine how that must feel."

"Right, well," AJ continues, "It led me to thinking, how could someone who has a privilege that so many other women in this world don't have, someone who was given a blessing, twice, that so many other women won't ever receive… how do you just take it for granted?"

The pain in my sister's face as she poses this question to our birthmother is louder than her voice.

"Oh Adel-"

"Her name is AJ," I cut off our mother, "No one calls her Adella. It makes her feel like someone's grandparent."

I swear, I'm not trying to act like a bitter teenager, and I know my sister could have set that boundary herself if it was that serious.

Her lips form a firm line in response to me, "AJ," She adjusts, "I understand why that question would be on your mind considering. I know it seems like I took it for granted, but I promise that isn't true."

I do my best to swallow the laugh that presents itself from my throat.

"It isn't true?" AJ repeats back to her, "How isn't it true? You gave birth, two times, to two healthy babies. You were a mother twice, and abandoned them. How is that not taking it for granted?"

I'm proud of my sister for calmly asking the question I don't think I could ask without disturbing every patron in the cafe.

"I…" Adeline searches for her words, "Okay. Maybe that isn't true, I can understand how one could say I took that blessing for granted and I can agree to that perception."

I hate that she speaks like she's trying to reason with a patient in therapy.

"I'm glad you can see it from the perspective of those that were abandoned," I respond to her.

She sighs.

"I was too young to realize what was going on around me before it was too late and I was in the thick of it all," She starts to explain, "I wasn't ready. I still had so many plans, I wanted to start my practice, I was barely finished schooling.

Your dad was ready for a wife and a homemaker, I wasn't ready for that."

"And you realized that *after* the two kids and living with him for seven years?" I ask her.

I sense AJ hold her breath, she's given up on silently trying to reel me in under the table and has switched to bracing for impact.

"Yes," she shrugs, "Yes, that's when I saw everything around me with me in the middle of it and I was able to pull myself out of the daydream and realize that I was nowhere near where I wanted to be before motherhood entered into the conversation. I just wasn't. I didn't want to abandon you guys, I didn't want to abandon your father, I cared about him so much. I panicked. I ran,"

"And never thought to look back," I retort, "Ready or not, you created that family and decided that it didn't align with where you wanted to see yourself at that time. So you just left, like you didn't have a responsibility or people that needed you."

My resolve to be level headed breaks and all the things that have built up inside of me are fighting for a way out.

"You're right," She says to my surprise, "You're right, Moriah. I completely failed taking care of the responsibilities I created for myself and I tried to escape them without consequence."

"But there were consequences, and big ones. Like our father having to give up his own dreams to fix what you did. Or, him trying to figure out what to do when we got our periods, thank God for MiMi being around. What about during high school? How do you think he fared with teenage girl mood swings, fights and boys?"

I rattle off a list of duties she should have been there to help with and she just lets me, so does AJ who hasn't spoken since my voice has found the light of day.

"I'm sorry," Is all she replies, "You're right and I'm sorry. I failed you both, and I failed your father and I can't imagine what that was like for all of you to deal with."

I don't know if I was preparing for a battle, but this doesn't feel like what I expected to hear.

"You're right, thank God for your Grandmother. While I knew she would fill in the gaps that she could, that's not justification for being so inconsiderate. I gave your father no time to adjust and I only saw my needs, not even the needs of the little humans that my very body created,"

She slumps her shoulders in defeat and it seeps into her voice as she speaks.

"It's true that I acted with selfish intent only, not seeing anyone else's perspective and what would happen after I choose what I did. But, not only that, I was scared, Moriah," Her voice cracks in the way AJ's does when she's trying to act like she's not on the brink of falling over.

"I was so, so, scared and the only thing I knew to focus on was something I could control. Myself, my career, my goals, that was familiar territory. Your father was talking to me about marriage and moving into a bigger house and really setting down roots and I didn't know what to do with that. I didn't know what he was seeing in me that would make him believe I could be what he was looking for. He wanted a family, a real one and thought I could give that to him, that was terrifying."

I watch as my mothers eyes morph from receiving to pleading, and I can't help but allow my defenses to weaken.

I look at her as she explains what truly led her away from the two girls that needed her, from the man that believed she was his happy ending, and I see how much we resemble each other.

Her hair falls on to her shoulders in tumbles of coils with gray strands throughout them. Her eyes tell a story that I'm sure began well before age started to become her narrator. Her mouth has the slightest lines beginning to frame it, but they're prominent as she speaks.

"I let fear lead me and disguised it as something else, it was a copout and I'm not proud of it," My mother continues, "But, I don't want you to for a moment believe that I was secure in that choice or that I went out living my best life, responsibility free, because that just isn't true. With every milestone I crossed, I never enjoyed it. I've never felt true fulfillment in anything I accomplished after leaving you girls and your father. I just felt empty."

This admission was something I didn't expect and as much as I want to argue it, I can't deny that I hear sincerity.

"Wow," AJ chuckles, speaking for the first time in a little while, "This all sounds a bit familiar, don't you think?" She turns to me.

I wish I could pretend that I don't know what she's talking about, but the more our mother gives us an explanation, the louder I hear Honey in my ear telling me that I may understand her more than I expect to.

I hate that.

I spent so many years believing our mother abandoned us because we just weren't enough for her, we didn't give her the thrill work did or that she was just a horrible person who couldn't own up to her own consequences and handle them like an adult.

When, in reality, she's the opposite… she's actually a lot like myself.

"Why couldn't you have just told him that?" I ask her, "Why couldn't you have just told him that you were scared, out of your element? You know he would've understood."

She looks to the table where her fingers fall over each other like uncoordinated dance partners, "I had too much pride," She says simply, "I couldn't admit that I had no idea how to follow through on something I started. Defeat isn't an easy thing to say you feel aloud, especially not to someone that you know thinks you hung the moon in the sky single handedly."

She chuckles, but there's nothing but truth in what she says.

From the stories my father told me growing up, you could tell my mother was a goddess in his eyes. Why? I'll never understand, but he loved her and that's not always something others need to get.

"I wish we could've heard this years ago," My sister says while words fail me, "It would've saved a lot of headache," She huffs out.

"And I'm sorry you didn't," Adeline finally allows her hand to give into the twitches she's been fighting for the last hour and touches the free hand AJ has laid on the table.

"I understand that the both of you are grown now with your own lives and I'm lightyears behind," Adeline continues, "I don't want to say that I want to make up for lost time because I worry that opportunity is long behind us now, but I would like to get to know the both of you better. If that is something that you want."

She looks at the both of us with nervous eyes, waiting for us to say something.

"I understand you aren't really in need of mothering anymore," she continues with a nervous laugh, "But-"

"Everyone needs their mother," AJ, with her kind and forgiving spirit responds to her.

I don't tell her that I want to be closer, I don't tell her that I need her despite what's happened. I don't say anything else at all.

All I know is, though things didn't go as planned and that a gap has been bridged between my sister and her mother, and even though my sister brought us here fueled with hurt, I know this is truly what she wanted.

While they speak of making amends, I'm left with my feelings about the fact that I relate to almost every word my birth mother said to us and try to figure out how I avoid walking down the same path, despite it possibly being too late.

# CHAPTER *FORTY-THREE*

## *Darrell*

**The** sounds of machines haunt me in the rare times I'm able to sleep.

Every time I close my eyes, I see only a few images.

It shuffles between how Honey may have looked as she collapsed out of her seat on the day that landed her in the hospital, and images of Moriah.

The way she looked through me when we first met, the first time I saw a smile reach her eyes, the first time I was given the privilege to touch her… and when she told me that we were over.

We'd barely even begun.

I haven't spoken to her, not even to update her about Honey, not there's much to update her on.

I don't know if she'd even want me to reach out, especially after so many days have passed.

Honey has been in and out consciousness for a little over a week. The doctors say her reason for passing out was her heart, they weren't lying when they told her she was declining quickly.

The small windows we've gotten with her have been filled with us just letting her know that we're here and we've got her.

I know that if she was able to give us more than a few sentences, she'd be scratching at the walls to go home and as much as I'd want to grant that for her, I know this is the best place for her to be.

I hear her take a deep sigh in her sleep and it takes me out of my thoughts.

I grab hold of her limp hand, and just imagine she's holding mine back.

My siblings and I have taken shifts staying here with her, Rayana and I being here the most while Anthony, Sy'Asia and Ang tend to the world that still goes on around us.

The tension that my brother and I once laid to rest found new breath the night Moriah followed us to the hospital for Honey.

I had so many conflicting thoughts in that moment.

I felt guilt because of not being there for my grandmother, I was upset with my brother for trying to make me feel worse than I already did, and I was hurt that the one woman I've taken a chance on letting into my life, into my heart, just told me that she didn't want the position.

I cared about Moriah, more than I realized before that moment.

I thought I'd found myself in a safe enough space to finally relax, to finally feel whatever my grandparents had always tried to prepare me for.

I thought I was closer to giving my grandmother what she wanted for me, to find my person like she did all those years ago.

"I don't know Honey," I say to her sleeping body in front of me, "You're usually right about a lot of things, but you may have struck out with this one."

Only the annoying beeping of the machines in the room responds to me.

"I know you think love is this grand healer of all that's wrong in the world, but… the way I'm feeling right now? Love may actually be what was wrong in the first place,"

I jump at her slightly stirring, wondering if I somehow have awakened her. I relax in my seat when her body goes back to its slackend state.

"Yeah, I'm disappointed too, granny. I really thought we'd found the one you were waiting for," I look down at here our hands are loosely joined together, "The one I'd been waiting for, I guess."

I lay my head on the arm that rests atop her beds guardrail, trying to stop the images of Moriah standing in my room, shaking her head at me as if she didn't believe her own words.

She wouldn't listen to me.

Me, of all people, trying to convince someone to give love a chance in any way. The most convincing person I know couldn't be convincing when it mattered the most.

I didn't know what else to do, but I couldn't let her go without feeling her one last time.

Without letting her feel me, one last time.

It was the most bittersweet moment I've ever shared with someone and thinking about it for too long makes me feel emotions I'm not comfortable with feeling.

"I think you and Gramps were just a rare case," I say again to no one, "I don't think that's going to be my story, as much as we hoped it would be."

I stroke Honey's hand with my thumb and after a few moments feel her briefly hold me back.

I'm not a man that believes in signs from above, but I'd be lying if I said I didn't take that as confirmation that something is going to turn around soon.

# CHAPTER *FORTY-FOUR*

*Moriah*

I'm spending my Wednesday night with my sister, my dad and Stasi.

We told our dad how the meeting went with our mother and just like the understanding man he is, he said he never faulted her for the choices she made.

That he understood that she may have been apprehensive because he was so ready to start his family and settle down, he just expected that she was too and even if not, that she'd soon get on board. It was his fault just as much as it was hers, for assuming she wanted the same things he did.

She and AJ exchanged information, I just waited at the car until they were finished.

We're sitting in the living room watching a movie and collectively sushing our father from asking his hundreds of questions when my phone rings.

I look at my phone to see who's calling, it's a number I don't recognize.

I walk into the next room to take the call so I don't disturb anyone else.

"Hello?"

"Hello, Moriah?" I hear a timid voice on the other end of the call.

"Rayana?" I've never given her my phone number.

"Yeah, hey. How are you?" Rayana responds

"Oh, hey," I say back to her, "I'm good, I'm good. How is everything with you guys?" I hesitate to ask my real question considering her oldest brother made it very clear that their family business is not mine to know.

"Things are… things, you know?" I can picture her nodding with her words, "Honey isn't nearly back on her feet. She's still in the hospital, they have her in the ICU. Doctors say it was her heart that made her pass out, they had to resuscitate her when she got here."

I let out the breath I was holding, "Oh god, that's so scary. I know you all are under a lot of stress then."

"Yeah, for sure. I don't think we've been this stressed since Gramps passed, maybe not even then. We knew what happened and couldn't do anything about it. This time around we don't know what the outcome could be and everyone's shifting blame to either themselves or someone else."

I hum, "Yeah, I get that," Is all I have to respond as her oldest brother's words ring through my head, telling Darrell that it was his fault for being with me that this tragedy happened to their grandmother.

"She's asked about you, once or twice," Rayana takes me away from my memories.

"Who? Honey?"

"Yeah," She laughs, "She isn't awake much but there were a few times she was able to ask *Where's Mo*?"

I smile.

"That makes me really happy to know, Ray. Thank you for calling me and telling me that"

"Of course, Mo," She says like it was a no-brainer, "You became like family in such a short amount of time. I know she'd want you to know, no matter what my erratic brother thinks is best."

My smile slowly fades and silence falls over the call.

"Um, so," Rayana says, "I know what happened… between you and my brother I mean."

I take in a deep breath, I was hoping to hear he was alright but I was also hoping we'd end the call after the update about Honey.

"Listen, Ray…" I try to find the right words, "I'm sorry if you hate me, I get it, it just wasn't a good idea and I didn't want it to get any deeper before someone got hurt, you know?"

She hums into the receiver.

"Yeah, and hurting him now instead of hurting him later, changes the hurt I guess?"

Damn, that's not the response I anticipated, and now I'm fully prepared for her to curse me out on her brothers behalf. I'd do the same thing.

"Moriah, look," I hear her take a breath, "I know I don't have much experience, not as much as you or my siblings. But, what I do know is what I see right in front of me. And, I saw you two. During the denial of liking each other and after the acceptance of it, you both changed."

I lean on to an end table as I listen to her speak.

"You both needed someone to take a chance on you, and you found it. I think the both of you were scared, but you were too scared to take the risk anyway. I've never seen my brother so happy with a woman, I've never seen him allow someone to get so close, and to let them around his family, around Honey?"

I know she isn't lying, it wouldn't take a genius to figure that out after seeing him with his family to know that they are what he keeps most sacred. It's a privilege to get close to them.

"He was just as scared, Moriah. I don't know much about your life outside of what you've shared with me, but I do know that the two of you don't have too different of an experience and that it's caused both of you to deny yourself of love from people outside of your family."

She takes a moment, I think to just allow me time to soak in her words.

"But he wanted to take that chance on you, and I know that you wanted to give him that chance. I'm no one to give out love advice, but…" Her voice trails off, "He just wants a chance to prove himself. He really, really cares about you Moriah."

I inhale as if I'm able to breathe in her words.

"Yeah… yeah no I care about him too, I hope you know that. I hope he knows that," I run my hands through my hair.

"I think he knows that you didn't believe in him, and that just caring about him wasn't enough to make you stay."

Fuck.

"I think you two should talk," Rayana suggests.

"I can't do that Rayana, you know that."

"I don't know that," She almost snaps at me, "Give me one good reason why you can't."

"Because he needs to focus right now," I throw my free hand in the air, "He needs to focus on Honey and you guys right now. He doesn't need me messing shit up for his head."

She scoffs, "You sound like Anthony."

"Maybe he wasn't so wrong this whole time," I shrug, "I mean, look what happened in the long run."

"Absolutely not," She says a little too loudly into the phone, "My brother means well in the grand scheme of it all, but he operates from a place of his own hurt. His heart was broken once some years ago and he projects his bitterness onto everyone around him and thinks that because he chose to bury himself in duty that everyone else should."

Rayana goes off.

"That has nothing to do with either one of you."

I sigh, the girl is a force.

"Still, I don't think he'd want to see me."

"I promise you that's the exact thing he needs right now. He'll be at the hospital Friday night, that's when his next shift with Honey is."

"I can't do this in the freaking hospital, Rayana."

"Yes the hell you can, you're not about to fuck the man. At least not in the hospital, I'd hope," She giggles.

"Oh my god," I cover my face with my hand as if she can see my embarrassment.

"Just go and talk to him, Mo. There doesn't have to be any heavy expectation on the outcome, just speak to him because he's too worried that you'd ignore him if he reaches out first. Plus, that way you'll be able to see Honey for yourself."

I let out a heavy breath, accept the defeat and brace myself for whatever is in store for me.

# CHAPTER *FORTY-FIVE*

## *Darrell*

*The* days that I do go into work feel pointless, I can't seem to focus on anything instead of everything that isn't work related.

It's friday and I just swapped off with Sy'Asia to take my shift with Honey at her bedside. She's only been awake for medication since I saw her last, two days ago.

The worst part is not knowing.

I try not to focus on that though, on the what if's and maybes and just focus on the right now, the time that I get to be by her side, where I should've been the day this all happened.

I can't imagine what I'd do without her, and I don't plan on finding out soon.

I hear footsteps enter the room while my back is facing the door, "Hey big brother," Rayana's voice greets me quietly.

I turn to see her fully.

"Hey," I sit my jacket on an empty chair on the opposite side of Honey's bed, "What's up?"

She enters the room fully and closes the door behind her.

"Not much, not much," She says, looking around the room like it's her first time seeing it.

It's not.

"What's wrong? You look suspicious as hell," I say eyeing her.

"How have you been feeling? Like, with the Moriah thing."

I sigh, "I'm not going to talk about this with you again, Rayana."

"You say that like we've been over it a thousand times, it's only been once DJ. I just want to check on you," She says with a scoff.

"One time too many, I'm the same as I was the last time we talked about it. I'm cool," I move around her and back to my seat at Honey's bedside.

"Have you tried talking to her?"

"No, Ray," I answer her frustratedly, "I'm not reaching out to someone who told me they don't want to be with me. I don't need a second round of rejection to understand what they said the first time."

"You should try, DJ," She presses, "I understand why you're nervous but-"

"But nothing Ray, just leave it alone man. I'm not even trying to think about all that right now, I have more important things to focus on."

"Like staring at our constantly sleeping grandmother?" She retorts, "I get how that's a pressing manner."

I roll my eyes at her, her mouth is sick.

"All I'm saying is DJ, we all say and do hasty things when we're scared. But, I also think we all deserve a second chance despite those hasty decisions, especially when we are truly acting out of fear. Sometimes even we ourselves don't understand what we're doing in the heat of it all."

"And how would you know that, Rayana?" I ask her. My younger sister has the life experience of an elementary school student, so I'm not sure where she gets off trying to impart this sudden wisdom.

"Call it a woman's intuition," She shrugs. "I know that you think you have to be hyper focused on all of us because you're trying to keep Anthony off of your back, but you have to remember he's making his own decisions from a place of pain that he hasn't resolved and healed from DJ. That pain isn't yours and has nothing to do with you."

I avert my attention from her and back to Honey who lays still in front of me.

"Don't let his pain and hurt cause your own by association. You treated anything Gramps said like it was written in the Bible," I turn my head slightly at the mention of his name, "Don't let that go, DJ. It's what sets you apart from everyone else, leading with your heart and your own compassion even though it's a little confusing sometimes."

I recenter my focus, trying to ignore my sister, no matter how right she sounds in this moment.

It's that heart and compassion she's talking about that partly led us here.

Silence falls around us, but I feel her still looking at me from the door.

"Darrell," She says, I only turn my head slightly, "I hope you don't hate me for this, but I figured it needed to happen,"

Before I can ask her what she's talking about, I turn to face her fully only to see Moriah enter the door and every sound around me stops at once.

She looks hesitant but even under these horrible hospital lights, she's breathtaking.

She's dressed in a pair of black leggings and a windbreaker jacket with a pair of yellow sneakers.

Her hair is pulled back into a low bun and she sports small gold hoop earrings with a hint of lipgloss.

I fight every urge I have to pin her against the wall and crush her lips with mine. But, just that quickly I realize I forgot our last conversation, and what she said to me, and I remember that I have to fight those urges for a different reason.

"Hi," She speaks first.

"Hi," I breathe out in reply.

I don't know what else to say, still wrapping my mind around the fact that she's in front of me right now.

I see her attention turn to Honey, but I can't take mine off of her.

"How is she? Still no update?" She asks, keeping her eyes trained on my grandmother.

"No," I swallow, "No update, not really. They're trying to keep her in a resting state until they can figure out a plan for her so she can recover at home."

She nods.

It's not until the silence that I'm reminded of Rayana being in the room with us.

"Um-"

"Can W-"

Moriah and I speak at the same time. If the room wasn't filled with awkwardness before, it surely is overflowing with it now.

"Can we talk? Like, somewhere else?" I ask her.

"Yeah," She rubs her arm, "Yeah, that's fine."

I look at Rayana who stands in the corner, eyes darting between Moriah and I, "Ray, do you mind-"

"No!" I don't get to finish my question before she responds, "No, by all means."

She opens the door for us to walk out.

Moriah exits first and I follow, we find an empty room close by.

I lead her in and close the door behind us.

"Can I start?" I ask her.

She almost looks thankful and nods yes.

I take a deep breath before I begin, "I understand that you're scared to give us an actual try, to give me an actual try. I'm scared too, but…" My words begin to escape me.

"Moriah, I've never felt the way I do for you, for anyone else. I've never lost all sense of reality the way I do when you make eye contact with me, or lose my breath as soon as you enter into the same room. I understand that relationships aren't exactly something you do, and that you're worried you'll find a fate like your father after finally trusting someone, I get that."

I start to close the gap that's between us, fighting between touching her and keeping my hands to myself.

"I've tried to fill my grandfather's shoes for so long when honestly, that spot has already been filled. I've needed to have someone or something to pour into, but it always felt forced or draining. It doesn't feel that way with you, if you let me, if you want me to… I'll take care of you. I swear that I will."

She doesn't speak immediately, she just looks at me as if she's trying to focus on me to keep herself steady.

"I believe you," She says, "I believe that you mean what you're saying and I'm sorry I made you feel like your effort wasn't enough, that I didn't have faith in you,"

She begins to meet me in the middle of the space that's left between us.

"I've had some time to think and I've had a lot of conversations and you were right. I was scared, I am scared, beyond it, of being heartbroken and left alone and not understanding why after feeling like I've done everything I could. But, I had to remember, that's sort of what love is. It's a gamble of trust, it's trial and error, and it's choosing the person you said you'd choose every day."

She looks down at her feet before she continues, "I tried to escape it, I really did. I tried to act like it was inevitable, that it was for the best anyway and that everything was fine before you so it would be fine without you… but I have never been so wrong in my life."

I take her by her hand, and allow my free hand to guide her chin up so that I could see into her eyes.

"Love isn't going to be easy for either one of us. You believe with love comes certain heartache, and before you, I thought it would only be a hindrance," I take her face into my hands hoping that I could make her feel all that she is to me, "You're the only source of light I have while I'm walking through the woods in the middle of the night. I've never seen clearer than I do now since you've come around. All I ask of you, is that you try loving me… because I can't stop loving you now that I've started."

She smiles up at me.

"That's the thing, Darrell… I never had to try loving you. I've fought to keep love at distance, it's like you saw that as a challenge and you took on head first without even trying or knowing. I never had to try loving you, I've been trying not to and it's seeming impossible."

I can only grin the way a kid does when presented with the very thing he's been asking to get for Christmas all year.

Finally, I get a reminder of what her lips feel like and I soak in the moment to make sure she knows just how much I appreciate it.

I didn't think it was possible for them to be softer, for her to be sweeter, but she is.

After a while we finally break our embrace and walk back hand and hand, to Honey's room.

We find Rayana sitting in the arm chair across from Honey's bed, scrolling on her phone.

She gasps, "Fingers intertwined is the best outcome I could've hoped for, please tell me this means what I think it does."

Moriah looks at me and smiles, "It means this was the only time I'll accept you meddling in my damn business," I respond to my giddy younger sister.

She squeals and hugs Moriah.

I love knowing that they enjoy each other as much as they do. Rayana deserves to have more people who care about her, and I'm sure she really wanted us back together just so she didn't have to feel guilty about wanting to hang out with Mo over me.

Some time passes with the three of us quietly talking and catching up. Moriah tells us about the meeting with her mother and how her sister and father have been since.

In the middle of Rayana rambling about some new show she's been binging, Anthony and Angeline walk in.

I swear you could hear everyone hold their breath at once.

His eyes immediately lock on Moriah, "You're not good at direct orders I take it?"

"Ant, calm that down man," I say from my seat next to Honey.

"I invited her, Ant," Rayana says timidly.

"I don't care who did, though you know better," He responds, "You've had your fun now it's time for you to leave. Only God knows what else could happen with you around and no one paying attention because of it."

"That's enough," I don't give Moriah a chance to react to my brother whose default as of late is asshole, "Nothing is happening just because she's here and she isn't leaving either."

He turns his body fully to me, "Oh word? Is that so?" He huffs out a laugh, "And since when in the hell do you tell me what is and isn't going to happen?"

I rise from my seat, "Since I remembered you aren't my damn father, Anthony."

"Darrell…" I hear Moriah's hushed voice, like if she speaks too loudly she'll set off a volcano.

Maybe she's right.

"Ah," My brother nods, "So you needed a little pussy in your life to grow some balls? Got you, got you."

"What the fuck did you say?" I get closer to his face, "You guys!" Ang shouts.

Just as he meets me in the space I stand, with our noses almost close enough to touch, we hear a voice that's foreign to the group in the room right now.

"That's enough," So weak we almost miss it, and if it hadn't been for Rayana's gasp, we may have.

"Honey?!" Rayana runs to my grandmother's side, "Hi granny," She says almost tearfully..

"You two," She struggles to turn her head towards my brother and I, but we know who she's addressing, "Come here."

We slowly walk to her side.

"I don't have much breath left to spare," She starts off, "But I know that the breath I do have left should not have to be used, reminding you two that you are brothers first before anything else."

She coughs for a bit and regains composure, "I do not care who is older or younger, who has seen what and who has done what. You are not rivals on the street and you are not bickering teenagers."

I look to my feet while Anthony struggles to keep our grandmother's eye contact as she chastises us both.

"I prayed that God would keep my heart beating long enough to see that at least one of my boys finally find a woman that can ease their troubles. You both wear the weights of your own worlds on your own shoulders and then you somehow make it heavier, you've made room for everything but love."

She grabs my hand with her own shaky one.

"God answered my prayers the day you met Moriah, and I am blessed to know that I'd leave your heart in capable hands, even if it took her a while to know that she was capable enough."

"Honey-" I want to correct her about leaving my heart with anyone.

"Not right now, DJ," She stops me, she knows I hate to hear her speak that way, even now in the state she's in. Maybe, especially now.

"Anthony," She speaks to my older brother, "I know your heart is harder to penetrate right now for reasons you may never give life to aloud," Now he looks anywhere but her face, "But I pray, my silent soldier of a boy, that you allow someone to let someone break your heart out of the cell you've put it in."

Her hand slides from it's place on his arm.

I didn't realize before this moment the heaviness that blankets the room and the sniffles I hear from those around me.

I try to ignore the reason why they're crying, maybe if I ignore it I can change it, it won't happen.

"Moriah," she tries to speak a little louder to get her attention from across the room, as if all eyes aren't already on her, hanging on her every word.

Moriah leaves her place on the wall and walks over to my grandmother's outstretched hand and I see Moriah biting back emotion, trying to be the strongest in the room as always.

"Thank you, for letting my boy find you," Moriah sticks out her chin just a bit, trying to fortify herself silently, "I want you to hear from my own mouth, that you have every bit of my blessing to be a part of this family. You've fit in from the first day."

Mo sucks in a deep breath and just nods her head, unable to allow words to escape her mouth in fear that they'll betray her. I see a firm squeeze between her hand and my grandmothers.

"You all do well to take care of each other, all of you. None of you are parents to the other, or a judge. Your only job is to love one another, help guide each other and hold on to each other as tightly as you can."

She slowly scans the room my siblings fill up.

"I don't want to see any more tears," She adds on, "Your Honey is an old coot, and I'm tired. I've raised you as best as I could and given you all the good sounding advice I could think of. My husband is missing me now, he let me stay as long as I needed to. It's time that I go spend the rest of my time next to him, where I belong."

I feel hands wrap around my arm and I think it's Rayana, but I'm too afraid to take my eyes off of Honey to confirm.

"Honey, I love you so much," Sy'Asia says, kneeled down on the opposite side of the bed, with her head laying on our grandmother's hand.

"Aw," Honey says, "My sweet girl, I was so blessed to get another chance at motherhood through you. And what a wonderful woman you've become, Sy'Asia."

My sister's cries begin to come out as sobs.

"We're going to miss you so much," Ang says from the foot of the bed, also joining in tears.

"You're not going to need to miss me girl, I'm not leaving you. You may not be able to touch me, but I'll be just as close to you as I've always been."

Her breaths are getting more shallow as she tries to talk.

"I just know your Gramps will tell me how proud he is of all of you, at the job you've done so far."

She looks at all of us one more time.

"I'm so blessed to be surrounded by love. I want you all to remember that you are too, anytime you look at each other."

Her eyelids start to look like they're too heavy for her to handle on her own.

"Wait, Honey-" Rayana leaves my side and rushes to the bed where our grandmother drifts in and out of consciousness.

"My kind girl, you've always been the strongest person I've known. Don't ever forget to fight for yourself the same way you fight for everyone else," Honey says to her with a lazy hand on my sister's cheek.

Rayana grabs hold of it and seconds later begins to sob, realizing the difference in alertness in Honey's body and slowly releasing her limp hand that falls back to the bed with a quiet thump.

And just like that, the woman who is the reason I know what love feels like, fades into a sleep that she will not wake up from.

Sobs rip through the room as my siblings hold on to each other for support.

Rayana hugging Moriah who still tries to hold on to her own tears.

My brother who is being used as a pillar for Angeline.

Sy'Asia, her cries are the loudest, she keeps her face to the bed while the mattress tries to muffle her heart wrenching sobs.

I'm frozen in my place, just a foot away from the bed.

After some time, my brother disappears down the hallway, and I feel a pair of soft hands turn my face from Honey.

I turn to meet Moriah, whose eyes are searching mine for something that I can't figure out.

She brushes away tears I didn't know were falling down my cheek, and gently guides me low enough to rest my chin on her shoulder.

The world went from the blurring noise of my family's pain to being able to hear only someone in the distance cry as if their heart has been ripped out of their chest.

It's not until I feel the violent shaking of my own body and the human shield of my siblings that I realize…

The distant mourner is me.

# CHAPTER *FORTY-SIX*

## *Moriah*

*It's* been 4 months since Honey's passing.

To say the Washington family has had a hard time adjusting would be an understatement for sure. Sy'Asia has only just started to resemble herself again, going from not uttering a word to allowing her snarkiness that we all have come to love slowly show itself again.

Anthony did what he's used to and buried himself in responsibilities.

Angeline and her two children have been around a lot more, I guess trying to stay true to her word to Honey and hold on to her siblings tightly.

Rayana, I think she understands a bit more than the rest about how precious life is and how quickly it can be taken from you, despite how hard you may try to hold on to it. So, I think she's dealing with it in her own way.

Darrell, well, he's still processing.

He never really had the chance to get over his grandfather, I believe he was only just coming to grips with it and now his only true mother figure has been taken from him too.

I'm doing my best to show up for him in the way he needs me to.

The dynamic in my household has seemed to do a little adjusting as well.

My mother and sister have started to form their relationship and it's been nice to be a witness to. Though AJ didn't admit it, she surely missed having a mother figure around.

I've been warming up to our mothers being present. I couldn't deny the parallels I see between the two of us, I'd be acting intentionally ignorant if I bypassed that.

I finally let Darrell meet my father.

After Honey, seeing how lost he and his siblings looked, I wanted them to know that the same way they opened up their family to me, though it was a bit reluctantly for some, I want to extend the same to them.

It took a little while but my father treats Darrell and Anthony like the sons he's never had.

He and Darrell bond over sports things I don't understand, while he and Anthony have their heart to hearts while doing projects around the house.

I truly don't think I've ever seen Anthony talk so much and not look like he wants to hit someone every second of the day. He even takes him to some appointments when he can so that AJ can get a bit of a break.

No one could replace their grandfather of course, but I'm happy that my dad could give them even an inch of the love they were missing.

Ang has actually, very unexpectedly, taken to my mother quickly, and she took to her as well as her children.

The Henderson family keeps in touch, though our work with them is done. The girls have started school on their correct grade levels, and their father has gotten an office job that he didn't realize he was qualified for.

It's nothing crazy but it absolutely sustains them the way they need.

I know I mentioned that my father has brought out a side of Anthony that I'm not used to, but he isn't the only one.

Neither Darrell or I can put a finger on it, but we're certain something very… odd is happening between his brother and Anastasia. Neither of us can put our finger on it and neither of them will acknowledge it whenever we bring it up, so we let it go.

For now.

We're all at my dad's home right now for Sunday dinner.

I look around and take a moment to observe the scene before me. Love is filling the room, smiles from ear to ear, laughter and conversations going so loudly you almost can't decipher the difference between their words and your own thoughts.

I can't help but to think how different life was just earlier this year.

We started as strangers with baggage that was barely ours to carry.

And while I do believe that what's meant to be will be, I can't help but to thank a little old, feisty woman who reminded us to follow our hearts and not the voices of others.

If it wasn't for her, who knows if we would've ended up.

Thank you Honey, for leading me to the one man who could change my outlook on everything I thought I knew about love.

# *EPILOGUE*

## Darrell

*It's* been a year since we've lost Honey and five years since Gramps.

We're nowhere near the way we were, but we've made it back to some sort of normalcy.

Sy'Asia has moved in with Ang and the kids. There was an emptiness she'd felt since losing Honey that caused us all to worry about her, after some convincing she agreed to move in with them. Being closer to the kids has done a lot of good for her.

Anthony gave up his apartment and moved into Honey's home with Rayana. It wasn't Rayana's first choice, especially with Anthony looking for someone else to care for with Honey being gone, but she appreciated not being left alone in the big house. Because she definitely wasn't going to move out of it.

As for me, I've been trying to keep my grandparents' words in the forefront of my mind, focusing only on what directly pertains to me and doing what makes me happy.

One of those things that make me happy just so happens to be the woman I'm standing next to.

Moriah has been my rock through all of this, keeping my head on straight and being a comfort to me on the nights where things feel a little too heavy.

I've done my best to be the same for her, as her mom has been slowly reintegrated into her family. Of course she isn't a child anymore so it doesn't affect her as much as it could, but it's been an adjustment for her to see her face so often after not seeing her for over 20 years.

She moved out of her fathers house also, after much, much convincing.

She's gotten her own place that isn't too far away from her family and also isn't too far away from me. It took her some getting used to. For the longest her sister, Stasi and myself were all on sleepover rotation so she could get adjusted.

We spend about every other night together, it's just a natural routine we've fallen into.

Currently we stand in the backyard of my childhood home, surrounded by family close and extended, and friends. Anthony mans the grill while Rayana and Sy'Asia tend to the kitchen.

Moriah busies herself entertaining the children as well as some cousins of ours and I'll never get over just how well she blends in.

"If someone handed me a mirror while I would watch her mother from afar, I'm sure my reflection would look exactly the way you do right now," Moriah's father, Jeremy, says from beside me. He creeps up so quietly these days with his walk slowed down and his cane as his aid.

"I don't even try to deny it anymore," I laugh, "I have it bad, Jeremy," I say to her father who has become a friend and a father figure wrapped into one.

"I could tell from the first day," He places a hand on my shoulder, "And there's no one else that I would've chosen to trust my daughter with. I've never seen someone penetrate that armor she had built around her and you did it with such ease that it even made her mad," The older man laughs softly, "You and your brother have truly become the sons that I never knew I needed to have around, though one will hold that title a bit truer than the other, I've come to love the both of you very much. All 5 of you, even as scary as Sy'Asia tends to be."

That makes me laugh, because she truly can scare a giant on the right day.

"Thank you, Jeremy. I hope I don't make you regret it," I place my hand on his shoulder in return, "I promise to make you and my grandparents proud."

He smiles and hobbles away to the seat nearest to the grill so he can feel like he's doing something along with my brother.

Anthony and I have yet to have a moment where we hash out our grievances totally and directly, but we've silently agreed to put aside all the things in the past and fulfill our promise to Honey by putting each other first as much as we're able.

I can't say he and Moriah are best friends, even with him now basically being a part of her family, but they tolerate each other more than they were able to initially.

I walk over to Moriah who stands with her mother and an aunt of mine, laughing about something I didn't catch.

"Do you all mind if I steal our favorite girl for a moment?" I ask as I approach the trio.

"Not at all," Her mother answers, "I think she was entertaining us out of kindness anyways," She laughs.

Moriah giggles and walks towards me.

"Hey," She grabs my hand as we walk towards the back porch.

"Hey beautiful," I give her hand a squeeze, "How're you feeling?"

"Pretty good I must say," She smiles and it easily reaches her eyes. They've been so genuine lately and I can't help but to take pride in having a hand in that.

"I love to hear that baby," We reach the steps and walk up so that we're elevated enough to see the group that fills our backyard. I take her other hand into my free one, and rub the back of them with my thumbs, "I love to see that smile on your face, you know that?"

She blushes, "Yeah, you don't let me forget," she giggles.

Rayana and Sy'Asia exit the house with the last of the tin foil pans of food.

"You see this?" I nod to the crowd, strangers who have become family for more than one reason, but one of the bigger reasons being us.

"Yeah," She gazes out onto the yard, "It's so nice. I'm not used to having big family gatherings, I could get used to it."

"This is all because of you, you know," I tell her, and she looks at me confused.

"How so?"

"Because you decided to give your heart a chance, to give me a chance. And because of that, so many people that didn't know they'd need each other, found each other. These are our people, together and they were bought together because of us. Isn't that beautiful?"

"Well, when you say it like that," Her smile grows, "Yeah, it's pretty beautiful."

"Could you see yourself expanding that family?" I ask her, testing the waters, "Adding a few additions of your own?"

She looks at me and takes a second to respond, "A few additions of *our* own, yeah, I could."

My smile deeps so much that it hurts my cheeks.

"I'm really glad you corrected that part, because I've been meaning to talk to you."

"Oh god, are you pregnant?" She gives a fake surprised expression.

I laugh, "No, I'm not pregnant. But, seriously Mo," I firm my grip on her hands to recenter her focus, "I'm so thankful for you Moriah."

"Aw," She grins, "I'm thankful for you too babe."

"You gave me purpose when I was fooled into thinking I'd already found mine. You teach me boundaries, that I can put myself first and still be the natural giver and provider that I am. That the world won't stop spinning and that I won't lose everyone I love just because I make a mistake."

She doesn't speak, she just allows me to continue speaking.

"You've given me a safety I never thought I'd find, and you show me time and time again that you're the person my grandfather prepared me for all those years ago."

Her face begins to morph into a confused expression, it only makes me smile because this woman will never understand the light she's brought into my life and how thankful I am for it.

"Moriah," I take a deep breath, "You're the person I've been waiting for without knowing that I was waiting. The way you make me feel, I can only imagine is the way my grandfather felt when seeing Honey for the first time, a sense of knowing.

Knowing that this is the woman he is bound to spend the rest of his life with, even if she didn't know or didn't believe it."

Her face changes from confusion to realization, and I know now that she knows what's coming.

"My country manners come with traditional tendencies, so rest assured, I spoke to both of your parents before I thought about talking to you."

Her breath catches in her chest and it's at this moment that she realizes all the eyes of those in attendance are on us.

"It didn't take me long to know that you were my one, even when we both tried to run from it," I take a small black box out of my pocket and kneel before her, "And I knew that once I started to love you, nothing in this world could make me stop. Not even you and your stubbornness."

She giggles through the tears that now stream down her cheeks, something she'd never let happen in front of a crowd on a regular day.

"Moriah Sha'neese Jackson," I open the black box and present to her an oval shaped 5 carat diamond ring, "Will do me the absolute tremendous honor, and marry me?"

Rayana squeals before Moriah can get out a sound.

She shakes her head wordless for a moment, "Yes, yes Darrell, I'll marry you."

After I place the ring on her finger, the cheers that erupt from below us fade to nothing in my ears as I scoop up the woman of my dreams into my arms.

Before Moriah, I knew without a doubt that the day I'd allow love into my life and believe the fairytale that my grandparents tried to feed me, that everything would fall to shit.

Little did I know that instead of taking my focus away, she'd not only sharpen it but help me realize what truly matters the most.

Taking care of my own heart, because if I can't do that, I can't fully show up for those that matter most to me.

After I place her back on the ground and kiss my now fiance, I look at the chair swing that sits just a few feet away from us.

Some may say it was the wind that made it swing with no one sitting it in, but I know it was my grandparents, the only parents I've truly known, smiling back at me. I know that I've truly made them proud.

# AUTHOR'S *NOTE*

Thank you so much for taking the time to read my debut novel. I hope that, even if you couldn't see yourself in the characters of this story, that it could serve as a comfy read for you anyway. Darrell and Moriah both have a special place with me, seeing a little of myself in each of them. I hope you're interested in continuing to follow their story through the series as we journey with the other couples that I hope will earn a spot in your heart.

Next up, we have Anthony and Anastasia and I hope you'll come along for the ride.

*XOXO,*

*E. L. Calloway*

Made in the USA
Columbia, SC
20 January 2025